# The New Bad A

# The New Bad Ass in Town
# © 2013 Mark A. Roeder

All rights reserved. No part of this book may be used or reproduced by any means, graphic, electronic, or mechanical, including photocopying, recording, taping or by any information storage retrieval system without the written permission of the publisher except in the case of brief quotations embodied in critical articles and reviews.

This book is a work of fiction. Names, characters, places and incidents are products of the author's imagination or are used fictionally. Any resemblance to actual events or locales or persons, living or dead, is entirely coincidental. All trademarks are the property of their respective owners and no infringement is intended.

Cover Photo Credit: Curaphotography (model) and Blackslide (background) on Dreamstime.com.

Cover Design: Ken Clark

ISBN-13: 978-1483913070

ISBN-10: 1483913074

All Rights Reserved


Printed in the United States of America

# Acknowledgements

I'd like to thank Ken Clark, James Adkinson, and Kathy Staley for all the work they put in proofreading this novel. Without their dedication this book would be a grammatical nightmare. I'd also like to thank Kathy for her creation of the characters Sadye and Female.

# Dedication

This book is dedicated to all the members of my yahoo fan group. They aren't just readers. They're also my friends.

# Chapter 1
# Caspian
# Bloomington, Indiana
# Late October 2009

"Well, helloooo..." Dylan said, as I sat down with my tray in the cafeteria of Bloomington High School North.

Dylan wasn't speaking to me. His head was twisted around in the opposite direction. I followed his gaze but couldn't make out who he was talking about.

"What are you going on about, Dylan?" I asked.

"I am checking out my next boyfriend, Caspian. Mmm!"

"Boyfriend?" Tyler asked. "Don't you mean hook up?"

Tyler and I grinned at each other. I gave him a high five.

"When have you ever had a boyfriend, Dylan?" Caleb asked from his wheelchair at the end of our table.

"I've had plenty of boyfriends," Dylan said, still not taking his eyes off whatever boy he was checking out.

"Five minutes with a football player in the laundry room doesn't make a guy your boyfriend," Caleb said.

"How'd you know about Cory? Did he tell you?" Dylan asked, whipping his head around so fast I expected his neck to snap.

"Cory Caldemyer?" Caleb asked.

"Yeah," Dylan said absentmindedly, his attention already returning to whatever boy he'd been checking out.

"I knew it!" Caleb said. "You owe me ten bucks, Jesse! Pay up!"

Jesse reluctantly dug into his pocket pulled out a ten, waded it up, and threw it at Caleb. Caleb caught it with ease. He had once been a star football player after all.

Dylan sighed and turned around.

"He's gone, but I'm gonna have some of that. What were you talking about, Caleb?"

"You on your knees for Cory Caldemyer in the laundry just off the locker room."

"Who told you that?" Dylan asked.

"You did about thirty seconds ago."

"I did?"

"Yes, don't you pay any attention to what you're saying?"

"He doesn't when he's checking out a guy," Tyler said.

"Did I really tell you about Cory?"

"Yes, Dylan."

"I did not. I wouldn't have mentioned his last name for sure."

"I asked and you told me," Caleb said.

"You tricked me!"

"By asking you? I don't think so."

"In all fairness, Dylan isn't responsible for his mouth when he's drooling over a boy," Tyler said.

"Which is practically always," I added.

"Hey! He was hot!"

A look of concern crossed Dylan's features. He looked each of us in the eyes as he spoke.

"You cannot tell anyone about Cory, guys. That was supposed to be top secret."

"I think we should make him pay us for our silence," I said.

"Well, if you want to get paid..." Dylan began.

"Do not go there," Tyreece said. "Any sexual favor would be a favor for you, not us."

"A lot you know. I am the best!" Dylan said. "You'd be begging for more!"

Dylan was talented. He was boy crazy and there were rumors he blew a lot of the jocks. My guess was he bent over for some of them, too. Dylan would never name names, except when he slipped up like today, but there was no doubt at least some of the rumors were true. I had some experience with Dylan myself, but I don't want to talk about that.

"Be that as it may," Tyreece said, "what I said is true. If you want us to keep quiet, you're going to have to make keeping silent worth it."

"Guys, please!" Dylan said.

"Quit begging, Dylan," Jesse said as he looked up from his latest fashion magazine. "We aren't going to tell and you know it. We're just messing with you."

"Thanks, guys!"

I should probably back up and make some introductions. I can't expect you to know all my friends. I haven't known any of them all that long myself. I only moved to Bloomington on September 1st, so a couple of months ago; I was as confused as you.

I'll start with Dylan. He's fifteen and a freshman like me. If I had to describe him in one word, the word would be flamer. Don't have a fit because I'm not being politically correct. I'm gay, so I have a license to say "flamer" if I want, just like I can say "homo" or "pillow-biter" without being offensive. Of course, I call them as I see them, and "flamer" really is the best word to describe Dylan. He has unnaturally blond hair and all the stereotypically gay traits. He's also a slut; not that being easy has anything to do with being gay. Dylan has probably done more guys than any girl in the school. Don't get me wrong. Dylan is okay and I more or less like him. He can be very annoying and he likes to hug way too much, but I think of him as a friend.

I already mentioned that Caleb was a football player and is in a wheel chair. He's a senior and he manages the football team. He also works with the coach and plans to be a football coach someday. Caleb is very good-looking with black hair, green eyes, and a muscular bod. Caleb is straight, which is a pity, but he has no problem with gay guys.

Tyreece calls himself the "token black" of our group. He is the only black guy, but that's just by chance. Tyreece is eighteen, very handsome, and has an incredible body according to Tyler, who has seen him without a shirt. It's rumored that Tyreece is majorly hung, as in ten inches, but no one knows for sure. I'm sure Dylan has tried to get into Tyreece's pants, but unfortunately, Tyreece is straight. We can't all be perfect.

Jesse is very gay, only he isn't. He's fifteen and a freshman. He has curly black hair, blue eyes, and everyone thinks he is the best-looking guy around, including Jesse. He's obsessed with his appearance, fashion, and money. I seriously thought he was gay when I first met him. I thought there was no way he could be straight, but I was wrong. Jesse also seems very shallow at first, but there's more to him than meets the eye.

Tyler is my boyfriend. He's eighteen and has reddish-brown hair and green eyes. He's very good-looking, but then I'm a little biased. Tyler is very friendly and cares about people he doesn't even know. We started out as enemies, but now we're dating. Yeah, it's a long story, but none of that matters right now. We just started dating a couple of weeks ago, but so far, so good.

That just leaves me. I'm not about to tell you everything, but I'm blond and I'm a Goth. I know blond and Goth don't seem to go together, but they do. I have my hair spiked, and it looks really hot with my spiked collar and wristbands. I wear black eyeliner and it really stands out because of my blond hair and fair complexion. I already told you I'm gay, but the boyfriend thing gives that away anyway. People don't know I'm gay until someone tells them. If Jesse and I stood together and someone had to choose which of us was gay, they'd pick Jesse every time.

Okay, now you know enough to go on. You'll have to find out the rest as we go along. If you find if the rumor about Tyreece is true, let me know. I'm curious.-

"So who is the boy *du jour*?" Tyler asked Dylan.

"Huh? Boy *du jour*?"

"It means 'boy of the day,' I think," Tyler said.

"Oh! I don't know his name. I've never seen him before. Did *you* see him?"

"No. I don't spend every waking moment checking out boys," Tyler said.

"Sure, you don't," Caleb teased.

"Hey! I happen to have a boyfriend!" Tyler said.

"The cutest, sexiest, most wonderful boyfriend *ever*," I said.

"What?" Tyreece asked. "You guys have broken up after what—two—three days?"

I glared at Tyreece and folded my arms over my chest.

"Why would you say that?" I asked, although I was pretty sure I knew what was coming.

"You said Tyler's boyfriend was the cutest, sexiest, most wonderful boyfriend ever. That obviously can't mean you."

"Ha-ha. Shut up," I said.

"I think Caspian is sooo hot!" Dylan said.

"Down, Dylan, or Tyler might punch your lights out," Caleb said.

Dylan curled his hands and panted like he a puppy. He was so weird sometimes.

"Didn't anyone notice him?" Dylan asked.

"Most of us aren't interested in boys," Tyreece reminded Dylan.

"It's okay. I won't hold your failings against you, but he's so hot even straight guys will want him."

"Straight guys aren't turned on by other guys, Dylan," Tyler said.

"Sure, they aren't."

I laughed. I don't think Dylan could wrap his mind around the concept of heterosexuality.

"No one noticed your newest obsession, okay?" I said. I was becoming slightly annoyed with Dylan. He was just too much sometimes.

"You've got to see him! He's so handsome! He has dark brown hair that's just a little curly, dreamy brown eyes, a hot, hot body, and the hottest ass."

"You can point him out sometime," I said. "When you find out his name, let us know and we'll add it to the list of boys you obsess over."

"Me? Obsess? There is no such list because I don't obsess."

"Hmm, let's see," Tyler said. "There's Brice Parker."

"Justin Schroeder," Caleb added.

"My uncle Percy," I said.

"My *dad*," Tyler said, shooting Dylan an evil glare.

"Don't forget Caspian," Tyreece said.

"Okay! Okay! Maybe I'm interested in a few guys..."

"A few?" Jesse asked, looking up from *GQ* for a moment. "More like thousands."

"Including my dad!" Tyler said.

"You already said that," Caleb pointed out.

"Yeah, but...*my dad*? I still can't believe you were hitting on my dad and his boyfriend at my birthday party!"

"They're hot! Besides, I hinted about a *three-way*. I wasn't trying to get him to cheat."

"I don't think that's the point, Dylan," Tyreece said. "I would never hit on your mom, Dylan. Unless… Is she hot?"

"Hey!" Dylan said.

"I'm just making my point, Dylan. I would never hit on a friend's mom. It's not cool."

"I couldn't help myself."

"I don't think we can argue with that," Caleb said.

I'll say one thing for Dylan; he's entertaining. I've never met anyone who was so boy crazy. When I first met him, I found him *extremely* annoying. More than that, I wanted to beat the crap out of him. I had some issues back then that I've dealt with, so I no longer want to bash Dylan's head in (at least not nearly as often). I still can't believe he gets away with the crap he does. Bloomington High School North is fairly accepting of gays, but Dylan openly checks out and propositions boys *all* the time. I think he mostly gets away with it because he has protectors. Several of the jocks look out for him, which is the main reason I believe the rumors about him blowing straight jocks. Why else would they protect a flamboyant homo? I guess they might like him for his entertainment value, but more likely they value him for his talent when he's on his knees. I shook my head and laughed for a moment.

"What?" Tyler asked.

"Nothing."

"Please don't tell me you're just thinking funny things. Your uncle tells me that."

"I'm not nearly as crazy as Percy," I said with a grin. I almost added something about Percy being crazy because he's a writer, but Tyler wanted to be a writer too and I wanted to stay on the good side of my boyfriend.

Our lunch period drew to a close so Tyler and I walked together to dump our trays.

I noticed three girls glaring across the cafeteria. I'd had run ins with them before. The Muffdiver Mafia. Most students detoured around them. As much as I thought of myself as a bad ass, these three were the true bad asses of the school and were the real force that kept things cool for us gay kids.

Precious looked me up and down and scoffed at me. Despite being all of 5' 3", she'd backed champion wrestlers against the wall. That might be because she'd pinned them all on the mat too.

She was North High's highest ranked wrestler. She was one strong girl. I'd seen her lift football players two feet off the ground just for the hell of it.

While Precious called herself a stud, her girlfriend Female was femme all the way. She wore pink mohair sweaters, feminine jewelry, high heels, and perfectly coiffed hair. The rumor was Precious had forced the cheerleaders to vote her as head cheerleader. She was voted this year's Homecoming Queen. She acted like a delicate flower most of the time but when I mispronounced her name as "female," she gave me a full dose of her famous attitude complete with head wag, "It's Fa-Ma-Lee, Goth Boy. Don't you know anything other than your damn Eurocentric worldview?" Two minutes later when the bell rang, she was still reading me out. I ran for the door.

The final member of the Muffdiver Mafia glared at Tyler's Justin Bieber hairdo so hard that I steered him far away. The drummer of local death metal band Killer Clits, Sadye wore combat boots, a crew cut, and more piercings than I wanted to know about. She's rumored to have her nipples pierced. Ouch! Somehow, Sadye'd become Dylan's biggest protector. She'd been suspended multiple times for pummeling his harassers. Unfortunately, she thought I wanted to beat him up! Don't know why.

I knew that if I could get in these girls' good graces I would be known as the Ultimate Bad Ass of North High. But did I really care? Hell yeah!

Tyler and I headed for our lockers. I looked at him for a moment and smiled.

"You know, you're very cute when you smile," Tyler said.

*That* made me blush.

"You give me a reason to smile."

That was an understatement if there ever was one. Tyler had helped me through some extremely difficult issues. There had been a whole lot of bad in my life recently. I had come to live with my uncle in Bloomington because both my parents were killed when our house burned to the ground. I was a messed-up kid when I arrived in this strange place where everything and everyone was unfamiliar. I barely even knew my Uncle Percy. I could only remember meeting him once before. Things are much better now, largely thanks to Tyler, but Percy has a lot to do with that too.  He stuck by me when I...um...was creating a few difficulties, but I don't want to say more about that.

"Are you okay? You stopped smiling."

"Sorry. I was just thinking about my parents."

Tyler wrapped his arm around my shoulder and gave me a one-arm hug.

"I'm okay.  I was mostly thinking about how much you've done for me. You and Percy."

Tyler grinned.

"Come on, I'll walk you to class."

"You're going to totally ruin my bad ass image," I said.

"That will never happen. Most of the school is afraid of you."

I laughed.

"It's mostly the spiked collar," I said.

"It's mostly the glare.  You can look very scary when you want."

"The glare is useful," I said.

We parted at the door to my classroom. I walked in and took my seat. Kids eyed me warily as if afraid I might lunge at them. I frowned at a boy as he walked past and he sped up. Tyler was right. I still had my bad ass rep.

All eyes turned to the front of the room as an unfamiliar boy entered.  Fresh meat.  This new kid didn't look nervous or uncertain like most when being stared at by two dozen strangers. He didn't seem to take much notice of us at all. He was very handsome and looked both sullen and sad. He had slightly curly brown hair and brown eyes. I checked out his butt when he turned around. Nice. Was this Dylan's new obsession? I thought it likely.

Mr. Holbrook entered and the kid handed him an add slip. I knew exactly what it was because I'd had a fist full of them only two months before.

"Class, we have a new student.  I'm sure you'll all make Brayden feel welcome."

Mr. Holbrook directed Brayden to the empty desk to my right. Brayden. At least he had a cool name. I pitied guys who went through life with boring names.

Brayden dropped into his seat beside Female with perfectly affected teenage disinterest. He didn't seem the type for creative writing. Then again, neither did I. I wanted to kill Percy when I discovered he'd signed me up for it, but it wasn't so bad. Mr. Holbrook let us write about things that interested us. He was forever stressing, "Write about what you love." I turned in a lot of assignments on skating because I kicked ass on roller blades and on the skateboard.

Brayden spared me one glare. I stared back, putting just a touch of menace in my eyes. I felt like we'd reached an understanding.

I smiled to myself during class. Some of the girls were checking out the new kid. If this was Dylan's new obsession, Dylan was going to have competition. He was also going to have to watch his step. I had the feeling Brayden would kick Dylan's ass just for fun if Dylan so much as looked at him funny. It was a wonder Dylan didn't get his ass kicked daily. I'd come close to pounding him myself on more than one occasion.

I won't bore you with the details of my class. It's bad enough sitting there. At the end, I shoved my books into my backpack and checked out Brayden's butt again as he left. Yeah, he did have a hot ass. As soon as Brayden was out of the room, the girls began talking about how hot he was. I guess they went for the brooding type. Brayden was hot enough, but I much preferred someone less like me, someone like Tyler.

When I walked out of the classroom, I noticed Brayden gazing up to one end of the hall and then the other. He didn't have the uncertain look of a new kid, but I could tell by his frown he was lost.

"What have you got next?" I asked.

Brayden looked at me. He didn't smile.

"World History. Room 185b."

He was a sophomore then, probably a year older than me.

"Down the hall, take a left, then it's the fourth door on the right."

"Got it," Brayden said then left without another word.

I was undecided about my feelings for the new kid. I kind of liked him because he wasn't scared of me. He met me on even ground. I kind of didn't like him because I almost felt he was challenging me. If he got up in my face, he was going to be very, very sorry. I didn't put up with crap from anyone.

My suspicion that Brayden was Dylan's new obsession was confirmed just a few hours later. I was heading for my last class of the day when I spotted Dylan leaning up against the wall gazing across the hallway. He looked like a hungry puppy staring at a T-bone. I followed his gaze and then laughed to myself. Dylan was staring at Brayden's butt.

Brayden turned, caught Dylan checking him out, and glared. I thought for a moment he was going to stomp over and kick Dylan's ass, but the glare turned into a sneer of disdain and Brayden moved on toward his next class.

"His name is Brayden," I said.

"Huh?" Dylan said, coming out of his daze.

"His name is Brayden."

"How do you know that?"

"Tyreece, Tyler, and I jumped him, tied him up, and tortured him until he talked. He told me his name, dufus! We have a class together."

"He's so, so sexy!"

"He's also going to kick your ass if you don't keep your eyes off him."

"I bet he's intense in bed. I bet he's the kind of guy who would throw me down, tear my clothes off, and…"

"Dylan! Wake up and quit fantasizing! This guy is not for you. Did you see the look he just gave you? I thought he was going to walk over and beat the crap out of you."

"He's so masculine. Mmm, I love bad boys."

Dylan looked at me. His eyes were glazed over with desire. He leaned toward me, but I put my hand on his chest and pushed him back.

"Dylan, snap out of it. If you try to kiss me, I'm gonna punch you. I'm dating Tyler. Remember?"

I reddened slightly as I spoke for it wasn't all that long ago that I'd cheated on Tyler with Dylan. I had my reasons for doing it and it's a long story, but Tyler knew I lied to Dylan saying Tyler and I had broken up. Yeah, I could be a bastard. Tyler understood and everything was cool between us now. Still, I felt remorseful and didn't even like to think about what I'd done.

"Sorry, I was still thinking about...Brayden." The dreamy lilt in Dylan's voice told me he was a goner. "You two give off the same bad boy vibe."

"Yeah, well, I'm not him and I'm taken. You need to forget about Brayden. That kid will kick your ass."

Dylan giggled.

"That's what Tyler used to tell me about you."

"He was right. There were several times I was two seconds away from bashing your head in. If you'd pushed it just a little more, I would have rearranged your face. You're right; Brayden and I are two of a kind, so I'm telling you to back off or he's going to pummel you. And, keep your hands off me or I will slug you."

"I'll take it slow and I'll be careful, but I'm gonna have him."

"Do you *ever* listen?" I asked.

"He's so hot," Dylan said, lost in thought.

I growled in frustration and walked away. I'd done my part. I'd warned Dylan off. If he was too stupid to listen, that was his problem.

After school, I met up with Tyler at his locker.

"What's up?"

I gave Tyler a mischievous grin.

"I don't mean *that*."

"I met Dylan's dream boy. His name is Brayden and he'll probably be getting detention soon or he might get suspended."

"Why?"

"Dylan is pursuing him. Brayden caught Dylan checking him out and glared at him."

"Let me guess. Dylan failed to take the hint?"

"He's oblivious to the danger. I warned him off, but he didn't hear a word I said."

"He's deaf to warnings and blind to danger when he's after a guy," Tyler said.

"He's going to get hurt."

"We need to keep him on a leash."

"No way! He'd enjoy it far too much and probably take it as an invitation for a three-way."

Tyler moved in and kissed me. I was pleasantly surprised. I didn't think he was bold enough to kiss me in school. We weren't secretive about our relationship, but if we were caught, we'd get detention for P.D.A.

I walked with Tyler to his car. That was one of the benefits of dating an older man. Tyler had a license and wheels.

"Your place or mine?" I asked as Tyler maneuvered out of his parking spot.

"Yours. I need Percy to look at a piece I'm writing."

"I think you date me just for access to my uncle."

"Hardly, you forget I knew your uncle long before you moved to Bloomington. Besides, there's plenty about you to like. I don't need any added incentive."

I checked out Tyler as he drove. I wondered what sex would be like with him. We hadn't done it yet. We hadn't been dating very long and Tyler said he didn't want to move too fast. For my part, I wanted to go all the way as soon as possible, but I was part of a couple now. Our relationship wasn't all about me. It was tough dating. I wasn't used to accommodating someone else. It was kind of a pain, as was having to make plans instead of just doing what I wanted. There were plenty of benefits too. I planned to take advantage of one of them as soon as Tyler stopped the car.

"Looks like Dad is here," Tyler said a few minutes later when he pulled up in front of the home I shared with my uncle.

Tyler's dad was dating my uncle. It made for an interesting situation.

Tyler began to get out of the car but I grabbed his arm and pulled him toward me. It was time for one of the benefits of having a boyfriend. I kissed Tyler on the lips, grasped the back of his head, and shoved my tongue into his mouth. We sat there and made out for a good five minutes before our lips parted. Tyler was breathing a little hard when we pulled apart. I wanted to jump on him, but I managed to control myself.

"Dylan is right about one thing," Tyler said.

"What's that?"

"Bad boys are hot."

I laughed. We climbed out of the car and headed inside.

I hadn't lived with my uncle long. Things were very rocky between us at first. Only recently had our relationship smoothed out. I hate to admit it, but the trouble was my fault. I had issues. When I first moved in and for a long time after, I didn't think Percy really wanted me. I expected to be sent to a foster home at any moment. I knew now I had been wrong about a lot of things. I was a messed-up kid, but Percy didn't give up on me. Tyler helped me deal with my issues too. I almost laughed when I thought of how much Tyler and I had hated each other such a short time ago. Who would have thought then that we'd one day be friends and would even be dating?

Percy and Daniel were sitting on the couch when we walked in. I think they'd been making out. I did not want to know. They were both nearly forty! The thought of old guys making out was just... eww!

"Hey, guys," Percy said.

"Hey."

"How was school?"

"Fine," I answered.

"No one-word answers, Caspian. How was school?"

I rolled my eyes.

"My classes were boring, my hamburger at lunch was made mostly of cardboard, and I tried to talk Dylan out of suicide."

Percy looked alarmed for a moment.

"Not suicide like you are thinking; He's got it bad for this new boy who is a bad ass and looks like he wants nothing more than to rip Dylan's head off."

"Dylan, of course, is oblivious to the danger and all warnings," Tyler added.

"Dylan...that's the boy who..." Daniel shook his head and laughed.

"Yeah, he's the one who hit on you and Percy at my birthday party," Tyler said.

"Talk about poor taste," I said.

"Hey!" Percy and Daniel said together. I loved messing with them.

"What's to eat?" I asked.

"Hamburgers made from cardboard after that remark," Percy said.

"Okay, I'm sorry. You're not totally hideous."

"I just love Caspian's apologies," Percy said to Daniel.

"How about pizza and a salad?" Percy suggested.

"Excellent," Tyler said.

"If there is pepperoni on it, I'm in," I said.

Percy looked at Daniel, and he nodded.

"I'll order a couple of pizzas in a while. It's a little early for supper."

"My stomach disagrees," Tyler said.

"Mine too."

"Okay, okay. I'll order now. Kids!"

"Young men," Tyler said.

"Kids," Percy retorted.

"Be fair, Tyler," I said. "When you're as old as Percy, everyone under 25 seems like a kid."

"Go to your room," Percy said, pretending to be angry.

"Okay, but I'm taking Tyler with me."

"Keep the door open," Daniel called out as we headed for my bedroom.

My bedroom was unfortunately close to the living room so there was almost no privacy with the door open. Why did parents always have to ruin anything that was fun?

"Let's get some homework done," Tyler said.

"Let's forget the homework and make out."

"Mmm. You are tempting me to the Dark Side. Let's make out for five minutes and then do homework."

Before I could argue in favor of making out for ten minutes, Tyler pressed his lips to mine. I slipped my tongue into his mouth and we picked up where we left off in the car. As we were making out, I slipped my hands up under Tyler's shirt. I ran my hands over his smooth abdomen and up onto his chest. I felt him all over. I wanted to pull his shirt off, but I didn't think he'd let me, especially with his dad and Percy in the next room. I grinned mischievously and tried to lift his shirt. Just as I thought, he stopped me, but he made out more fiercely than ever.

It was about ten minutes before we parted and only then because we heard footsteps coming. Tyler quickly sat down on my bed and I dropped into the desk chair. It wasn't because we'd get into trouble for making out, but we were both noticeably aroused.

I thought the front of my jeans might rip and I had felt Tyler's bulge pressing into me as we tongue-wrestled. That's not the kind of thing you want a dad or uncle to see. The footsteps retreated and we were left in peace.

"Okay, now we get some homework done."

"Aw, man!"

Tyler gave me "the look." He gave it to me whenever I didn't want to do something that I really did have to do. He knew I'd crumble.

"Okay! Okay! Why is it you can make me do things that Percy can't?"

"Because you don't make out with your uncle."

"Oh, God! Eww! Bad mental image! Eww! Eww!"

Tyler laughed. I quickly shifted to thoughts of chocolate cake. I always kept an image of chocolate cake in my mind for times like this when I desperately needed to get a particularly disturbing image out of my head.

"I will get you for that," I warned.

"I shall live in fear," Tyler said, his bright eyes shining.

I lunged and grabbed him before he could escape. I got him in a headlock.

"Say you're sorry."

"Never!"

"Say it!"

"I cannot be broken!"

Percy stuck his head in. From the other room, it probably sounded like we were getting it on. I wish!

"Oh, hey," I said, releasing Tyler. "I was trying to make Tyler do his homework. I think we should get it done, but all he wants to do is make out."

"Uh-huh," Percy said. "The pizza should be here in about fifteen minutes." Percy left us alone again.

"You're such a liar," Tyler said, but then laughed.

"Do you think he bought my story?"

"Did he sound like he bought it? Percy isn't stupid, Caspian. When have you ever wanted to do homework?"

"Okay, we'll do some now. Happy?"

"Yes."

I smiled as I got to work. I smiled a lot now than Tyler and I were together. I didn't smile much at school because that would ruin my bad ass rep and once that's gone it's gone, but I smiled when I was alone and especially when I was alone with my boyfriend.

Mercifully, about fifteen or twenty minutes later, Percy called out that the pizza had arrived. I was starving. Tyler and I rushed into the kitchen. The table was already set with Percy's Blue Willow plates. Two steaming pizzas sat on the counter. Tyler and I both grabbed a plate.

One of the pizzas was double-pepperoni. Yes! The other had pepperoni, but also sausage, pineapple, and green peppers. I went for the double-pepperoni. Tyler got a slice of both.

Percy was all smiles when he sat down. He loved it when we were all together. I looked at Tyler's dad. He was smiling too. Tyler told me Daniel looked exactly like him when he was Tyler's age. I had a preview of what Tyler would look like he was really old. Daniel was still kind of hot, so Tyler would still be looking good for years. Percy was no preview at all of how I would look. We looked nothing alike. We didn't even have the same color hair.

The pizza was great and even the salad wasn't bad, although I'm not fond of eating green stuff. Percy and Daniel each had a couple of slices of pizza, and Tyler and I finished the rest.

Percy moaned about having to put his roadster in storage for the winter. I will admit the Shay was a cool car. It looked just like a 1929 Model A Roadster, but it was built in 1980. Whenever we rode around town, people gawked at it. I kind of missed the car too although I wish he had a Lotus or at least a Corvette instead.

After we finished eating, Daniel stood.

"I have to get going. I take it you're staying here for a while?" he asked Tyler.

"Yeah. I have something I want Percy to look at and I want to hang out with Caspian."

"Sure, stick me with babysitting," my uncle said.

I glared at Percy, but my bad ass rep didn't go anywhere with him.

Percy stood up, and then he and Daniel kissed.

"My eyes! My eyes! Old guys kissing! Yuck!" I said.

"Who are you calling old?" Percy said.

"You! You've got to be sixty, right? Or is it seventy?"

"It's time for a post-natal abortion," Percy said, moving toward me. I wasn't quite sure what that meant, but Percy pretended to reach for my throat.

"Hey! Hands off my boyfriend!" Tyler said.

Percy backed off but still eyed me as if he might lunge at any moment.

"Just remember. I know where you sleep," Percy said.

"I'm sorry. You don't look a day over fifty."

Percy shot me a fake evil glare, and I laughed.

"I'll see you later," Daniel said and kissed Percy again.

When Daniel had gone, Percy sat back down.

"How are you two doing?" he asked.

"I think I might be pregnant," I said.

Tyler's eyes widened, and he choked on his Coke. It took several moments for him to stop sputtering and coughing. Percy looked at me and then at my boyfriend.

"We haven't!" Tyler said. "I mean...not that he could...but we haven't, uh..."

Percy grinned. He enjoyed seeing Tyler flustered.

"I wasn't referring to that aspect of your relationship, but while we're on the subject..." Percy began.

"I have homework," I said. I got up and tried to make a break for it.

"Sit!"

I sat back down.

"Please, no sex talk. I know about the birds and the bees," I said.

"Obviously not if you think you might be pregnant."

"Ha-ha. Old people should not try to be funny."

"You call me old again and I'm putting icy hot in your shorts."

"Oww!" I said, fighting the instinct to cover my crotch. Tyler looked as if the statement gave him pain too. "Save me, Tyler. Call Child Protective Services."

Tyler gave me his "whatever" look.

"There is something we need to discuss," Percy said.

"Uh-oh," Tyler said.

"I just want to talk to you about using protection."

"We haven't...um...done *that* much. Caspian and I plan to move slowly. We might...I mean...man, I can't talk about this. It's embarrassing," Tyler said.

"Let me make it easy then. I remember what it was like at your age so I'm not going to make any unrealistic demands, but I do think you should take things slowly."

"How slowly?" I asked.

"It would be best if you at least waited until you were sixteen, Caspian."

"I am NOT waiting ten months!" I said.

"Calm down, Caspian. I'm just saying take things slowly and consider the consequences. You both know how to be safe, right?"

"Yeah," Tyler said.

"Will you buy me some condoms?" I asked. I was hoping for some shock value.

"Yes, I will."

"And lube?"

"I will buy you some tomorrow, but I encourage you not to use them until...well until you're older."

"So, you're buying me condoms, but you don't want me to use them? I'm getting a conflicting message here."

"I know. I would like you to wait until you are eighteen, Caspian."

"Now it's eighteen? What happened to sixteen?"

"Let me finish. I would like you to wait, but I'm fully aware that's not very realistic, so I want you to be able to protect yourself and Tyler. And to further embarrass you, I'm going to require you to listen to a lecture on how to properly put them on because almost 20% of condom users don't do it right."

"Okay, I guess I get it."

"Just be careful guys and make your decisions ahead of time and not in the heat of the moment."

"Well, thank you for an uncomfortable and embarrassing talk, Percy," I said.

"Any time."

"Oh no! Once is enough."

"Wait 'til the condom talk. It'll be fun!"

Percy began to clean up.

"I want to get Percy's help on something. Why don't you do homework while I'm talking to him and then I'll join you," Tyler said.

"Everyone is against me!" I wailed.

"What horrible overacting," Percy said. "I hope you don't plan on a career in the theatre."

"Bite my...I mean shut up! Join me as soon as you can, Tyler. Maybe Percy will run out and buy condoms, and we can try one out later."

Tyler turned red and Percy pointed to the door. I laughed and left the kitchen.

I enjoyed giving my uncle a hard time, but I didn't push it too far. He had put up with a lot since I'd arrived and I do mean a lot. I don't really see why he didn't kick me out. I cringed when I thought of the things I'd said and done, but at the time I was so scared and lonely and in so much pain that I lashed out without thinking. Percy had been patient. He'd put up with all my crap when few others would. I knew I owed him and I just plain wanted to please him. Of course, I could only go so far. I had to be me. I laughed evilly at that thought.

I didn't like homework. That probably goes without saying. I thought schoolwork should remain in school. Most adults didn't bring their work home with them. There were exceptions, sure, but waiters and mechanics and people who worked in factories didn't have to bring work home so why did I? Percy did all his work at home, but he didn't count. He was writer. It's not like that's a real job. I laughed to myself when I thought of what Percy would have to say about that.

I set to work so I could get my homework finished as soon as possible. I wanted to be free to spend some time with Tyler before he had to go home. Tyler usually ripped through his homework, but he was a lot smarter than me. I suspected seniors didn't have as much homework as us freshman anyway. I almost couldn't believe I was dating a senior! I was one of the few freshmen dating a senior. I was a god!

I finished my homework before Tyler and Percy were done with whatever they were doing. When I walked into the kitchen, they were sitting at the table. Percy was marking up Tyler's manuscript and making notes as he gave Tyler pointers. They were both so engrossed in their work they didn't notice I'd entered.

I felt kind of jealous. The pair almost seemed like father and son. Tyler shared a love of writing with Percy that I couldn't. Percy and I didn't share any interests. He collected antiques, which was just junk to me. He was obsessed with Star Trek and I didn't care for it all that much. I did like his vintage car, but I was more into sports cars and muscle cars. Percy wasn't into anything cool like skating, or fighting, or good music. Percy and I didn't have that much in common, but Tyler and Percy did.

I got a Coke out of the refrigerator and tried to force my feelings of jealousy away. It was stupid to be jealous of my boyfriend and Percy. Tyler and his dad were close. Percy cared a lot about me. He sure wouldn't have put up with so much for so long if he didn't. It didn't matter than Percy and I didn't share many interests. We cared about each other and we were a family, so what was there to complain about?

I sat my Coke down and rubbed Tyler's shoulders. I gave him a massage partly to make him feel good and partly because I wanted to touch him. I was not accustomed to having someone I could touch whenever I wanted. This whole boyfriend thing was new to me.

Tyler's muscles were tight, but they began to relax under my fingers. He even turned his head, leaned back, and gave me a quick kiss on the lips as he and Percy continued work.

"Mark Twain said that a writer should never use two words where one will do," Percy said. "You have to learn to adapt that to your own work, but it's good advice. Often, an awkward sentence can be made to flow by simplifying it. Using fewer works to say the same thing often does the trick."

"Isn't there a letter or something on the wall in our office that has something to do with Mark Twain?" I asked.

"Yes, it's a letter written by him. I bought it at an autograph auction."

"You mean that letter was really written by the guy who wrote *Tom Sawyer*? How can that be? The signature on it is something else... Samuel something?" I asked.

"Mark Twain was the pen name for Samuel Clemens. Writers often use pennames," Percy said.

"It sounds like lying to me," I said.

"Yes and no. Writers sometimes write under different names when they are known for one kind of writing but are publishing something that is different. It was well known in Twain's time that his real name was Samuel Langhorne Clemens."

"Langhorne?"

"Yes. Of course, Twain did often introduce himself as a professional liar," Percy said with a grin.

"Why?" I asked.

"He primarily wrote fiction. A work of fiction isn't true so one could say that it is a collection of lies. Therefore, a writer of fiction is a professional liar."

"Ha! I'm telling everyone from now on that my uncle is a professional liar. I think I'll leave out that you're a writer."

Percy just shook his head.

Percy and Tyler wrapped things up soon, and Tyler and I went back to my bedroom. I pulled Tyler to me and pressed my lips to his. We began making out and fell onto my bed.

Kissing Tyler made me want to do a whole lot more. If we had been somewhere alone, I would have ripped off his shirt and probably his pants too. I couldn't do that in my bedroom. I had argued that I should be allowed to keep my bedroom door shut when Tyler was over, but I didn't get anywhere. Daniel made Tyler keep his bedroom door open when I was over there too. It was a conspiracy to keep us from having fun.

At least Percy wasn't nosy. He didn't stick his head in every five minutes. He rarely stuck his head in my room when Tyler was over at all, unless it was to announce that dinner was ready or to ask if we wanted to go out with him or something like that. He did give me my privacy, but there was still only so much Tyler and I could do with the door open.

It was probably a good thing that I couldn't close my bedroom door. Tyler said we should go slowly and I didn't think I could do that if the door was closed. I needed sex so bad! The bulge in Tyler's pants told me he did too, but he had better control than me.

I guess there was something sexy about not going further than making out and groping. I guess sex wouldn't be as special if we just went straight to it. At least that's what I told myself, but I was hoping I could talk Tyler into doing a lot more soon. If I could get him alone somewhere, I had the feeling I could take things further. I just wanted to be careful not to go too fast and make him mad.

By the time Tyler had to leave I was so worked up I couldn't stand it. We were both getting aggressive and it was all I could do not to rip his clothes off. Tyler grinned at me when we pulled apart at last.

"You Goth boys sure are wild," he said.

"You have no idea."

I sighed when Tyler left, then yawned. It was getting kind of late. I decided to go to bed right then. If I went to sleep immediately I might have a good Tyler dream. If he thought I was wild making out with him on my bed, he'd be shocked by what we did with and to each other in my dreams!

I brushed my teeth, said "goodnight" to Percy, stripped, and climbed into bed. I lay there and thought about Tyler until I fell asleep.

# Chapter 2

I grinned the next morning when I woke up. I had dreamed about Tyler and it was a *very* good dream. I wondered if I should tell him about it. He would blush for sure.

By the time I finished breakfast, I decided to tell Tyler about my dream, but I chickened out when I slipped into the passenger side of his car and gave him a kiss. There was no way I could tell him the things we'd done in my dream. He might think I was a freak!

Still, it was a good dream and put a smile on my face all the way to school. I dropped the smile when I got out of the car. Bad asses cannot smile often or they cease to be bad asses.

The first thing Tyler and I spotted when we entered the school was Dylan standing by the water fountain drooling over Brayden. Dylan was so obvious it wasn't even funny. Okay, maybe it was funny.

Tyler and I reached Dylan just as he started to move toward Brayden. We each grabbed an arm and pulled him backward down the hall.

"What are you doing? Let me go! I was just getting ready to make my move!"

"You were just getting ready to commit suicide," I said.

"No way! I'm the master of seduction. Lemme go!"

"If you're this intent on getting beat up, I can slug you in the face a few times," I said. "At least I'll stop when you ask me to. Maybe."

"Hello?" Tyler said. "You can't be this oblivious to reality."

"In my reality, Brayden will be naked soon—with me!"

"Oh man! He needs professional help," I said.

"He's completely delusional," Tyler replied.

"I'm right here, you know! I can hear you!"

"You can hear, but I doubt you're listening," Tyler said.

"Come on, guys! We're friends."

I moved my free hand in a "so-so" gesture.

"Not funny, Caspian! We're friends, so let me go."

We were well down the hallway by then. Brayden was nowhere in sight. We released Dylan.

"Thanks to you two I'll have to wait who-knows-how-long for my next chance. You owe me!"

"Get that look out of your eyes, Dylan, because it's not going to happen," Tyler said.

"Come on, a three-way would be so hot!"

"No, Dylan," Tyler said.

A couple of boys near us wrinkled their noses and looked at us in disgust. I glared at them and lunged in their direction. They scurried off.

"You can't stop me. He's going to be mine," Dylan said as he walked away, no doubt in search of his current obsession.

"I say we start a pool. We can pick the hour and day that Brayden beats the crap out of Dylan," I said.

"In that case I'll take 11 a.m. today, but it's not funny, you know. Dylan is going to get himself hurt. If that kid even finds out what Dylan's been saying, he'll kick his ass."

Tyler's words were only too true. At the end of third period I turned the corner by Dylan's locker just in time to see Brayden slam Dylan back into the lockers. There wasn't a teacher in sight, but there were a few onlookers.

"Oh, crap," I said under my breath.

"What have you been saying about me?" Brayden asked, or rather yelled.

Dylan had the oddest look of both fear and desire upon his features.

"I just said I thought you were hot and you *are* hot."

I walked forward quickly. Dylan was about to get himself killed. Brayden punched the locker beside Dylan's head and a loud, metal clang rang out.

"Stop talking about me, faggot, and stay away from me!"

"You're really hot when you're angry," Dylan said. The kid was clearly suicidal.

Brayden drew back for a punch and this one wasn't going to be a warning shot. I launched myself at Brayden, grabbed his arm before he could kill Dylan, and shoved him away. I'm not sure who hit who first, but the next thing I knew we were beating the crap out of each other.

The fight only lasted a few seconds. I felt myself bodily jerked backward. I struggled until I realized a teacher had me. Brayden and I were marched straight to the office, still glowering at each other.

We sat on opposite sides of the waiting room. I was tempted to jump up and punch Brayden in the face. I was so mad I wanted to rip his head off and piss down his neck. I kind of lost it when I was angry. I'd been told I had anger control issues.

Brayden glared at me and I glared right back. I muttered under my breath. Brayden flipped me off and I was up out of my chair in a flash. He jumped to his feet as I lunged for him.

"Stop!"

We both looked around. Principal Maclaine stood in her office door and she was not happy.

"Both of you, in my office, now," she said firmly and sternly.

Once inside, she pointed to two chairs in front of her desk. They were so close together Brayden and I were nearly touching. We glared at each other as we sat down. Both of us were just itching to fight. No matter what, I planned to get him after school.

"I want to hear why this happened," Principal Maclaine said.

Brayden and I began talking at once.

"One at a time. Caspian first. You will get your chance next, Brayden."

"I had to step in because *he* was about to punch Dylan in the face."

"I was not, but he would have deserved it if I did. The faggot was..."

"Brayden, that is not an appropriate word to use here or anywhere else and I told you that you would get your chance to speak."

Brayden snapped his mouth shut and glared at me while shaking his head.

"Dylan isn't very strong and he's not a fighter. *He* was picking on him and was going to punch him."

"Brayden?" Principal Maclaine asked.

"That kid has been saying stuff about me. He was going around telling people he thought I was hot and that he *wanted* me. Kids were laughing behind my back! I told him to knock it off. I wasn't going to hit him. I only wanted to scare him."

"Liar!"

"Shut up!"

"Quiet!"

We both looked back to the principal.

"I'm giving both of you Saturday detention for fighting."

"That's not fair!" I shouted.

"He attacked me!" Brayden yelled.

"If either of you raise you voice again, I will double your punishment."

I closed my mouth and gave Brayden the nastiest look I could manage. He shot a similar look right back at me.

"I am being very lenient. This is your second day here, Brayden and already you've been involved in a fight. Caspian, this isn't the first time you've been hauled into my office for fighting."

She was right. I knew I was standing on shaky ground.

"If you can't get along, I want the two of you to stay away from each other."

"I'll be glad to stay away from *him*," Brayden said.

I was steaming, mostly because that's what I wanted to say and Brayden beat me to it.

"I will be happy to stay away from him, but what about Dylan? Am I supposed to just stand there while some punk attacks him for *no* reason?"

"You..." Brayden began, but the principal held up her hand.

"I will be speaking to Brayden momentarily about Dylan, but if you do witness something you think is wrong, you are to report it to a teacher and not take matters into your own hands."

I nodded.

"Your uncle will be receiving a letter about this incident, but I suggest you tell him yourself first."

"You're not going to call him in?"

"I don't think it's necessary this time, do you?"

I shook my head.

"You may go now, Caspian. Stop by the nurse and get an icepack for your eye."

While Principal Maclaine wasn't looking, I scratched the side of my head with my middle finger. Brayden ground his teeth. He wanted to return the gesture so badly, but it was already too late. Principal Maclaine was looking right at him. I shot Brayden a smirk as I departed just to piss him off.

I headed for the nurse's office and told her student helper the principal sent me for an icepack. I hissed when I applied it to my face. I hadn't realized until then that Brayden had gotten in such a good punch.

I went to the restroom to check out my face in the mirror. Yep, my left eye was already turning black. That really set me off. Brayden didn't have a mark on him and I'd landed some good punches. I should have gone for his face instead of his stomach.

The bell rang as I walked to my locker. The halls filled with kids rushing in all directions. I dumped my backpack and waited on my boyfriend. He wasn't long in coming. Tyler slowed as he neared me.

"What happened?" he asked, looking just a little scared.

"I got in a fight. Sorry, but I ruined the pool for you. You were really close on the time, but I stopped Brayden before he could beat the crap out of Dylan."

"Are you okay? Is Dylan okay?"

"I'm fine except I have detention. Dylan was untouched. I got Brayden before Brayden could get Dylan."

"I guess it couldn't be avoided?" Tyler asked doubtfully.

"Well...maybe I could have just pushed in between them, but Brayden was getting ready to pound him. I lost my temper and well..."

"I get the picture."

"Percy is going to be pissed," I said.

"He's not going to be happy, but at least you did have a good reason this time. Come on. Let's go eat. I'm starved!"

Tyler and I went through the lunch line together, as we usually did. Lunch didn't look too bad: grilled cheese, chili, salad, apple wedges, and vanilla cake.

"Rough sex?" Caleb asked as we sat down.

"I wish," I said. "I..."

That's as far as I got. Dylan came out of nowhere and hugged me.

"My hero!"

"Get off me, homo!"

"Caspian saved my life!"

"Only because I was bored and had nothing better to do," I said.

"I'm getting a psychic image," Tyreece said. "Dylan ignored all warnings as well as common sense and put the moves on the boy he spotted yesterday. The kid reacted violently and Caspian had to save Dylan's skinny butt."

"That's not psychic. It's what we all knew would happen, except for Caspian saving Dylan," Jesse said.

"He saved me!"

Dylan kissed my cheek before I could stop him.

"You! Sit!" I commanded, pointing at Dylan and then at his usual seat across from me. "If you kiss me again, I'll punch you in the face!"

I glared at Dylan. It took all the control I could muster not to slug him. He was so infuriating.

"Dylan, sit down or we'll have to rescue you from your rescuer and perhaps his boyfriend too," Caleb said.

I glanced at Tyler sitting beside me. He found the whole thing amusing.

"What did you learn from the events of today, Dylan?" Tyreece asked.

"That Caspian is ferocious!"

"Everyone knows that. He's borderline psycho. I mean, what did you learn about going after boys who are not interested in you?"

"That I'm going to have to put a lot more effort into getting Brayden than I thought!"

"Brayden?" Tyreece asked.

"That's the kid who wanted to rearrange Dylan's face," I said.

"So, you learned nothing," Tyreece said.

"I learned that Brayden will be aggressive and dominant when we have sex! I bet Caspian is just like that. He is, isn't he, Tyler?"

The question caught Tyler with a spoonful of chili half way to his mouth. I was glad it was only half way. He might have choked on it if Dylan had asked the question five seconds later. My boyfriend turned completely red.

"Yeah, Tyler. Is your little freshman boy toy wild in bed?" Tyreece asked, a mischievous grin turning up the corners of his mouth.

"I think that's why he's into younger guys," Caleb said. "He likes them wild."

Tyler looked like he wanted to hide under the table.

"I think he dates Caspian because he can get him into movies for half price," Jesse said.

"Hey!" I said.

"I just wonder if Caspian is tall enough to ride on the rollercoaster at the fair," Tyreece said.

I gave Tyreece my evil glare.

Tyler put his arm around me.

"You're all just jealous because my boyfriend is so hot and sexy."

"Yes, he is," Dylan said dreamily.

"Yeah. Yeah. Hot and sexy, but you never answered the question. Is Caspian wild in bed?" Tyreece said.

"You're just a little too obsessed with our sex life, aren't you, Tyreece?" Tyler asked. "Thinking about experimenting with a guy or are you just not getting any?"

"Point to Tyler!" Caleb said.

"Who says I haven't experimented already?" Tyreece said.

Dylan jerked his head in Tyreece's direction.

"Don't even think about it, Dylan."

I doubted Tyreece had ever messed around with a guy, but I wasn't surprised he had the balls to say he did. I'd always liked Tyreece. I admired his strength and courage.

"I'll be thinking about it all day," Dylan said. "If you ever wanna experiment, Tyreece…"

"Do not go there," Tyreece warned.

"I have detention thanks to you, Dylan," I said. "I should kick your ass for getting me into trouble."

"Wouldn't it have been easier to just let Brayden do the ass kicking?" Jesse said when he could free himself from his *Details* magazine. "That would have eliminated the middle man."

"If anyone is going to kick Dylan's ass, it's going to be me," I said.

Dylan grinned. He almost looked as if he liked the idea. He was a very odd boy.

My black eye drew a lot of attention and reinforced my bad ass reputation. Eyewitness accounts enhanced my rep further. Word was spreading that I'd jumped Brayden. Rumor took things even further. The story that made its way back to me was that I'd tried to kill Brayden and would have done so if a teacher hadn't pulled me off him. I rather liked that rumor. Of course, many now assumed that I stepped in to protect Dylan because he was doing me sexual favors. I would have been concerned about that rumor if I wasn't out, but I made no secret about dating Tyler. Why should I? It was no one's business who I dated. I was on the receiving end of some nasty glares now and then, but I glared right back. In some ways, being out further boosted my bad ass rep because it took courage to be publicly out. Even Dylan was respected for being out and he flitted around like a fairy.

I laughed for a moment, but then stopped myself when someone noticed. I'd pictured Dylan flying around with little wings and a magic wand and the image was just too funny. I wasn't going to tell him about it because knowing him he'd show up at school dressed like a fairy. He had the courage and the lack of common sense to do it.

Near the end of the day, Brayden and I passed each other in the hallway. I scowled at him. It was his fault I had Saturday detention. Brayden shot me a nasty look. Some kids hurried to get out of the way because they didn't want to get caught in the middle of round two. It was like a scene in a Western where everyone clears off the street because there is going to be a gunfight.

Other kids slowed down hoping for a fight. I would've liked nothing better than to punch Brayden in the face, but then I'd be in real trouble. Brayden was too smart to go after me so we passed each other and went on.

I noted a few guys looking at me fearfully as I made my way to classes. Despite getting detention, getting in a fight was a good thing. It was just what I needed to secure my bad ass image. There probably weren't many guys brave enough to mess with me. My rep protected me from anyone who wanted to cause trouble because I was gay. It protected Tyler too because I'd go after anyone who tried to hurt him. I'd seen guys eye us with distaste and then look away fearfully after I glared at them. Yeah, being a bad ass was worth a lot in high school. I didn't have to work at it too hard. It wasn't in my nature to take crap off of anyone and I'd rather use my fists than words to settle disagreements.

Tyler drove me home after school and we made out for a few minutes in the car before I went in to face my doom. Getting in trouble didn't bother me much, but I knew Percy would be disappointed. I didn't like to disappoint someone who had done so much for me.

I found my uncle writing in his office. He looked up and stopped typing the moment he spotted my black eye. He stood up quickly.

"Are you okay?"

"I'm fine, but, uh... I have detention."

Percy led me into the living room and we sat down on a couch.

"Tell me what happened."

I told him about Brayden and Dylan and the teachers having to pull us apart. I told him what Principal Maclaine said.

"Are you disappointed in me?" I asked.

"No. I'm not. I don't like you fighting, but I think it's admirable you stepped in to protect someone who is weaker."

"You got mad when I got in trouble for fighting before."

"You picked a fight for no reason the last time. This situation is different. It would have been better to let a teacher handle it, but..."

"There were no teachers around!"

"Then, I'd say you did the right thing."

"I still got detention."

"Look at it from the principal's point of view. You've been in her office for fighting before and she cannot allow fighting. She may even agree you did the right thing, but that doesn't change the fact you were in a fight *again*."

"Saturday detention sucks."

"No good deed goes unpunished."

"What's that supposed to mean?"

"It means that doing something good, like protecting Dylan, often has a cost."

"Well, it shouldn't."

"I agree, but that's the way it is. I don't think you would have done things any differently if you had known for sure you'd get detention."

"No, I didn't want to see Dylan get hurt. I wasn't worried about getting punished. The only thing that worried me after the fight is that I'd let you down."

"Standing up for someone who needs you is always the right thing to do. There is no way you can let me down by doing that. I want you to try to solve problems without resorting to violence, but sometimes violence is a necessity."

"Thanks, Percy."

We stood up and hugged. I held on for a few extra moments. I missed my mom and dad a lot, but knowing Percy cared about me helped. It had taken me a long time to trust that he did care about me, but now that I did I felt a lot better about many things.

# Chapter 3

Saturday detention sucks. Just getting up early on a Saturday sucks. Not riding to school with my boyfriend sucks. Tyler offered to drive me, but why should his Saturday morning be ruined too? Percy drove me. Like most old people, he gets up early anyway.

I'd been in Saturday detention before. The last time was for picking a fight with two bigger guys. I did it because I thought Percy didn't really care about me. I was expecting him to toss me out on the street eventually so I figured I'd get myself suspended and get it over it. That didn't work out like I'd planned. I got detention instead of a suspension and Percy saw right through my plan. He knew exactly why I did it, which proves he's not as dumb as I thought he was. I'm not sorry I did it. It allowed me to figure out that Percy really did care about me. I figured I had detention coming for picking a fight. I guess I understood why I had it this time too, but it sure wasn't fair.

Saturday detention was in the cafeteria. On this Saturday there were five inmates: Brayden, a girl who looked capable of murder, two burnouts who had been harassing Dylan, and me. Four out of five of us were here because of Dylan. I really wanted to blame him, but then he didn't ask to be harassed or attacked. I guess he did ask for it in a way. He could've toned down his gayness a bit and he certainly could quit checking out boys so openly, but why should he? Dylan was just being Dylan. If he toned his gayness down, he wouldn't be Dylan anymore. What right did any of us have to ask him to stop being himself? I did think he should stop being so obvious when he was checking out guys, but that was just my opinion. I guess if I had to be in detention, standing up for Dylan was a worthwhile reason for being there. That didn't mean I wasn't going to slug him if he kissed me again! There were better ways to show gratitude!

Coach Hawkins was the lucky teacher who had detention duty this week. He looked less happy to be there than any of us.

"You're here until noon," Coach Hawkins announced when I joined the others. "No talking, no cell phones, no getting out of your seat. You can read or study."

That was it. I was glad I didn't have any questions because the coach looked ready to bite the head off the first person that spoke. I didn't have any classes with Coach Hawkins so I didn't know if he was always so charming or if he was just royally pissed off that he had to get up early on Saturday morning too.

I'd brought along my backpack filled with books. I figured if I had to suffer by sitting there I might as well get all my homework done and work on book reports and other projects so I wouldn't have to do them later.

I got to work since I figured that would make the time go faster. It was a warm and sunny autumn day; the perfect kind of day to be outside. Why couldn't the weather be dismal today? Detention wouldn't be half as bad if it was cold and rainy out. I looked up and glared at Brayden. If it weren't for him I'd be outside, maybe making out with Tyler in a pile of leaves.

Brayden glared back at me, but I noticed something as I sat there working. Whenever I looked up, Brayden was either frowning into a book or glaring at one of the other inmates with baleful hatred. It wasn't just me he had it in for; he didn't like anyone.

Detention was BORING! I think I would've rather been locked up in a cell somewhere. Maybe those convicted of minor crimes should be sent to detention instead of jail. I bet there would be a lot less crime. The silence in the cafeteria was deafening. I had an overpowering urge to scream just to see if my voice still worked.

I became adept at watching Brayden over the top of my book without him knowing it. While I was delving into freshman English and math, I observed the new bad boy of North. Sometimes, he looked like he wanted to beat the crap out of everyone in the room. He even gazed at his books as if he wanted to pummel them. Sometimes, he looked so dejected I almost pitied him. Once, I even saw him wipe away a tear. What was that about? Sure, detention was lethally boring, but I couldn't imagine anything making that kid cry. I was so stunned I stared at him and he caught me. I caught just a glimmer of fear in his eyes before he glared at me. He looked quickly down at his book and proceeded to ignore me.

I eyed the pair who had harassed Dylan and shot them a threatening glare. They knew I was in for attacking Brayden, and they looked away fearfully. I smiled to myself. If they messed with Dylan again, I'd give them a good scare. They thought they were bad, but they were amateurs compared to me. I wasn't going to let anyone pick on Dylan. If someone was going to punch him, it was going to be me.

Great! Where did that come from? What was it about Dylan? Half the jocks protected him. Well, I knew what *that* was about. Maybe I shouldn't be so quick to protect him. Everyone would think I was looking out for him because he was blowing me. Then again, what did I care what everyone thought? I was going to do what I wanted and if others didn't like it they could go screw themselves. I laughed quietly but evilly. I enjoyed being me.

Brayden and I stayed well away from each other as we exited the cafeteria at noon and walked outside to wait on our rides. A woman that I guessed was his mom pulled up in only a couple of minutes. I saw her caress Brayden's cheek as soon as he got in the car. I bet he'd hate it if he knew I saw that! I caught a glimpse of his mom's face. She looked sad and worried, probably because Brayden was a problem child. I was willing to bet this would not be his last Saturday detention.

I grinned when Tyler pulled up. I hopped in his car and we took off.

"You're much better looking than who I was expecting," I said.

"I thought we would celebrate your release by going to McAlister's Deli. I'm buying."

"Thanks, but I just got out of detention, not prison."

Tyler drove us to the eastside and parked at the west end of Eastland Plaza across the street from College Mall. I had never been to McAlister's before, but I'd eat anything, except sushi. What was up with eating raw fish? I heard some of it was cooked, but it still looked nasty to me. As far as I was concerned, sushi was nothing but fishing bait.

I liked McAlister's as soon as we walked in. There was lots of brass and wood and it was all shiny and new. We walked up to the counter and looked at the menu. There was so much stuff! We stood there a good long time in indecision before we stepped up to the counter.

Tyler ordered a grilled chicken Caesar salad. I went for a "choose two" and picked chicken tortilla soup and half of a sweet Chipotle sandwich. We both ordered Cokes and took them to a table while we waited on our orders.

I loved going out with Tyler. He was much more than just a guy I wanted to get naked with. He was a friend. Sometimes, he felt more like a friend than a boyfriend. I don't mean that I didn't care about him or desire him. He just seemed more like a best friend than anything else. Maybe that's the way it was supposed to be. I didn't know. I'd never had a boyfriend before.

"So how was detention?" Tyler asked.

"Extremely boring! I did finish all my homework, as well as the next book report I had due and I even started on the next book report after that."

"Good, then we have the whole day to do whatever we want. I finished most of my work last night and did the rest this morning before heading over to your house to do yard work."

"I'm glad Percy pays you to do the yard instead of making me do it," I said.

"Well, I was his lawn boy before you came along. He overpays me. I kind of like doing it too."

"You like mowing the lawn and raking leaves? You are a sick, sick puppy, Tyler."

Tyler just giggled.

"I noticed something when I was in detention. Four out of five of us were there because of Dylan."

"He is a mover of events," Tyler said.

"Maybe we can have him fixed and he won't be so boy crazy."

"Good idea, but I don't think he'd go for that."

"Someone is going to mess him up bad someday. He's going to leer at the wrong boy and POW!"

"He already looked at the wrong boy, but you were there to save him. You're his hero now."

"Great. That's just what I need," I said rolling my eyes.

"Dylan is mostly harmless. He's just... Dylan."

"I think he's his own species—homo over-the-topus."

"I'm glad you stood up for him. I'm just sorry you got hurt doing it."

"This," I said, pointing to my black eye. "This is nothing. It's the detention I didn't like."

"At least that's over."

"Thankfully!"

Our orders arrived. My soup came with long, thin tortilla chips. Our waiter, a cute college boy with curly brown hair returned in a minute with a big chocolate chip cookie for both of us. He smiled and winked.

"I think he's one of us," Tyler said.

"Let's tell Dylan about him and he'll eat here all the time."

The food was delicious. I wished the cafeteria food at school could be so good. It would almost make school worthwhile.

As we were eating, I looked up to see none other but Brayden enter McAlister's. This time he was with both his parents. He spotted me sitting with Tyler, but he didn't glare. He just looked sad.

"There's Brayden," I said.

"Dylan's crush? The boy you fought?"

"Yeah, just going up to the counter."

Tyler turned and checked him out.

"Yeah, I've seen him at school. So that is the infamous Brayden. Dylan is right. He does have a hot ass."

"Agreed. That kid confuses me."

"Well, you are blond," Tyler teased.

"Funny! I was watching him some in detention. He looked so unhappy."

"Well, he was in detention, not visiting Disney World."

"Yeah, but I even saw him shed a tear once and I'm sure that wasn't because he was stuck in detention."

"Oh."

"Yeah, and he was looking at everyone in detention as if he hated them. I expected him to give me that look but not the others. He doesn't even know them."

Tyler looked at Brayden again, this time with more compassion.

"Don't," I said.

"What?"

"Don't take him on as a project."

"I'm just looking!"

"Yeah, but it's the way you were looking. You used to look at me like that when you kept coming over and trying to sit with me and be nice."

"Well, that worked out okay, didn't it?"

"Better than okay, but that's not the point. I don't want him hurting you."

"You didn't hurt me and you're far more dangerous than he is."

"Thanks, but you don't know that for sure. Maybe he's a sociopath. I'm just a bad ass."

"He looks lonely. Look at his parents. They look worried about him."

"Maybe they found the human hearts he hid in the freezer," I said.

"You're the one who pointed out he looked sad in detention."

"That doesn't mean I want you hanging around him. Everyone is sad sometimes."

"But look at him. He looks really..."

"Caleb warned me about you," I said.

"What?"

"He said you can't help but take a lost puppy home. I didn't much care for being referred to as a puppy when he said it, but I can see it's true. Don't get involved. There is something seriously wrong with that boy."

"That's what everyone told me about you," Tyler said with a grin.

"They were right, too. You were in danger. If things had played out just a little differently..."

"But, they didn't and here we are."

"Stay away from him. Please? For me?"

I wasn't good at puppy dog eyes, but I did my best.

"Okay. For *you*."

I grinned.

"I'll give you a special reward later, if you'll let me," I said. Just speaking the words made me breathe harder.

"What reward?"

"Let's just say that we will have to be alone and leave it at that."

Tyler arched an eyebrow and I wiggled mine.

I saw Brayden watching us while pretending he wasn't. He seriously looked like he was about to cry. I was so shocked I had to fight not to stare at him. His parents kept up a pleasant conversation as if trying to draw him out, but it wasn't working.

I forced myself not to think about Brayden. I had just warned Tyler off and here I was focusing on him. I suppose it didn't matter. I wasn't getting involved. The only likely interaction between Brayden and me was a fistfight, and I intended to avoid that if possible. I did not want another Saturday detention.

Tyler and I talked and laughed and ate. Despite the presence of Brayden, I wasn't worried about my bad ass persona. I figured punching him repeatedly in the gut was enough to preserve my rep with him. I thought he might point me out to his parents, but he didn't.

Tyler and I went to the mall next. I made the ultimate sacrifice and went inside Hollister with Tyler. I would not have been caught dead wearing any of those clothes, but I had to admit Tyler looked sexy in the shirt he tried on. Best, he tried it on right there by the rack and I got to see his sexy body. He wasn't built, but he had some nice muscles. I'd run my hands up under his shirt before, but I liked seeing what I'd been feeling.

Tyler made his purchase and I escaped from preppy land. Next, he dragged me into Yankee Candle. I had to admit they smelled good, but candles??? I had a feeling Dylan would make a better shopping companion for Tyler than me, but I was happy as long as I was with my boyfriend. I loved the sound of that—boyfriend.

Tyler popped open lids and had me smell scents like Autumn Leaves, Buttercream, and Garden Sweet Pea. The Buttercream smelled good enough to eat. It smelled just like the icing on a birthday cake.

The mall was fairly crowded and we spotted a lot of kids from school. I was glad we weren't trying to hide our relationship because it would have been impossible. We saw Caleb's girlfriend, Brittany, pushing him in his wheelchair. I wasn't sure if she was really his girlfriend, but she acted like a girlfriend.

Caleb pointed us out and Brittany waved.

"What are you doing here?" Tyler asked.

"Looking for racing stripes for my wheelchair. We're *shopping*, Tyler," Caleb said as if Tyler was an idiot. Caleb turned to me. "I don't think your boyfriend is too bright."

"At least he's cute," I said.

"Hey, no ganging up on me, especially you two!"

"Caspian said you're cute. That's a compliment, Tyler."

"Uh-huh. Be nice to me or I'll sabotage your brakes."

"See what kind of friends I have?" Caleb asked Brittany. "I'm nice enough not to mention that Tyler is dating a grade school boy and he threatens me."

"Hey! I happen to be a freshman. I'm not in grade school," I said.

"Oh yeah! That's right. It's just that you're so much younger than Tyler that I forget."

I growled at Caleb, but my anger was only an act. He was merely jerking us around.

"Boys," Brittany said, rolling her eyes.

"Want us to hang out with you and Caleb all day?" I asked.

"No!" Caleb and Brittany said together. Tyler and I laughed.

"We'll see you at school, Caleb. Later, Brittany," Tyler said.

We walked into Target where a couple of older ladies stared at me. I was used to being stared at. My spiked blond hair and Goth-look drew a lot of attention, especially from the older crowd. I thought about kissing Tyler right there in the store to shock the onlookers, but I didn't want to embarrass Tyler.

"I'm glad to see Caleb and Brittany working out so well. I knew they would if Caleb would just give himself a chance."

"What do you mean?" I asked.

Tyler suddenly looked slightly fearful.

"Well...his accident damaged his confidence with girls and Ashley didn't help. She dumped him while he was in the hospital."

"What a bitch."

"She's a social climber. She's obsessed with being popular. Anyway, after his accident, Caleb's girlfriend dumped him, he was stuck in a wheelchair, and he felt he was no longer in shape."

"No longer in shape? What did he look like *before* the accident? He's hot!"

"It was mostly in his head. He put on five pounds or so and said his abs weren't defined anymore. We had a little talk about that and I pointed out he was still extremely hot. Anyway, Brittany is good for him. I'm glad she's able to look past the wheelchair."

"I rarely see it. When I look at Caleb, I see his hot bod!" I said.

"You're going to make me jealous soon."

"Jealous of a straight boy? Come on. You notice hot guys *all* the time. I saw you drooling over that poster at the entrance to Hollister. I thought you were going to run over and lick it."

Tyler grinned.

We bought a big bag of peanut M&Ms and opened them up as we walked back into the mall. We strolled along talking, checking out cute boys, and browsing in store windows. I had never been that much into hanging out in a mall, but I enjoyed it now because I was with Tyler.

We returned to the car. I grabbed the door handle and pulled on it.

"It won't open."

"It's locked."

While Tyler unlocked his door and climbed in, I kept trying the handle and saying, "It won't open" over and over. It was the beginning of a running gag. From then on, whenever we were getting in the car, I'd keep trying the locked handle and saying "It won't open." It made Tyler laugh.

We stopped by McDonald's and got a couple of large dollar drinks, then Tyler drove me to Cascades Park. The park wasn't too far from home, but I'd never even been on Old State Road 37.

"I love driving through here," Tyler said as we descended into the valley and followed the narrow, twisting road.

Tyler drove us through a golden tunnel of autumn leaves. The trees hugged the road and their branches intertwined overhead. To our left clear water rushed through a rocky streambed. Here and there were small waterfalls. I understood how Cascades Park got its name.

The stream ran over a shallow paved area that led to a small parking lot. Tyler drove through the stream and we parked under the trees.

We had the park to ourselves. We walked north over a footbridge and then followed the stream closely. The streambed was mostly one big area of rock with large stones here and there. Whenever we neared one of the cascades, the water roared. The waterfalls were rarely more than three feet in height and more often only one, but I loved the sound of the running water.

"This is really cool," I said.

"I come here sometimes to walk and think. It's almost as if this valley is in the past."

Golden leaves flowed down the steam as we walked. It was cooler down in the bottom of the valley, but no wind stirred. We walked for a good, long while without speaking. I watched Tyler as he gazed at the trees and the stream. I appreciated the beauty of the place, but I had the feeling he saw a lot more than I did. I guess I was more of a city boy. I liked busy streets, cars rushing by, and people hurrying along. It if wasn't for the stream it would've been too quiet for me in this place. Tyler and I were so different.

"This would be a good place for a picnic," Tyler said.

"You mean eat *outside*?"

"That's the definition of a picnic, Caspian."

"I prefer my picnics in Taco Bell or KFC."

Tyler shook his head.

"What am I going to do with you?"

"Tie me up and..."

"You're beginning to sound like Dylan."

"Well, I like his ideas about some things, like sex."

"You don't like moving slow?"

"I guess there is something hot about making myself wait, but mostly it's just pure torture. We're both gay and we're dating. We need sex so why shouldn't we do it?"

"I'd feel...like I was taking advantage."

"How can you be taking advantage when I'm the one who wants to do it? I wanna get it on right now!"

"Calm down there, Tiger," Tyler said.

"Don't you want me?"

"Yeah, I want you. I just want to make sure I'm thinking with my head and not with my dick."

"You think way too much! We should be doing it *all the time*! This is when we're supposed to do it. We'll probably lose interest when we're really old. You'll be thirty in twelve years. You won't even want sex by then!"

"I'm pretty sure I will."

"Come on, we don't have to go all the way, but I need to do something or I'm going to explode."

"I don't know, Caspian."

"What's the point of dating if we can't have sex?"

"There is a lot more to dating than sex."

"Yeah, but sex is a big part of it. We've known each other for two months and all we've done is make out and feel a little."

"We've only been dating for two weeks. Most of that two months we barely had anything to do with each other."

"We still knew each other! Maybe we didn't get along so well..."

"We had a fist fight, Caspian."

"Yeah, yeah. I remember, but it's not like we just met. Come on, I need it."

Tyler looked uncertain. Words weren't getting me anywhere so I dropped the subject for a bit and steered us toward a shelter building made of stone. When we walked around the back and were out of view, I pulled Tyler to me and kissed him.

He resisted at first, but I slid my tongue in his mouth and he surrendered to me. I kept making out with him and then slowly let my hands roam up under his shirt. I took my time, kissing and caressing him, getting him good and worked up. I knew the effect I had on him. I could feel the evidence poking into my leg. Tyler needed it just as bad as I did.

I kept kissing Tyler and touching him. I ran my hand down over the front of his jeans and rubbed him there. As I suspected, he didn't have the willpower to stop me. I knew I wouldn't stop someone who was touching me there. Well, not if I found him attractive.

I kept rubbing and kissing Tyler deeply. I worked his belt loose and with one hand made my way through his button and zipper. It took me a few minutes, but as soon as I'd freed him I slipped to my knees and drew him in. Tyler moaned. There was no way he was going to stop me now.

I was consumed with the desire to do exactly what I was doing. There had to be some instinct at work. The force was too powerful to be anything else. Tyler ran his fingers through my hair as I gave into my desires.

Tyler did make me stop after a couple of minutes. He pulled away from me and I thought our lovemaking was over, but he ripped through the front of my jeans and soon I was the one moaning.

I didn't last very long after that. Tyler's lips and tongue felt too good.

"Tyler, I'm gonna…" That's as far as I got before I lost control. The only further warning was my loud moan.

When I finished, I dropped to my knees as Tyler stood. I picked up where I'd left off. I could feel Tyler's body reacting to the sensations I created for him. He whimpered and moaned. I felt powerful and wonderful at the same time. I was making Tyler feel better than he had probably ever felt before. I loved the control I had over him just then, but even more I loved my ability to give someone who meant so much to me so much pleasure. Tyler began to breathe faster and moan louder.

"Caspian, I'm close. I'm gonna…"

I didn't pull away. I kept right on going, just as Tyler had done. Tyler moaned loudly. I felt him throbbing in my mouth. I didn't care for the taste all that much, but swallowing was so hot!

We pulled up our jeans and looked around, but we were still alone. I guess we'd taken a fair risk, but there was no one around. I wasn't thinking about the possibility of getting caught while we were doing it. I wasn't thinking about anything but satisfying my overpowering need.

I gazed into Tyler's eyes, trying to figure out what he was feeling.

"You're not mad, are you?" I asked.

He shook his head.

"If I'm mad with anyone, it's with myself for being weak and not resisting you, but I don't think I'm even mad with myself. You were right. There's no good reason why we shouldn't have some fun. Just don't tell Percy or my dad."

"Awwww! I was going to run straight home and tell Percy all about it."

"Sure you were. Come on, let's walk some more. Before we know it, days like this will be gone."

"Then we can walk in the snow," I said. "What's with all the walking, anyway? Sitting in front of a TV playing a Wii is easier."

"You can't be as lazy as you pretend."

"But this is exhausting," I fake whined.

"You big liar."

I smiled in response.

"You are so different when we're alone," Tyler noted as we kept walking.

"You mean because I sometimes act goofy?"

"That and you're nicer."

"I don't act goofy around anyone unless I know and trust them. I don't act silly at school because it ruins my bad boy image."

"Oh, yes. Your all-important bad ass rep."

"I'd get in a lot more fights if I didn't act like a bad ass."

"How's that?"

"As I'm sure you know, I have a temper, sometimes a hair-trigger temper. I also have a little difficulty controlling my mouth."

"I've noticed."

"Most guys don't mess with me because they are afraid of me. I give them a glare and they scurry away, saving both of us a fight, detention, and possibly suspension."

"You could just control your temper and your mouth."

"If you were me, you'd know how hard that is. Sometimes, I get so angry I think I'm gonna explode!"

Tyler laughed and I knew why. I had a furious expression on my face because just thinking about getting mad made me mad. My anger passed quickly.

"So that's why you're nicer when you're with me?"

"That and I try to show you my good side because, well, I like you a lot."

Tyler smiled at me. I felt closer to him than ever.

# Chapter 4

Brayden kept to himself. He didn't initiate conversations and didn't talk much when someone else tried. I noticed that about him during our shared class and whenever I spotted him in the hallways. He wasn't quite unfriendly, but he wasn't friendly either. He wouldn't even have much to do with girls. I heard girls talking about Brayden a lot. Mostly, they spoke about how hot he was, but their interest was only increased by his lack of interest.

I didn't like Brayden. He would have attacked Dylan if I hadn't been there to stop him. I'd landed in detention because of him. I also thought he was a jerk. No, I didn't like him, but I did find him interesting. What interested me the most was that watching him was like looking into a mirror that reflected me in the not-so-distant past. I wasn't the same Caspian I had been a couple of months before or even just a couple of weeks ago. Much had changed in my life, but not all the pain had gone away. Some of it would never go away.

Percy was great, but I missed my mom and dad and I knew they were never coming back. I understood now that they didn't die in the fire that destroyed our home because I was gay, but they were still gone. The life that I had known had vanished. If it wasn't for Percy and Tyler, I'd still be the boy I had been when I arrived in Bloomington. I'm sure Brayden had not experienced the same tragedy I had, but everyone had their own problems. Everyone had their own pain. I didn't like Brayden, but I did feel just a little sorry for him.

I saw Brayden give Dylan the evil eye as they passed in the hallway. I balled my hands into fists and moved forward, but they passed without incident. Maybe I didn't feel sorry for Brayden. I didn't like homophobes. I didn't like them at all. If he made one move toward Dylan, I would kick his ass, detention be damned.

I noticed Tyler watching Brayden at lunch. Dylan followed Tyler's eyes to where Brayden was sitting alone.

"He's so, so sexy," Dylan said.

"Don't even think about it," I warned Dylan.

"What?"

"I know what you're thinking. That kid almost kicked your ass just because you drooled over him. Knock it off. I don't want to get detention again for stepping in to save your butt. I'm not sure I'll even bother next time."

"I wouldn't," Jesse said.

"You wouldn't because you might get your hair messed up," Caleb said then laughed.

"There is that, but I wouldn't step in to save Dylan again if he can't take a hint that Edward Cullen over there isn't interested," said Jesse.

"Ohhhh, maybe he's a vampire," Dylan said.

"If you start talking about *Twilight*, I'll beat the crap out of you myself," I warned. "I hate that shit. This is reality, Dylan. There are no vampires. Brayden didn't merely give you a hint he's not interested. He was going to rearrange your face. I'm telling you right now, you're on your own if he attacks you again."

Tyler gave me a look that said I needed to calm down. He was probably right, but it wasn't easy.

"It was really sweet of you to save me last time," Dylan said, looking at me dreamily.

"Don't start!" I warned. "I told you if you kiss me again, I'll slug you! Don't even try to hug me!"

"Whoa! Someone hasn't been getting any lately," Tyreece said.

Tyler and I looked at each other and grinned slightly. It was a big mistake.

"Well, well. Maybe I'm wrong," Tyreece said.

"Details! Give us details!" Dylan said.

"No details, please," Jesse said, looking up from his phone for a moment. I was willing to bet he was looking at pictures of himself.

"Yes, spare our hetero ears," Tyreece said.

Tyler had gone red, confirming for everyone that he had messed around.

"What did you guys do? Did you go all the way? Who was the bottom?"

"It's none of your business, Dylan!" I said.

"Oh! That means Tyler is the top," Caleb said.

"He is not! I mean, we didn't do that anyway, but...it's none of your business!"

"Calm down, Caspian," Tyler said.

"We're just jerking you around," Caleb said. "You know we're all homo-friendly or homos in Dylan's case."

"I am THE HOMO!" Dylan said too loudly.

"Like everyone doesn't already know that!" some kid called from a nearby table.

That made me laugh and much improved my mood.

"Come on. I *really* want to know," Dylan said.

"Dylan, that's personal. You don't...forget that. I was going to say you don't go around revealing the details of your sex life, but you would if anyone would listen," Caleb said.

"I'm very discreet."

"Only about who you do it with."

"Except Cory Caldemyer," Jesse said.

"That was a slip up and you guys promised to keep quiet about that," Dylan said.

"No one outside our group will ever know," Tyler said.

"I would never have guessed Cory is bi," Tyreece said.

"He's not," Dylan said.

"Are you sure?" Tyreece asked.

"Yeah, I'm sure. I offered to do other things with him and he wasn't interested. He's not even interested in a blow unless he's really horny and can't get a girl."

I could just imagine what the "other things" were. I noticed no one asked for details because Dylan would tell us all about what he wanted to do with Cory.

"So you're just a substitute girl for him," I said.

"Yeah," Dylan said, getting that dreamy tone in his voice again.

"He could just replace you with a blow-up doll," I said.

"I am MUCH better than a blow up doll. I'm MUCH better than any girl! I can..."

Jesse reached over and held his hand over Dylan's mouth. After a few moments he began to pull his hand away, but Dylan immediately tried to speak so Jesse put his hand over Dylan's mouth again. It became a game and soon Dylan was giggling too much to talk.

"On behalf of us all, thank you, Jesse," Tyler said.

I wondered if Dylan would back off Brayden or not. He had to realize the object of his obsession had no interest in him. We had all warned him to stay away from the kid. I'd even told him I'd let Brayden beat the crap out of him next time. I still had the feeling Dylan would keep after him. I think he'd still be after me if Tyler and I weren't dating.

I wondered if I could keep from intervening if Dylan got himself in trouble again. It would serve him right if he got his ass kicked, but Dylan had a puppy-like quality that made it hard to not want to protect him. I guess I'd decide when the time came. Maybe my warning that Dylan was on his own would discourage him. Ha! That was a laugh. All I could do was try.

Tyler drove me home after school like he always did. We made out in the car before I went in, which we also always did. I wished we could do in the car what we'd done at Cascades Park, but anyone walking by could've seen us. Perhaps if it was dark…

"You're on your own for supper tonight," Percy said when I entered the house.

"Abandoned again!" I said.

"Don't get too dramatic. Daniel and I are going out. Here is a twenty. You can order a pizza or go out if you want."

I liked how Percy treated me like an adult sometimes. He didn't order a pizza for me or tell me not to blow the money on junk food like I was a little kid. He also didn't humiliate me by suggesting I needed a babysitter. I was fifteen after all!

As soon as Percy left for his date, I called up Tyler. We made plans and he picked me up at six. He wanted to go to the Irish Lion for coddle. I wouldn't have known what that was, but Percy had taken me there and ordered coddle in a bread bowl. It was a kind of Irish stew. Since I had cash to pay my own way, I told Tyler the Irish Lion was fine although I would rather have just gone to Taco Bell.

There was nowhere to park downtown, which wasn't unusual. Tyler finally found a spot a few blocks west of the Irish Lion. Once again he was forcing me to walk! We headed for the pub.

"There's your buddy," Tyler said when we'd walked only a block and a half.

Up ahead I spotted Brayden just passing the Irish Lion. He hadn't seen us because his attention was focused on an alley. Suddenly, he darted into the alley. I heard a voice yell "faggot!" and then heard Dylan scream.

Tyler and I looked at each other for just a second and then bolted toward the alley too. I no longer had to wonder if I'd step in and save Dylan's butt if Brayden attacked him again. Dylan had stalked Brayden and now Brayden was kicking his ass for it. What the hell was wrong with Dylan any way? After we saved him, I was gonna kick his ass myself.

Tyler and I turned into the alley. We expected to find only Dylan and Brayden, but Justin Schroeder and Cory Caldemyer were there too. Dylan had really done it this time. Brayden was a bad ass and both Justin and Cory were big and built. Fists were flying and so much was going on at once it was hard to sort it out

I started to rush Brayden, but that's when I got the shock of my life. Brayden clocked Cory in the face and then pounced on Justin. Brayden wasn't attacking Dylan. He was after the other guys. He was about to get jumped from the back, so I darted in and slugged Cory in the face.

Justin was a wrestler and a good one at that. He had Brayden on his back in no time. I was too occupied with Cory to help, but Tyler tackled Justin and Brayden squirmed free. Cory clocked me in the face and I went down, but I came right back up and delivered a flurry of quick blows to his stomach, face, and chest. My quick temper had kicked in and I was one pissed-off kid. I didn't care about anything but hurting that bastard.

It took both Tyler and Brayden to handle Justin. I wasn't doing so well with Cory. The football player was about five inches taller and at least fifty pounds heavier and was all muscle. Cory slammed me into a brick wall. It hurt—bad. I was dazed. I saw a fist flying toward my face, but I couldn't move out of the way in time. Suddenly, a blond blur jumped on Cory from behind and threw him off balance. It was Dylan.

I shook my head and rushed Cory. Dylan was all over him, but he wouldn't last long. Dylan punched and scratched and kicked. He fought like a cat, but he was like a cat on a Doberman. I nailed Cory in the side of the face, then punched him in the stomach. I got a fist in the stomach for that and doubled over in pain, but Dylan was on Cory again. This time, Dylan kicked him right in the nuts.

That was it for Cory. He screamed in pain and dropped to the pavement. I staggered toward Tyler, but he and Brayden had Justin down and were pounding him with their fists.

"I give! I give!" Justin yelled.

Tyler and Brayden backed off. Brayden's eyes were smoldering. I could tell he didn't want to stop pummeling Justin and controlled himself only with extreme difficulty.

"Let's get the hell out of here," Tyler said.

The four of us limped out of the alley. Tyler led us in the direction of his car. I don't think any of us wanted to chance Cory or Justin coming after us. If there hadn't been four of us, we would've been dead meat.

I eyed Brayden as we walked along. Why the hell was he fighting to protect Dylan? Only a few days before, I'd had to jump on him to keep him from kicking Dylan's ass. Now, he'd come to Dylan's rescue? It made no sense at all.

"Thanks, guys," Dylan said when we reached Tyler's car. "I thought they were going to kill me."

Now that the fight was over, Dylan was visibly shaken. He was, in fact, trembling and tears were flowing down his cheeks. His pretty face was marred by a black eye.

"You're okay, now, Dylan. We'll keep you with us. I don't think those two will be a problem any time soon, but just in case, I say we go somewhere else," Tyler said.

"I'm gonna head out," Brayden said and started to leave.

"Wait!" I said. "Don't go. Stay with us. We need to talk. I've got to know what happened. Besides, it may not be safe for you here alone."

Brayden shrugged.

"Let's go to my place and get cleaned up," Tyler said.

I looked around. We were all a mess, smeared with dirt and blood. We couldn't exactly walk around in such a state and I was eager to get an ice pack on my face. My newest black eye stung!

We all climbed in Tyler's car, and he drove us to his place. Daniel was out on his date with Percy so we had the house to ourselves. We took turns in the restroom cleaning up. I observed Brayden as he sat in Tyler's living room. He was as brooding as ever and seemed extremely sad. He almost looked as if he could cry, and I couldn't figure it out. It wasn't the fight or the pain. He was too much like me to let that get to him. Brayden confused the hell out of me.

While we all cleaned up, Tyler got us Cokes from the refrigerator and then we all sat around the living room. Awkward silence reigned, so I broke it.

"Okay, so what did you do *this* time, Dylan?" I asked.

Dylan looked at me like a frightened rabbit.

"I...um...kind of flirted with Cory. Justin laughed at him and that's when Cory came after me."

"How many times have we told you not to do that?" Tyler asked. "You never listen!"

"He's sooo hot!" Dylan said.

"So what happened next?" I asked.

"They chased me into that alley. I tripped and they grabbed me. Cory punched me in the stomach and called me a faggot and that's when Brayden appeared and jumped him."

Tyler, Dylan, and I all gazed at Brayden. He wasn't uncomfortable under our gazes, but he appeared uncharacteristically indecisive.

"I'm really confused. I thought you hated Dylan," I said.

"I don't hate him. He just pissed me off because he was stalking me and always leering at me," Brayden said.

"Why did you jump in to save him this time?" Tyler asked.

"I don't like bullies and I don't like homophobes."

"Whoa. Wait. You are a homophobe!" I said.

Brayden clinched his fists and glared at me. For a moment I thought he was going to jump on me, but he controlled himself.

"You don't know anything about me," he said and scowled.

"I know what a dick you were when you tried to beat up Dylan."

"Caspian, he just fought to protect Dylan," Tyler reminded me.

"Listen, thanks for giving me a ride, but I'm going to get going," Brayden said.

"Please stay," Tyler said.

"I...that's not a good idea."

"We'd...like to get to know you," Tyler said. "We appreciate what you did for Dylan and...well, you're new and probably don't know anyone so..."

"Listen, you guys seem pretty decent, but I don't really want to get to know anyone."

"But..." Tyler said.

Brayden got up and left, leaving us all confused. We just sat there for several moments after Brayden shut the door.

"He's soooooo hot," Dylan said.

Tyler and I glared at Dylan.

"What? Don't you think he's hot?"

Tyler shook his head, and I rolled my eyes.

I rode along as Tyler drove Dylan home. We dropped him off and then Tyler looked at me.

"Are you okay?" I asked.

"Yeah. It's a good thing it was four on two. Justin is strong!"

"I didn't know you were such a wild man," I said. "You're kind of a bad ass yourself."

Tyler laughed.

"As if! You know you can kick my ass any day, even if you are a little freshman."

"I'd rather kiss you."

I slid over and did just that.

"Are you okay?" Tyler asked when our lips parted.

"Yeah, but I wouldn't be if Dylan hadn't jumped in. That dude was huge!"

"I've never seen Dylan fight before," Tyler said. "I didn't get to see him much this time, but I caught that furious look on his face. He was pissed off. I don't think he liked Cory hurting you."

"The way he fights is almost funny. There can't be much power in his skinny arms, but he punched and kicked and scratched. I might have laughed if I wasn't in so much pain. I think he surprised Cory, especially when he kicked him in the nuts."

"Dylan did that?"

"Oh, yeah. He dropped him."

Tyler and I both laughed.

"You sure you're okay?" Tyler asked.

"What I am is starved! Still want to go to the Irish Lion?"

"I think I'm hungrier than that now. Let's hit the China Buffet and eat *everything*."

"I'm in!"

Tyler drove to Eastland Plaza on the east side. The China Buffet was several doors down from McAlister's where we had eaten not so long ago. I paid for my own this time since Percy had given me a twenty. I had a lot of change left. The China Buffet was inexpensive.

I loaded up on different kinds of chicken, some cheesy crab stuff, and rice. I didn't know what most of it was, but I didn't care as long as it tasted good. Tyler got a salad, but his plate was loaded with chicken and shrimp too.

Once we had our drinks, we began eating. Everything was so good. Yum!

"So what do you think is up with Brayden?" Tyler asked as we ate.

"I can't figure him out. I thought he yelled "faggot" right before Dylan screamed, but it must have been one of others. When we came around the corner and I spotted the other two, I thought we were screwed. Can you imagine us fighting Justin, Cory, *and* Brayden?"

"That would not have been pretty, even with my tough boyfriend."

"Ha! Those dudes are massive! I don't think anything ever shocked me more than seeing Brayden jump on them instead of jumping Dylan."

"I was shocked by something more once."

"Yeah? What?"

"The first time you kissed me."

"Oh, yeah!"

I bet that did shock Tyler more, since I'd attacked him and was beating the crap out of him. It's a long story, but I doubt anyone else has the same first kiss story.

"We can rule out homophobe for Brayden," Tyler said.

"Yeah, I was completely wrong about that."

"Easy mistake."

"Did you see him after the fight? I thought he was going to cry, and I don't think it had anything to do with getting pummeled."

"I wasn't paying much attention. I just wanted to get the hell out of there."

"Something was really bothering him," I said.

"He was in a rage when he was fighting. I saw his face. He had the same look you get when you completely lose it."

"Me?"

"Don't act innocent. You know you're a bad ass and when you lose it, you're scary. It was like he had all this rage stored up and it came bursting out all over Justin."

"It's a good thing. Brayden is tough, but he's not very big."

"You didn't have much trouble with him."

"Well, yeah, but that because we're about the same size and I'm a badder bad ass."

I grinned.

"I'm glad he was there and that we came along too. I hate to think what those guys would have done to Dylan."

"Yeah and you know? I don't think Dylan would have learned his lesson even if they'd beaten him senseless. He would've been hitting on male nurses from his hospital bed."

"If those guys didn't kill him," Tyler said.

We both grew quiet at that. It could have happened. I doubt Cory and Justin would have tried to kill him, but they could have easily gone a little too far.

"I'd miss the little fairy if he was gone," I said.

"Should I tell him that?"

"Don't you dare!"

We talked about other things, but my mind kept going back to Brayden. There was something about that kid...

# Chapter 5

At school on Monday, the whole lot of us had black eyes and bruises. It was soon all over school that Tyler, Dylan, Brayden, and me had tangled with Cory and Justin. I wondered if the two jocks would come after us, but when I passed Cory and later Justin in the halls, they didn't look like they had it in for me. They probably liked that fact that fighting four of us made them look like studs. I bet they didn't tell anyone we left them moaning and bleeding in the alley. Tyler thought it wise not to say much about that. I didn't agree, but then I didn't like the thought of those guys going after my boyfriend.

"My heroes!" Dylan said as he ran up from behind and wrapped an arm about each of our necks.

"Get off me, pest!" I said.

"Don't pretend you don't like me. You've saved me twice now."

I shoved Dylan off, but he clung to Tyler.

"We all make mistakes."

"It wasn't a mistake. You like me."

"I just like to fight."

Dylan made a move to hug me.

"Stay!"

Dylan did his puppy imitation, curling his hands into paws and panting.

"You are so pathetic! Get away from me."

Tyler laughed. I glared at Dylan, lunged toward him, and stomped. Dylan squealed and hid behind Tyler.

"Go away now or I will hurt you," I said.

Dylan threw me a kiss and raced off.

"He's so annoying!"

"I like to think of him as entertaining," Tyler said.

"You're nicer than I am."

"Well, there is no getting rid of him..."

"Or killing him."

"...so I figure I might as well enjoy him as much as possible."

"Just keep him away from me."

"Come on, you know you like him, at least a little."

"Yes, but I'll never tell him that. Mostly, he's just a big pain in the ass. I should rename him Hemorrhoid."

Tyler and I walked down the hallway together. Heads turned as we passed.

"So, what do you think?" Tyler asked. "Do they see us as homos who got bashed or guys brave enough to take on jocks who could break us in half?"

"Who cares?" I said and meant.

"I love that. You really don't care, do you?"

"Why should I care what a bunch of losers think? As far as I'm concerned, they can all kiss my..."

"Be that as it may, I just wonder how we're viewed."

"Planning on running for class president?"

"Hmm, a gay class president, but no, it's too late for me. I am a senior, you know."

"True. Dylan should run. He could give head in return for votes."

"You are terrible."

"Like he wouldn't do it and enjoy it!"

"I don't think I'll argue about that. How would he get the female vote?"

"Haven't you noticed that girls love him? He's the puppy they never had."

"He is cute and cuddly and the girls know he has no ulterior motives. Maybe we could clone him and sell Dylans."

"Bad, bad idea! One of him is more than enough."

"Hundreds of Dylans running around would be disturbing."

"One running around is disturbing. Hundreds would be a nightmare."

I spotted Brayden later when I was walking alone. Instead of glaring, he nodded to me. It was the friendliest he'd ever been to me, perhaps to anyone. He did get along okay with girls but was standoffish even with them. There was a lot of me in Brayden. I was him not so long ago.

Caleb, Tyreece, and Jesse eyed Tyler, Dylan, and me as we approached our table together at lunch. Dylan had latched onto us on our way down to the cafeteria and there was no getting rid of him. I sat down and waited for the jokes about rough sex and three-ways, but none came.

"Are you guys okay?" Caleb asked.

Tyreece watched us intently, waiting for our answer. Jesse even put down his latest fashion magazine.

"We're fine," Tyler said.

"You look horrible," Jesse said.

Leave it to Jesse. With him, it was all about appearance.

"So what happened?" Tyreece asked. "We've been hearing weird rumors all day."

I let Tyler do the talking because I was hungry and the chicken nuggets, mashed potatoes, and cinnamon roll on my tray looked too good to resist. I was less excited about the green beans and canned peaches, but they didn't look too bad either. I ate and listened until Caleb interrupted the story.

"Whoa! Whoa! Wait. Brayden was fighting off two guys who were after Dylan? The two of you fought *with* Brayden *against* Cory and Justin? Isn't Brayden a basher? Isn't he one of the bad guys? Shouldn't he have been on the other side?"

"We were kind of wrong about Brayden," Tyler said. "He isn't so much a basher as a bad ass who got tired of being stalked by someone we all know." Tyler stared at Dylan, who put on his best "who me?" expression.

Tyler went on with the story, making me sound very heroic. He even made Dylan sound courageous and that's not easy.

"I didn't know you could fight, Dylan," Tyreece said.

"I don't so much fight as go spastic," Dylan said.

I laughed.

"I think Dylan scared Cory. Dylan was a crazy boy. He was all over him," I said.

"I think Dylan just wanted to grope him," Jesse said.

"He's done more than grope him already," Tyreece pointed out.

"Well, I did get a couple of good feels," Dylan said.

I rolled my eyes and went back to my chicken nuggets.

The level of attention directed toward Tyler and me increased after lunch. I guess everyone who hadn't heard about the fight got the story at lunchtime. Even in the cafeteria, I'd noticed kids looking at us and at Brayden who sat alone at a distant table. I wondered what Brayden thought of the attention. He was a confirmed bad ass now. I saw some guys take the long way around to get to their table instead of getting near him. The girls were more enamored of him than ever. The brooding bad ass thing worked for Brayden.

I was already a confirmed bad ass, but the latest fight added to my rep. I think Tyler gained the most. Guys looked at him with new respect. I don't think they thought him as the kind of a guy who would get into a fight, let along tangle with one of the toughest wrestlers in school.

Tyler couldn't hang out after school. He'd promised to do something with his dad. I didn't mind too much since I got to spend a lot of time with Tyler, but I had hoped for a hot make-out session. We made out a little when he dropped me off, but I could've used a lot more. I wanted to go somewhere alone with him so we could continue to explore. Now that Tyler was more willing, I wanted to take things a little further. I hoped he'd be up for going all the way soon.

Since I couldn't get it on with my boyfriend, I started in on my homework right after Tyler dropped me off. School was actually becoming kind of fun. My grades were up and it was nice to see a B and even an occasional A on my assignments instead of the Cs and Ds I'd often received in the past. I began to get even a little interested in some subjects. Tyler had a way of making things interesting. Percy kept on me about my schoolwork, but I put in a lot more effort because Tyler encouraged me and was always willing to help me. I wanted to please Tyler, so I found myself paying way more attention to my homework than in the past.

After I finished my schoolwork, I sat and gazed out the window, wondering what I was going to do with my evening. It was weird. Now that I had a boyfriend, I had trouble doing things by myself. I hadn't had that problem before. I thought I might just be lazy and watch some TV, but when I walked into the living room, Percy was watching *Star Trek*. I didn't want any part of that. I didn't know much about *Star Trek*, except that if a security dude wearing red went down to a planet he was a goner.

I told Percy I was going out for a walk and then headed outside. It was the beginning of November now, but fairly warm still. I headed toward the stadium and Assembly Hall. That seemed as good a destination as any.

I walked around aimlessly, thinking random thoughts, such as Dylan groping Cory while he fought him. I wondered if Cory knew he'd been violated. I wondered if Dylan fantasized about it. I wouldn't be at all surprised if he did—the little pervert.

Cory and Justin were both rather good looking and had great bodies. Their pecs pressed against their shirts and their biceps looked as if they might rip through their sleeves. Why did hot guys have to be such jerks? Of course, the fight was still mostly Dylan's fault. He should have known better than to flirt with Cory in front of one of Cory's buddies. The kid was not too bright sometimes.

There wasn't much going on at the stadium. It was quite a contrast to game weekends. When IU was playing a home game, there were thousands of people everywhere! Percy always tried not to drive when game traffic flooded the streets. Once, we were coming home as a game was letting out. The drive that usually took ten minutes took over an hour!

The stadium was eerily quiet, almost ghostly. Where tens of thousands sometimes sat there was no one. I walked past Assembly Hall next. That's where all the basketball games were played. There were a few students going in and out, but not much was happening there either. I walked on, across Fee Lane, and up 17th Street. I passed the outdoor pool, which was closed now, and then turned toward Armstrong Stadium, where IU soccer games were played. It was also where the Little 500 was held. I had no idea what the Little 500 was when I moved to Bloomington, but Percy told me it was a big deal. It was a bike race. I thought that sounded pretty lame, but then Percy forced me to watch *Breaking Away* and both the movie and the bike race were pretty cool.

I walked to Armstrong Stadium and looked down toward the field. The grass was so green and well kept I wondered if it was real. This stadium was deserted too, but no, there was a lone figure sitting on the bottom row of bleachers, staring out at the field. I looked closer. I wasn't sure, but it looked like Brayden. Whoever it was had the same hair and was wearing the same jacket Brayden had worn at school. I walked down the stairs to check it out.

As I neared, I could tell it was Brayden. He couldn't see me yet, but I could see the side of his face. He was just sitting there, staring out at the soccer field. He turned his head when I drew closer. He jumped to his feet and quickly wiped away the tears that had run down his cheeks. His eyes were red. He'd been crying hard.

"Why are you spying on me?" he asked angrily.

"Dude, I'm not spying on you. I was out walking. How would I even know you were here?"

"Well, just leave me alone then!"

"Don't be so hostile. We aren't enemies, you know."

"I just want to be alone, okay?"

"Listen, I can see that something is bothering you. If you want to talk about it..."

"I don't want to talk about it! Can't you get that or are you too stupid?"

Brayden glowered at me with clinched fists. His body was tensed and ready to spring into action. Brayden's features were a mask of rage, but I wasn't going to ignore the tears running down his cheeks.

"Come on, talk to me."

"Leave me the fuck alone! I don't want your help! I don't like you or your prissy little friend or your pussy of a boyfriend!"

My eyes narrowed. I didn't care what he said about Dylan, but no one talked about Tyler like that.

"Tyler isn't a pussy."

"Yeah, right. That's exactly what he is. He's a senior and he's dating a freshman? Isn't he hot enough to get someone his age? He's probably too afraid to approach a guy his age because he might get his ass kicked. He's a pussy."

I snapped. I flew at Brayden in a rage and slugged him in the mouth. My head snapped back as he clocked me a good one and we tumbled to the ground. Our fists were flying as we rolled over one another, slugging away viciously.

We broke apart for a moment, climbed to our feet and went at it again. I slammed Brayden into the chain link fence, but he came right back at me. My neck popped as Brayden landed a right cross to my chin. I was dazed, but came back with a hard punch to the gut. Brayden doubled over. I rushed him and took him to the ground. We spent the next couple of minutes pummeling each other until we were both grasping for breath. We broke apart and glared at each other while our chests heaved and our fury slowly diminished.

We reached an unspoken agreement that the fight was a draw. With a final glare, we turned away from each other and went our separate ways. I wouldn't have turned my back on a guy like Cory or Justin, but I knew Brayden wouldn't jump me. He was a jerk, but he wasn't a coward. I had a grudging respect for his fighting abilities.

I walked back the way I'd come, thankful that Percy wasn't home. I could feel a trickle of blood running down my chin and I was sure I looked quite a mess. I grinned when I pictured Brayden's messed up face. Our fight was a draw, but I still think I'd given better than I'd taken.

I limped toward home as my breathing returned to normal. I wasn't afraid of a fight, but I didn't enjoy how I felt after one was over. That's when the pain really hit me. While I was fighting I pushed the pain aside, but when it was all over—owww!

I wondered who would've won if we'd kept going. I liked to think I would have, but I wasn't sure. Brayden fought a lot like me. The more we hurt each other, the harder we came back at each other. I don't think either of us walked away because of the pain. I know I didn't and Brayden didn't look like the pain fazed him either. I was willing to quit because I was exhausted and couldn't catch my breath. I had a feeling that's why Brayden was willing to call it quits as well.

I was back home in a few minutes. I walked into the bathroom and checked myself out in the mirror.

"Damn, I look tough."

I grinned for a moment. I now had two black eyes and a busted lip. The dried blood looked particularly nasty and I was once again thankful Percy was not home. I grabbed a washcloth and cleaned up. My face wasn't nearly as much of a mess when I finished, but I still had two black eyes, a messed up lip, and a bruised cheek. I admired myself in the mirror and grinned.

***

"What happened to you?" Tyler asked as I climbed in his car the next morning.

"I...uh...got into a fight."

"I can see that. Are you okay?"

"I'm fine."

"Are you sure?"

"Yeah, I'm sure. It was just a fight."

"Caspian!"

"Hey, I didn't go looking for trouble."

"You managed to find it without difficulty, didn't you?"

"Why are you jumping on me?"

"Because I worry about you, okay?"

I grinned.

"I had no choice. I had to hit him."

"So you started it?"

"No. He did. He called you a pussy."

"Who?"

"Brayden."

"Brayden?"

"What did I just say?"

"You shouldn't have hit him just for calling me a pussy."

"No one talks about my boyfriend like that!"

I saw Tyler grin before he could hide it. He liked that I stood up for him.

"You should have just let it go. So what if he calls me a pussy? Caspian, you have to stop fighting so much. You're going to get hurt."

"It's just another black eye and a busted lip and a bruised cheek."

Tyler took his eyes off the road and looked at me for a moment. He looked so worried about me that I felt guilty.

"I'm sorry, okay? Like I said, I didn't go out looking for a fight."

"You don't go looking, but you always find one."

"I do not!"

"Yes, you do!"

I narrowed my eyes. I stared straight ahead, trying to calm myself down. It took me several moments.

"You say you don't want me to fight, but you're starting a fight right now," I said.

Tyler laughed for a moment.

"Yeah, I guess I am. I just don't want you to get hurt. I know you're tough, but... I worry."

"I'm sorry. I don't mean to get into fights, but I get so mad. Even when I just think of Brayden shooting his mouth off..." I ground my teeth and began to breathe harder. I looked quickly toward Tyler when he began laughing.

"I'm sorry, I don't mean to laugh, but you should see your face right now. You sat there and worked yourself into a rage, just by thinking about Brayden."

"I kind of have a temper, don't I?"

"Kind of?"

"It's one of my charms?" I asked doubtfully.

Tyler looked at me and cocked his head to one side.

"I don't think so...."

When we arrived at school, Tyler gave me a delicate kiss on the lips.

"I won't break, you know."

"Yeah, but your lip."

"It's fine. Kiss me."

Tyler leaned in again and kissed me harder. Our tongues entwined. I wished we could ditch school and get it on, but I knew Tyler wouldn't go for it and Percy would be pissed off. He was none too happy I'd been in another fight. He wasn't proud of me for this one.

We kissed for a few moments and then reluctantly drew apart. We climbed out of the car and walked toward the school. Kids were checking us out. Tyler still had a black eye from the fight with Cory and Justin and I was sporting new battle scars.

The first person I saw in the hallways was Brayden. We glared at each other. He mouthed "pussy" toward Tyler. I took a step toward him, but Tyler put his arm across my chest.

"Don't even think about it," Tyler said, then leaned in close and whispered. "If you get into another fight, you aren't getting any."

Instead of being angered by the blackmail, I was intrigued by Tyler's statement. Did he mean we would go all the way soon if I behaved myself?

"If you're a good boy, I'll give you a special treat," Tyler whispered.

I forgot all about Brayden. The front of my jeans bulged and I began to breathe a little harder. Maybe I could control my temper after all.

I did my best not to even look at Brayden in class. Our eyes met only a couple of times and we glared at each other. I was going to try to keep from getting into another fight with him, but I wasn't about to take any crap from that jerk.

Word spread that I had been in yet another fight. It wasn't long before most of my classmates knew Brayden and I had tangled. I liked the attention but had to pretend I didn't when Tyler was around.

I was the center of attention at lunch. Everyone stopped what they were doing and stared at me as Tyler and I sat down.

"What did you do this time?" Caleb asked.

"Why do you assume *I* did something?"

"Because I have grown to know you in the short time you've lived in Bloomington. This makes what, four fights?"

"Actually, five." I looked at Tyler quickly. "Oops."

"What?" Tyler asked.

"I didn't tell you about the one a week ago. There was this drunk college boy and..."

"I don't want to hear about it," Tyler said. I was glad because he would've been mad for sure. That fight was my fault.

"I do! I love to hear about Caspian fighting. It's so hot!" Dylan said.

"I heard you got into it with Brayden," Tyreece said.

"You heard right."

"My Brayden? You didn't hurt him, did you?" Dylan asked.

"Just a little more than he hurt me."

"Yeah, I'd call it even. I got a look at Brayden's face earlier," Caleb said.

"Yeah! I really..." My voice trailed off when I noticed Tyler scowling. "It was a draw."

"You should have told us you were going to fight Brayden. We could have sold tickets! We could have advertised it as the ultimate bad ass showdown!" Tyreece said.

"Don't encourage him," Tyler said.

"Tyler thinks I fight too much."

"You think?" Caleb asked. I stuck out my tongue at him.

Tyler was probably right. I did fight too much. I couldn't help it. I got so angry! Sometimes, I just wanted to... I stopped myself. I was doing it again. I was working myself into a rage just by thinking about guys who pissed me off. I willed myself to calm down. Tyler gave me an encouraging smile.

I was going to do it. I was going to control my temper for Tyler—and for the special reward he promised me.

\*\*\*

He was at it again. Dylan. He was drooling over Brayden as Brayden bent over to get a drink from the water fountain. Brayden turned and noticed Dylan checking him out. I tensed, ready to spring into action, but Tyler already had his hand on my bicep. I willed myself to calm down as I waited to see if Brayden would make a move toward Dylan.

Dylan winked at his obsession. He truly was an idiot. Brayden scowled, shook his head in disbelief, and walked down the hallway. He noticed Tyler and me just in time to mouth "pussy" to me again. I clinched my fists, but Tyler still had his hand on my arm. I had to fight myself to keep from tearing after Brayden, but I willed myself to calm down. I slowly counted to ten.

"That's it. Let it go."

"Please let me kill him?" I grinned. I was kidding... mostly.

"Maybe for Christmas."

Dylan walked over to us, still watching Brayden as he walked down the hallway.

"I bet he looks magnificent naked," Dylan said.

"You'll never know unless you kidnap him," I said.

"Oh! I like that idea!"

Me and my big mouth.

"Don't even think about it. You wouldn't enjoy prison," Tyler said.

"I bet he would."

Tyler shot me a warning glance.

"Okay, okay. Dylan, kidnapping BAD."

"Oh, I wouldn't really kidnap him. I'm just going to fantasize about it. Now, if Brayden would kidnap me. Mmm."

"The only thing Brayden is going to do is knock your teeth out if you don't leave him alone. Go stalk someone else," I said.

"Just wait. I'll get him. He's resisting, but he's weakening."

"I wouldn't call scowling instead of kicking your butt weakening."

"I bet he's hung."

"Arrggh!" I said. I grabbed both sides of Dylan's face in my hands and made him look at me. "Brayden is not interested. He will never be interested. If you keep stalking him, he will kick your ass. Get it?"

"You have such beautiful lips."

"I give up," I said, releasing Dylan and shaking my head in disgust. "Go. Stalk Brayden and get yourself beat up, but I'm not coming to visit you in the hospital. On second thought I will, but only to say, 'I told you so!'"

Tyler pulled me away.

"I think you're losing your temper again."

"Wouldn't you?"

"Probably." Tyler laughed. "Come on. I have to get home. I have way too much homework tonight."

"Want to take me to your place and give me that special reward you mentioned?"

"You haven't earned it yet."

"At least tell me what it is."

"No. If you knew, it would drive you insane."

"You are a cruel, cruel person, Tyler Keegan."

Tyler laughed and led me to his car.

# Chapter 6

Tonight was the night. Percy and Daniel had gone to a play at the IU Auditorium, so Tyler and I had a minimum of two hours to ourselves with no chance whatsoever of being interrupted. Neither of us had spoken the words, but we both knew something was going to happen tonight. I'd been a good boy and hadn't been in a single fight since battling it out with Brayden in Armstrong Stadium. Tonight, Tyler was going to give me my special reward. We both knew we were going to go further than ever before and I hoped that meant going all the way.

Tyler came over shortly after Percy and Daniel left. I had no intention of letting our precious time slip away, so I took Tyler by the hand, pulled him into my bedroom, and closed and locked the door. I panted slightly as I gazed at him.

"You look like a wild animal right now," Tyler said. I noticed his voice was husky as he spoke the words. He was just as worked up as me.

"I feel like an animal and I'm definitely wild. I'm ready to pounce. So, do I get my special reward? I've been a very good boy."

"Yes, you have been a very good boy and tonight you get to be a very bad boy."

I loved it when Tyler talked to me like that. I pulled him to me and kissed him hard on the lips. Our tongues entwined and our hands roamed.

I was three years younger than Tyler, but I was the aggressor. I grabbed Tyler's shirt and pulled it over his head, then ripped off my own. I loved feeling his naked torso rubbing against mine as we made out. I could feel something else rubbing against me too and it was getting harder by the second.

Tyler wasn't shy. He shot this tongue into my mouth, then pulled away and nibbled on my earlobes and my neck.

"That's driving me crazy," I said.

Tyler smiled and then licked his way down my chest. When he flicked his tongue over my nipples, I pressed his head against my chest. The sensations Tyler created were so intense I feared I'd lose control even before I got my pants off.

We ripped our way through each other's jeans and soon our clothing was scattered about my room. We fell onto the bed, hugging, kissing, and groping. We panted and moaned. My need for Tyler increased by the moment, and he became increasingly aggressive. He shoved me onto my back, leaned over, and drew me into his mouth. I moaned even louder than before.

I enjoyed Tyler's talented mouth until I was about to bust, then pushed him off, and returned the favor. It was Tyler's turn to moan now. I derived extreme pleasure from making him feel good and from the way he panted, moaned, and writhed on the bed I was making him feel very, very good indeed.

I kept going until Tyler began to moan harder than ever. I could feel his body tense and I knew he was close. I pulled back, then reached over and opened the drawer of the stand beside my bed. I took out the box of condoms Percy had given me.

Tyler and I hadn't discussed whether or not this was the night we would go all the way. We also hadn't discussed who was the top and who was the bottom, but Tyler didn't object as I tore open the condom and unrolled it onto my penis. I could tell from the expression on his face that he wanted this as much as I did.

I tried not to let my uncertainty show as I prepared. At least I looked like an expert as I put on the condom. I'd practiced with one the night before and it was a good thing too. Even after reading the directions, it took practice to put it on right.

I moved toward Tyler and lifted his legs over my shoulders. I wanted to see his eyes as I entered him. I wanted to share this moment with him. This wasn't just sex. This was a significant moment in both our lives, an once-in-a-lifetime event. There would never be another first time.

I'd like to say everything went perfectly. I'd like to make myself sound like a porn star. The truth is I had some…uh…difficulties. Tyler was really tight and I couldn't get in. I got so nervous I began to lose my erection and then I really couldn't get in. Tyler sensed what was going wrong and pulled my face to his and kissed me deeply. We made out and my erection returned full-force. I forced myself to calm down and relax. This was Tyler. He wasn't going to laugh at me if I couldn't do it. Tyler was patient and kind. He was also very, very hot! I burned with need for him.

I pressed against Tyler and suddenly I slid in, too fast and too far. Tyler cried out in pain.

"I'm sorry! I'm sorry! I didn't mean to…it just…"

"It's okay. Just hold still for a moment."

I held perfectly still, fighting the instinct to thrust. It was a powerful instinct, but Tyler had tears in his eyes. I never meant to hurt him.

Slowly, the look of pain on his face lessened. He took a couple of deep breaths, then looked me in the eyes and smiled.

"Okay, go very slowly."

I barely allowed myself to move, but ever so slowly I pushed myself into Tyler. My mind exploded with pleasure and again I had to fight the instinct to thrust all the way into him. I inched myself in, stopping whenever the least sign of pain crossed Tyler's handsome features. I pushed in deeper and deeper until I was all the way in. I moaned with the pleasure of it. Tyler pulled me down and kissed me while I was still inside of him.

We kissed then smiled at each other. Tyler nodded. I drew back and began to thrust ever so slowly. I let Tyler's expression guide me. I increased my tempo as his face contorted with pleasure instead of pain. We both moaned as I went at it harder still. Ever so slowly I increased my speed until Tyler grasped my buttocks and pulled me into him.

I gave into instinct then and we both moaned and groaned with wild passion. I fought to keep from going over the edge. I wanted to experience the ultimate release more than anything, but I also wanted to keep going forever.

My breath came faster and faster and my heart pounded. Sweat trickled down my bare torso. Tyler's moans made maintaining control harder than ever. I think I could have got off just listening to him. I didn't think I could hold back much longer. I had never felt anything so intensely pleasurable in my entire life. I nearly cried with the effort of holding back and then Tyler moaned loudly, his body tensed, and he shot all over his abdomen and mine.

Tyler's orgasm sent me over the edge. I moaned in unison with him and cut loose. My mind exploded with pleasure. My orgasm ripped through my body like a shockwave. My vision blurred and blacked out for a moment and the sensations continued. I felt like my orgasm was going to go on and on forever, but it moments it was over and I collapsed on top of Tyler, gasping for breath, my heart pounding in my chest.

I pulled out and rolled over onto my back beside Tyler. We panted as our breath slowly returned to normal. I lay there, staring at the ceiling. My mind was still spinning with what we had just done.

Tyler and I turned to each other. We kissed, then lay facing each other, gazing into each other's eyes.

"Was I good?" I asked.

"You were magnificent."

"I was so nervous. I'm sorry I hurt you. It just...slipped in."

"It's okay. It hurt bad but the way you made me feel after made up for it."

Tyler grinned.

"I guess I'm not a virgin anymore," I said.

"Me either."

"I'm glad my first time was with you. I love you, Tyler."

"I love you too."

We kissed again, then sat up.

"You can have the bathroom first. I guess we both need to clean up," I said.

"Yeah."

I watched as Tyler walked toward the bathroom. He had the hottest ass! I almost couldn't believe I'd just gone all the way with him.

When Tyler returned all fresh and clean from his shower, I took my turn. Tyler was dressed when I returned to my room, so I pulled on my clothes. We smoothed out my bed and I hid the used condom deep in the trashcan. There was no evidence of what we had just done.

"Are you okay?" Tyler asked as we sat down on the bed again.

"I'm great!"

"Good. I was a little worried you'd have regrets after we did it. I had planned to go all the way tonight, but I wasn't entirely sure until you pulled out the condom..."

"...you wanted it bad," I finished.

"Yeah."

"I don't have any regrets. It was incredible. I'm also glad to have it over with. I don't mean "over with" as in it was like a test or getting a vaccination. It's just... I was afraid I wouldn't do it right or that I wouldn't be any good or that I couldn't do it, and I almost couldn't."

"You were just nervous. Now, you have nothing to worry about. You were incredible."

"I'm sorry I hurt you."

"Forget it, Caspian. You couldn't keep that from happening. My virginity didn't yield easily." Tyler laughed.

"That was one special reward. It was well worth not fighting," I said.

Tyler and I looked at each other, then leaned in and kissed. I felt closer to him than I ever had before.

When Percy and Daniel came back later, they found Tyler and me sitting together watching TV. My heart raced with fear for a few moments when they first looked at us. They seemed to sense something had gone on in their absence. I had the strangest feeling they knew Tyler and I had gone all the way, but that was crazy. The feeling passed as quickly as it had come. We turned off the TV, and Tyler and I helped Percy and Daniel carry in groceries, which was mainly milk for me – Percy insisted I was a growing boy – soft drinks and snacks. Percy didn't cook.

"You guys really know how to have a romantic date," Tyler said. "I thought you were going to see a play, not go grocery shopping."

"We did. We stopped by Kroger after."

Tyler shook his head in disgust.

"Am I going to have to teach you how to date?" Tyler asked. "Kroger is not the place to end a date."

"When you're as old as them, what does it matter?" I asked, mostly to be a smart-ass.

Percy gave me the evil eye and it made me laugh.

Percy and Daniel looked at each other and shared a smile. For a moment, I wondered if they had sneaked off and gone all the way too. I doubted that was it, but they were up to something. Old people could never be trusted. Tyler picked up on it too.

"What?" he asked.

Percy and Daniel looked at each other again.

"Do you two have any plans for Saturday?" Percy asked.

Tyler and I shook our heads.

"Keep it that way."

"Why?" Tyler asked.

"We're going to go out to eat and then we have something to discuss with you," Percy said.

Tyler and I looked at each other.

"What?"

"We will tell you then," Daniel said.

"Tell us now!" I said.

"It's too long a discussion to start now. Besides, we want to take you somewhere nice," Daniel said.

"I guess that means no Taco Bell or KFC," Tyler said to me. "It must be big."

"They are probably going to send us both to boarding school. I don't trust them," I said.

"You know, we're standing right here," Percy said, then grinned. "While the boarding school idea is tempting, that isn't it."

"So what is *it*?" I asked.

"You'll find out this weekend and not a moment before," Percy said.

I growled in frustration. Percy and Daniel laughed. I glared at them, but they knew I wasn't really angry so it did no good.

Tyler went home with his dad, so that left Percy and me alone in the kitchen. He looked at me curiously for a moment.

"You look...different," he said.

"Me?"

"No, that boy standing behind you. Of course, you."

"I'm the same delightful boy you've always known."

"If you're delightful, then you have changed."

"Funny!"

I yawned. It was getting kind of late and I'd had a very strenuous night. I grinned with the thought.

"I'm going to bed. Good night, Percy."

I started to leave.

"Not so fast."

My face paled for a moment. Could he tell by looking that Tyler and I had done it?

Percy pulled me into a hug and I hugged him back.

"Good night," he said, and then kissed my forehead.

I smiled and headed to the bathroom.

After I'd brushed my teeth, undressed, and climbed into bed, I lay there and gazed at the ceiling. I almost couldn't believe I had lost my virginity. I was glad it was with Tyler. There were some hot, hot guys at school, but with them it would have been only sex. Tyler and I had shared something special.

I pictured it all in my mind again. I wanted to remember every moment of my first time, even the parts that didn't go so well. I knew only too well that this time would never come again.

I fell asleep thinking about Tyler and it gave me very pleasant dreams.

***

When I awakened the next morning I lay there trying to remember if Tyler and I had really both lost our virginity last night or if it was all a dream. I had dreamed about making it with Tyler before so it took me several moments to figure things out. Slowly, I realized that Tyler and I had gone all the way. I grinned.

When I hopped in the passenger seat of Tyler's car, we smiled at each other. Tyler's smile was shy, but mine wasn't. Why be shy around someone who had seen me naked, who had licked all over my body, and who had bottomed for me? I had never been as intimate with anyone as I had been with Tyler.

"How are you?" I asked.

"Sore."

I had been fastening my seatbelt, but I turned my head quickly toward Tyler.

"Are you okay?"

"I'm fine. I expected to be sore. You are kind of big, you know."

I laughed.

"I'm not that big."

"Big enough and it was my first time."

"You're sure you're okay?"

"Yeah, but I was thinking about something that worries me."

"What?"

"Well, what if the condom failed somehow? I could get pregnant."

I punched Tyler in the arm.

"You are so not funny!"

Tyler laughed.

Maybe it was just me, but people seemed to look at Tyler and me differently as we walked into school together. Could they tell just by looking that we'd done it? In a way, it didn't matter. I didn't much care what anyone thought, as long as my bad ass rep was intact. If I'd bottomed, maybe I would've wanted to be more secretive, but maybe not even then. The eerie sensation that others could read my mind intensified as we passed more and more of our classmates. Jesse paused as we walked by and just stood staring at us.

"I feel like everyone knows we had sex," I said quietly as we walked along.

"That's really weird. I was thinking the same thing."

"They couldn't know, could they?"

"I don't see how. Do I look any different?"

"You do have a kind of glow to you. I must be good."

"Oh, you're very, very good, big boy."

I grinned.

"I think we're just being paranoid, but while we are on the subject, I don't think it's really anyone's business but ours and maybe the guys."

"Works for me," I said.

"You don't mind if Caleb and the others know?"

"Why should I mind? I'm surprised you don't mind. You're a much more private person than me," I said.

"True, but I just really, really want to share this with someone."

"Hey, I was there, remember?"

"Oh, I remember. I'll always remember. I mean someone else."

"You could tell your dad."

"Not funny."

"We could put it in the daily bulletin."

"That would be telling *everyone* and everyone doesn't need to know…"

"…that I tried to get you pregnant last night?" I finished for my boyfriend.

A girl walking past overheard us and gave us the strangest look. I laughed, but Tyler wasn't amused.

"You aren't very good with secrets, are you?" Tyler asked.

"Okay. I'm sorry. I'll be more careful."

The feeling that everyone could tell Tyler and I had gone all the way persisted throughout the morning. I knew the idea was ridiculous, but I could have sworn people looked at me differently.

When Tyler and I sat down with our trays at lunch, Dylan looked back and forth between us.

"You guys did it, didn't you?"

Tyler and I looked at each other, our mouths hanging open. Tyler turned slightly red.

"You did!" Dylan said. "What was it like? Who was the top?"

Caleb and Tyreece were watching with amused interest. Jesse had his face poked in a fashion magazine, but I knew he was listening.

"Let's take a poll. I say Tyler was the bottom," Caleb said.

"Yeah, Tyler was definitely the bottom," Tyreece chimed in.

"No question. Tyler's the bottom," Jesse said without looking up.

"Oh yeah! I think so too!" Dylan said. "I love to bottom."

"Tell us something the entire school doesn't know," Caleb said.

Tyler blushed a little more as each of our friends spoke. By the time Dylan voted, he was beet red. There was no need for us to announce anything. The guys knew.

"Congratulations," Caleb said. "This is a big step for you guys."

"Thanks. Now if you're all done embarrassing me, perhaps we can talk about something else," Tyler said.

"Not a chance," murmured Jesse.

"What's embarrassing about sex?" Caleb said.

"You're kidding, right?" Tyler asked.

"Most guys brag," Caleb said.

"I talk about having sex all the time!" Dylan said.

"We know!" the entire table said in unison.

"Are you embarrassed because you were the bottom?" Caleb asked.

"Yeah, kind of."

"Don't be. You're the same Tyler you were yesterday. We already knew you were gay. Remember? We all know what gay guys do. Everyone has their little sexual kinks and I'm not even sure bottoming counts as kink."

"I have sex with a girl who likes to pretend she's my sister," Jesse said, still without looking up from his magazine.

"*What?*" Tyler asked.

"Who?" Tyreece asked.

"I'll never tell."

"I used to do it with a girl who would only have sex with me if I wore my football uniform, including the shoulder pads," Caleb said.

"One of the soccer players is into role-play rape. He climbs through my window at night when my parents are gone..." Dylan started.

"Too much information, Dylan!" Tyreece said.

"Why is that too much information? You guys are talking about pretend incest and a football uniform fetish."

"He does have a point," Jesse said.

"The point, Tyler, is that everyone has their own sexual kinks and fetishes and bottoming is pretty tame, especially compared with Dylan's role play," Caleb said.

"It's soooooo hot!" Dylan said. "Sometimes, I'm actually asleep when he comes in and..."

"Shut up, Dylan!" everyone said in unison.

"You guys are so tame, except you, Caspian. I bet you were an animal when you are on Tyler."

"He was," Tyler said with a grin, then immediately turned red again. He was so cute when he was embarrassed.

"Okay, let's all take pity on Tyler and change the subject, but I am happy for you guys," Caleb said.

84

"Thanks," murmured Tyler. He was staring at his food, trying not to make eye contact with anyone.

"I have a new topic!" Dylan announced too loudly.

We all looked at Dylan, just waiting for some inappropriate sexual comment.

"What is this?" he asked, spearing a golden brown, fried object about the size of a hot dog. "I thought it was chicken, but maybe it's fish. It doesn't look natural."

"The less you know, the better," Tyreece said mysteriously.

"Didn't the menu say something about fried eel?" I asked, looking around the table.

Dylan eyed me suspiciously.

"Eel?"

"Yeah, I think eel was listed on the menu," Caleb said, taking a bite out of his whatever-it-was. "It's kind of slimy on the inside, but not bad."

Dylan gulped.

"You know what, Dylan?" Jesse asked.

"What?"

"You're way too gullible."

"I am not! What does that mean?"

"It means you're easily fooled," Tyler said. "Like when Caspian tells you a chicken plank is eel and you believe it."

"I didn't believe it! I was just acting."

"Uh-huh."

Poor Tyler. He was still embarrassed. Even though the topic had changed from losing our virginity to today's mystery meat, Tyler still looked like he wanted to crawl under the table. I moved even closer to him so that our shoulders were touching. He looked at me and grinned shyly.

"Oh! My! God! Look at him in that tight shirt!"

I looked up at the sound of Dylan's voice to see Brayden carrying his tray across the cafeteria to an empty table. His shirt was way too tight. It made him look ripped.

"I wanna lick him all over," Dylan said.

"Do you ever think about anything besides sex?" Tyreece asked.

"Chocolate. I think about chocolate. Chocolate syrup. I know a college boy who likes me to take chocolate syrup and..."

"Congratulations, Dylan. It took you less than five seconds to turn your thoughts from chocolate to kinky sex."

"Oh! Oh! Have you ever taken whipped cream and..."

"Dylan!" Jesse shrieked. "You're going to ruin dessert for me forever."

"You want to know what I do with bananas or a cucumber?" Dylan asked.

"That's it," Jesse said, pushing his tray away. "I'm never eating again. There isn't a food that Dylan hasn't perverted into a sex toy."

"I've never quite figured out what do with an artichoke," Dylan said thoughtfully.

"I have a suggestion for you, Dylan," Caleb said.

"Ha. Ha."

Tyler finally relaxed. I was glad I wasn't such a private person. I didn't want to have sex in front of an audience, but I really didn't care who knew Tyler and I got it on. Well, yeah, I did care. I didn't want Percy to know because he'd probably give me a lecture about safer sex. I didn't want Daniel to know because I wasn't sure how he'd feel about me topping his son. Mostly, I didn't care who knew. I wasn't embarrassed. I was proud!

After school, I went home with Tyler. We mostly worked on homework, but we took a few make-out breaks. I didn't mind studying so much when I was with Tyler. Being with him changed a boring solitary task into a social event. Tyler was into anything involving reading or writing and his enthusiasm was somewhat contagious. I say somewhat because I didn't think I could ever get as excited over reading a book as Tyler. I sat and gazed at him as he read a passage of *The Catcher in the Rye* out loud. His eyes were lit up and he was consumed by the words on the page. I smiled as I watched him.

"What?" he asked, pausing for a moment.

"I just realized my boyfriend is a geek," I said, then giggled.

"You're going to pay for that," he said.

Tyler sat the book down, then pounced on me. I thought for a moment he was going to kiss me so I willingly let him get on top of me, but it was a trick. He ran his fingers over my sides, tickling my ribs. I giggled, laughed, and then squealed. I squirmed to get away, but I couldn't break free. I was laughing so hard it sapped my power. I writhed helplessly under Tyler as he tormented me with his fingers.

"Stop! Stop!" I pleaded with what breath I could manage between giggles.

Daniel appeared at the door. Tyler looked over his shoulder, then climbed off me.

"Your son is out of control," I said, getting up.

"I just learned Caspian's Achilles heel. He is ticklish, very ticklish," Tyler said.

It was true. I couldn't stand being tickled. What Tyler didn't know, and what I was never going to tell him, was that the bottom of my feet were even more ticklish than my ribs.

"I'll learn your secrets and then you will pay," I said, using my best evil villain tone.

"Or, I could tell you Tyler's weaknesses," Daniel said mischievously.

"Don't you dare!" Tyler said.

"So, you have weaknesses that I can exploit," I said thoughtfully, looking at Tyler. I turned my attention to Daniel. "Tell me."

Daniel began to open his mouth.

"No, you don't! Out! Now!" Tyler said.

Daniel began to open his mouth again, but Tyler pushed him out the door. I could hear Daniel laughing as he walked down the hallway.

"So, what *are* your weaknesses?" I asked Tyler, closing in on him.

"Don't make me tickle you again."

I gave Tyler the evil eye but came no closer.

"That's better. Now, let's finish this chapter. You want me to keep reading or would you rather read it yourself?"

"Keep reading. You make it much more interesting."

Tyler began to read. The sound of his voice was comforting. I loved making out with Tyler and sex with him was incredible, but I think I liked the companionship best of all. I felt secure and content when he was near me. I'd lost so much in recent months—

my parents, my home, and my old life—but Tyler made me feel like everything was going to be okay.  He made me feel like I was home.

# Chapter 7

Brayden sat alone every day at lunch. I don't know why I cared. He had mostly been a jerk. I'd had to save Dylan from him once and then there was our slugfest. He hadn't mouthed "pussy" to me in the hallways for a while, but when he looked at me, he either scowled or looked angry and upset. He was a jerk, but I couldn't help but remember that he'd jumped in to save Dylan's butt from Cory and Justin. The kid did not make sense.

I noticed Tyler gazing over at Brayden's lonely table now and then. Whenever I spotted him looking at Brayden, I did my best to distract him. Tyler had a habit of taking on hard luck cases and my greatest fear was that Tyler would try to make nice with Brayden. It's not that I had any reservations about them becoming friends (like that would ever happen!). I feared Brayden would explode and beat the crap out of my boyfriend.

Tyler wasn't stupid. He was a good deal smarter than me, but he unfortunately possessed the courage to approach someone like Brayden when he knew he might get hurt. That was actually a good quality and one I admired in my boyfriend, but I was afraid Brayden might mess up Tyler bad. Tyler wasn't the toughest guy around and didn't know that much about fighting.

I wanted to just forget about Brayden, but some people can't be ignored. Dylan was one of those. He was over-the-top, talked way too much, and was always excited. Brayden was nothing like him, but he was just as hard to ignore. Every time I was near him I thought back to the day at Armstrong Stadium. He'd been crying and I knew that most of his anger wasn't directed at me. He was mad at the entire world. I could have dismissed it, but I sensed he was in pain. Whatever was eating at him on that day troubled him still.

My own life was coming together nicely, mostly thanks to Tyler, although I have to give credit to Percy and even Daniel as well. Percy didn't try to replace my dad and yet he felt like a dad. Daniel did too up to a point, although I wasn't around him nearly as much. I didn't really want to think of him as a dad since I was dating his son. That made it too weird. It was bad enough that Tyler's dad was dating my uncle. Tyler was the one who really made the difference. We had become great friends. Finally having an outlet for my overwhelming sexual needs was incredible, but just being with Tyler, the closeness and the companionship, was more valuable. That had surprised me a lot. I'd always thought of sex as the ultimate goal. Sex was everything I thought it would be, but all the rest that came with the relationship was even more special to me.

I was on my own after school. Tyler was busy with Caleb. I didn't mind so much. Tyler and I both had our own lives and as much as I loved spending time with my boyfriend I needed time alone too.

I laughed grimly as I left the house. I laughed because it had just occurred to me that I'd finished all my homework before setting out to do what I wanted to do. Percy wasn't home and Tyler wasn't there to prod me either. I did it all on my own without even thinking about it. I think somewhere in the past few weeks Percy and Tyler had tamed me—then again, maybe not. So what if I finished my homework first thing? I was still a wild boy!

The wild boy wasn't quite sure what to do. If was summer, I could've gone swimming in the IU outdoor swimming pool, which was only a couple of blocks or so from home. I obviously wasn't a student, but for $2 anyone could swim there. It was November now so the pool was closed and it was too cold for swimming anyway. I headed for the Memorial Stadium. It was even closer to home than the pool. There was no football game going on, but maybe the players would be practicing. Sometimes I watched them through the chain-link fence.

When I arrived at the stadium, it was empty. I guessed the team was working out in the weight room or practicing elsewhere or maybe they had an away game. I couldn't remember the schedule. The gates were open so I walked into the stadium itself. Since there was no practice I doubted if anyone would chase me off.

I walked down near the edge of the field and looked up at the stands. I felt tiny standing alone in that huge stadium. The seats went up to dizzying heights and there were thousands of them. I hadn't attended a game yet, but I'd walked over for the tailgate parties. There were people everywhere then and there was free stuff like posters and boxes of popcorn. The roar of the crowd was deafening during games. Now, all was still and I was completely alone where thousands sometimes sat.

I looked across the field. I wasn't alone. There was one other person in the stadium, sitting on the first row of bleachers. I wasn't completely sure, but it looked like Brayden.

I felt a sense of *déjà vu* as I walked around the edge of the field toward him. The last time I'd walked to a stadium I'd happened on Brayden. Did the kid have an obsession with stadiums?

As I drew closer, I was more and more certain I had found Brayden in a stadium again. I wasn't sure why I approached him, but then again maybe I was. The image of him sitting alone day after day was burned into my mind, as was the memory of him crying in Armstrong Stadium.

Brayden looked up as I neared. His eyes were red again and his face was puffy. He had been crying once more. He wiped his tears away and glared at me.

"What do you want, stalker?" he asked gruffly.

"Why are you crying? Why do you sit alone every day?"

"It's none of your fucking business!"

"No, it's not, but sitting alone when you could have friends isn't much fun. Believe me, I know."

"Just go away or I'll..."

"You'll what? You'll fight me? I'm just as big of a bad ass as you, Brayden. I'm sure you remember the last time we tangled."

"You wouldn't understand anyway!"

The slightest crack in a door that had been sealed shut appeared. I sat down close to Brayden.

"I might. Who else can you talk to? You sit alone at lunch and you don't let anyone near you."

"Maybe I like it that way."

"Don't try to bullshit me. I used to be you! Not very long ago I sat alone at that same damn table. I wasn't there because I wanted to be. I was there because I thought I had to be. I thought no one could understand what I was going through."

"Well, you can't understand what I'm going through! No one can so just leave me the fuck alone!" Tears ran down Brayden's cheeks.

"Maybe I can't understand what's bothering you, but you can't keep shit all to yourself. It will eat you alive if you do. Believe me. I know."

Brayden looked at me, his eyes filled with tears, his lower lip trembling. He didn't say anything for a few moments. He just sat there and looked like his life was coming to an end.

"He killed himself, okay? My boyfriend killed himself! Six months ago today! He fucking killed himself!"

Brayden lost it. He buried his face in his hands and bawled his eyes out. My mind was spinning as I scooted closer. I reached out and put my hand on his shoulder, but he jerked away. He turned and looked at me with pure hatred even as he continued to cry.

"Are you happy now? You don't know anything about what I'm going through!" It was hard for Brayden to speak through his sobs, but I could feel his pain and his rage.

"Yes, I do," I said.

Brayden shook his head and glared. If looks could kill, I would've been dead.

"My parents burned to death in a fire a few months ago," I said.

Even as I spoke the words I began to choke up. The old pain returned. The pain I had to deal with every single day welled up with renewed force. Brayden's fury softened into sullen anger. He didn't yell at me so I continued. I don't exactly know why I continued. Maybe I just needed to tell someone. I hadn't even told Tyler the details of the night. The memories were just too painful.

"I woke up one night, coughing. My room was filling with smoke. I hurried to my door, but when I grabbed the doorknob, it seared my hand. I ran to my window, but it was stuck. I grabbed my desk chair and smashed my way through the window. I climbed out..."

I had to stop for a moment because I was beginning to sob. Speaking of that night made me see it in my mind. More than that, I could feel the searing heat, smell the acrid smoke, and feel the sting of the smoke in my eyes. I had to take a deep breath before I could go on.

"I ran to my parent's window, but... There was nothing but flames. There were flames everywhere. The whole house was a ball of fire. I couldn't get in. I couldn't even get close! My parents burned to death in that house and I couldn't help them."

I lost it then, crying so hard I couldn't speak. Brayden just sat there and stared at me. When I got myself under control, I looked into his eyes.

"Don't tell me I don't know what it's like to lose someone I love," I said when I could once again speak. My voice was filled with anger, but I couldn't help it.

We sat there in silence for several moments.

"It's not just losing him that hurts, is it?" I asked quietly. "You feel guilty, so guilty you want to die."

Brayden jerked his head toward me. The shock on his face was clear to read.

"I thought God took my parents away from me because I didn't appreciate them," I said. "I used to get into a lot of trouble and I mean holding-up-a-convenience-store trouble. On top of that, I'm gay so when my parents died in the fire, I figured it was my fault. I was the one who killed them. It wasn't the fire. It was me."

Brayden gazed at me. Neither of us said anything for a few moments, but then slowly Brayden began to speak.

"Things were bad at my old school, after they found out about Stuart and me. I used to have a lot of friends there. We both did. Stuart and I were popular, two of the most popular guys in school. We were jocks—soccer players—and we were good. Everyone wanted to be our friend, but then..."

"They found out you were homos," I said.

Brayden nodded.

"Everything went bad then. We went from popular to outcasts overnight. We tried to keep going, but they wouldn't let up on us. Every day we went to school and they called us names. They threatened us and made fun of us. I thought my teammates would be there for me. I grew up with those guys, but...they were the worst. They...well...they did some horrible things to us. We had to quit the team. It made me feel like a coward, but my teammates hated me and every day I went into the locker room fearing what they might do to me, and worse, what they might do to Stuart."

"So...what happened? What made him..."

"He hung himself, right in the locker room, but it wasn't really Stuart that hung himself. They did it to him."

I looked at Brayden confused and for a moment afraid.

"You don't mean..."

"No, but he couldn't take their cruelty anymore. Even after we quit the team, they hounded us and they weren't alone.

"I am the most to blame. If it weren't for me, he'd still be alive. I was his boyfriend. I was the one who knew him the best. I should've known. I should have read the signs. We could have run away together. He'd still be with me then. He'd still be alive."

There was another long moment of silence. Brayden cried quiet tears.

"I punished myself for what I thought I'd done," I said, filling the silence. "I wouldn't let anyone close to me. I didn't think I deserved to have any friends and I knew no one would like me. I knew no one would ever care about me again, but... I was wrong. My uncle and especially Tyler made me see that. I wasn't a very good son, but I know now my parents loved me and they knew I loved them. What happened wasn't my fault. It was just a horrible, horrible tragedy."

"That's where we *are* different. You didn't start that fire. You didn't cause it. I killed Stuart because I wasn't smart enough to know that he couldn't take it anymore."

Brayden shook his head and tears ran down his face.

"I loved him! I loved him and he's dead because of me! Because of me!"

Brayden began sobbing again. I pulled him close and this time he grabbed onto me, hugged me hard, and cried into my shoulder. Tears stung my eyes.

"You're wrong, Brayden. You can't tell what someone is thinking. No matter how close you are to them, you can't read their mind. You didn't kill Stuart. He killed himself. It's like you said; he couldn't take it anymore. The others are to blame—your teammates and all those who tormented him. They killed him, as surely as if they forced him to hang himself because that's what they did. With words and cruelty, they drove him to take his own life. Blame them if you want, but not yourself."

"I tried to help him," Brayden said, lifting his head and looking into my eyes. "I tried to make things better for him. I tried to be there for him. I tried to make him happy. I loved him so much! Why couldn't I save him?"

Brayden's eyes pleaded with me.

"You're only one person, Brayden. No matter how much you love someone, you can't protect them from the world. All you can do is…what you can do. You've got to stop blaming yourself. Do you think Stuart would want you to blame yourself? Do you think he'd want to see you suffering like this?"

"No. I know he wouldn't, but…"

"There is no but. I never met Stuart, but he must have loved you. There is no way he couldn't love you when you so obviously loved him. I know that my parents want me to be happy. They don't want me to blame myself for what happened. They want me to live and find whatever happiness I can in life. I know that's what they want because if our situations were reversed that's what I would want for them. If you had killed yourself instead, wouldn't you want Stuart to be happy? Wouldn't you want him to make friends and find whatever joy he could?"

Brayden nodded. Tears streamed from his eyes.

"The pain will never go away," Brayden said quietly as he looked out over the green football field.

"No, it won't. It won't ever go away."

"How did you stand it? How do you deal with it?" Brayden asked me, his face a mask of pain. "It hurts so bad I want to die. Sometimes, I think I would have been better off if I'd killed myself too. Sometimes, I feel guilty because I didn't."

"Don't think like that. I thought about killing myself too, but one thing I've learned is that suicide is never the right answer. I read somewhere that suicide is a permanent solution to a temporary problem. There was a time…not long ago at all…that I hurt so bad inside I wanted to die to escape the pain, but I held on and things got better.

"The pain will never go away, but it will dull. You can learn to live with it. You just have to take each day as it comes and grab onto whatever happiness you can. When your life is so desperately painful, the tiniest little bit of pleasure is like…like a brilliant light in the darkness. It's as if the universe knows you have nothing and makes even the littlest thing seem wonderful. You've got to stop blaming yourself. You've got to stop punishing yourself. You have to start living and grabbing each little bit of happiness that comes your way. When you do that, life begins to get better.

"Not long ago, I didn't have anything to live for…at least I thought I didn't, but now I have a home, an uncle who cares about me like I am his son, and a boyfriend who is not only a boyfriend, but a best friend. The pain is still there. I miss my parents so bad sometimes I cry. Sometimes, I have nightmares. Sometimes, I get so sad I don't think I can make it, but I know I can make it because every day I look for what's good. I grab onto it and I won't let it go. That's what you've got to do, Brayden. You've got to start living again. You've got to look for those little bits of happiness, grab onto them, and never let go."

I didn't realize it, but I was trembling slightly. I understood Brayden's pain only too well. Talking to him made me feel my own pain more intensely, but it also made me feel better because I knew I could deal with that pain. My life wasn't perfect, but I did have a life now and it was a good life. I knew Mom and Dad were happy for me and that made me happy.

"So...you still want to fight?" I asked.

Brayden smiled for just a moment.

"I've had my ass kicked enough here lately."

"Me too. Listen...um...let's get out of here. Let's do something. Let's go out to eat. My treat. We'll just hang out and talk. After all, I'm the only friend you've got...so far."

Brayden's eyes lit up with a ray of hope at the word "friend."

"We were enemies a few minutes ago, you know," Brayden said.

"Yeah, we were, but I don't feel that way now. Do you?"

Brayden shook his head.

"How about it then?"

"Won't your boyfriend be jealous?"

"Wow, don't we think highly of ourselves? No. Tyler trusts me. I'll call and tell him right now."

I pulled out my cell phone before Brayden could object and called Tyler.

"Hey, I found a really hot guy and I want to take him out to eat. Is that okay?" I asked.

"Another one? You slut."

I laughed.

"It's Brayden."

"Brayden? Seriously? At least you're right about the hot part."

"Yeah, long story, but I want to hang out with him. I might even talk him into sitting with us at lunch."

I looked at Brayden as I said that. He didn't give any indication of whether he liked the idea or not.

"Um... is it safe? I mean..."

"It's all good, Tyler. Brayden and I won't be fighting today."

"Just be careful."

The concern in my boyfriend's voice made me smile.

"There is nothing to worry about. Trust me. I love you."

"I love you, too."

"So, your boyfriend thinks I'm hot, huh?" Brayden said after I'd put my cell away. He could obviously hear both ends of our conversation.

"Well, you are, so yeah, but don't get any ideas. Tyler is taken."

Brayden smiled for a moment, but then looked very sad. I knew he was thinking about his dead boyfriend. I hopped up. I didn't want to give Brayden the chance to slip into depression.

"Come on. I don't have a car so I hope you don't mind walking."

"I don't mind," Brayden said.

"I'll take you to the Bakehouse. It won't be crowded at this time of day."

"We're going to eat in a bakery?"

"No. It's called the Scholar's Inn Bakehouse. They sell bagels and cupcakes and cookies, but they also have pizza, burgers, and good breakfast stuff. It's downtown. Percy has taken me there."

"Percy is your uncle, you said?"

"Yeah. He hates to cook so we eat out a lot."

We walked to Fee Lane and then headed south. We passed Briscoe, McNutt, and Foster dorms and then walked on. We didn't speak for a while. I think we both needed a little break. We had talked about some heavy stuff. I'd told Brayden things I hadn't planned on telling him, but sometimes things just come out. I felt like I needed to tell Brayden and not just because I wanted him to know he wasn't alone.

I was pleased with myself for getting Brayden to open up. I think I was probably the only person who could make Brayden spill his troubles. He needed someone who would get in his face and not back down even under the threat of violence. There were a couple of times Brayden looked ready to punch me in the face, but once I started I was determined not to back down. If it came to blows then that's what happened. It's not like I would've earned more detention. The worst outcome would have been getting my ass kicked, but I could hold my own with Brayden.

The anger had gone out of Brayden, but he looked so sad I pitied him. He had been through something truly horrible. I wasn't sure what I'd do if something happened to Tyler, but if he died in a way that made me blame myself, I knew it would be a thousand times worse. Brayden had been in his own private Hell. I wasn't so cocky to think I'd saved him and that everything was okay now, but at least I'd drawn him out. Now, he had someone he could talk to about his problems. I knew that was worth a lot. Just knowing I could talk to Tyler or Percy or Caleb made my problems seem smaller.

I hoped to draw Brayden into my circle of friends, as Tyler had drawn me in. Friends were always good, even if one of them was Dylan. I wondered what Dylan would say if he knew I was eating out with his dream boy. I looked at Brayden walking beside me. I could see why Dylan was so infatuated. Brayden was extremely handsome and the bad boy vibe he gave off made him extremely sexy.

"What?" Brayden asked when he caught me looking.

"I had no idea you were gay."

"Well, blonds aren't known for being bright."

Brayden didn't smile, but I had the feeling he was teasing me. *That* was a very good sign.

"We're not especially bright, but we're majorly hung. It's nature's way of evening things out."

"Blonds are hung?" Brayden said, raising a dark eyebrow to express his doubt.

"*Majorly* hung. It's not widely known. We try to keep it a secret. Our blond hair gives us an unfair advantage as it is."

"You're so full of shit, Caspian."

I gave Brayden my best devilish grin.

"So, back to you being a homo…"

"What about it?"

"You hid it really well."

"I didn't hide it."

"You sure went after Dylan for drooling over you."

"I told you. I went after Dylan because he pissed me off. He was so annoying! Every time I looked around he was there. I felt like I was being stalked. He was getting on my nerves."

"You *were* being stalked. Dylan is relentless."

"Does he really blow as many guys as everyone says?"

"Why do you want to know? Thinking of trying him out?"

"Have you?"

I hesitated a moment too long before answering.

"You have, haven't you? Dylan has given you head!"

Brayden's smirk made me want to smack him, but I calmed myself down.

"Just once."

"Was he good?"

"Actually, he was incredible."

"So why just once?"

"It's a long story, but I'm with Tyler now so I can't hook up with Dylan."

"Would you if you weren't dating Tyler?"

"I probably would. I know Dylan will do it and he does give incredible head and I do get really horny."

"You're a guy. Of course, you get horny."

"True."

"I don't think I like Dylan. He gays it up too much," Brayden said.

"Gays it up?"

"He acts like such a stereotype. I don't like guys who can't be themselves."

"Dylan is being himself. That's not an act. That is just how he is. Dylan is probably more himself than anyone else in the whole school."

"Really?"

I nodded.

"He's more himself than you? So, you put on an act?" Brayden asked.

"I'm mostly myself. I try not to smile too much, and I throw in a glare here and there I'm not feeling. I do have a rep as a bad ass to maintain."

"I guess you're not a fake. I hate fakes."

"I figure, why bother pretending to be something I'm not? If someone doesn't like me, they can go fuck themselves."

Brayden nodded.

"I like that. So...the Goth-thing? That's the real you?"

"It is, but...I haven't been feeling it as much lately. I stopped wearing the eyeliner 'cause of the black eyes. I'm getting a little tired of the eyeliner anyway so I think I'm going to drop it. I can't give up my collar or wristbands. I'd feel naked without them."

Brayden and I were actually talking. I was amazed. The guys would be astounded.

We walked downtown to the square, and I took Brayden into the Bakehouse.

"Order whatever you want. I'm buying and I'm seldom this generous so take advantage," I said.

I gazed at the menu boards written in chalk. The burgers at the Bakehouse were incredible, but then so was the pizza... I liked the Euros too..."

"What's a Euro?" Brayden asked.

"It's a sandwich sold on the streets of Paris. It's served on a baked baguette. They're really good."

"Next question. What's a baguette?"

"It's sort of a long, narrow bun."

"Gotcha."

Hmm... Did I want a Euro? Maybe a honey club Euro? I looked over at the breakfast menu and made my decision.

"I'm getting the Sriracha scramble," I announced.

"What's that?"

I pointed to the board.

"It's scrambled eggs with sausage, red and green peppers, Monterey Jack cheese, and spicy Sriracha chili sauce. It comes with home fries and Bakehouse toast. Oh! The toast here is extra good."

"I can't decide so I'll get that too."

I went up to the counter and ordered. I gave my name, then handed Brayden a cup. We walked over to the soda fountain and filled our cups with Pepsi and ice.

I liked to sit at the counter that looked out the windows, but I wanted to talk with Brayden, so I picked a booth instead. We slid in and drank our Pepsi's while we waited.

"Thank you for trusting me enough to tell me what happened," I said.

"It's not a secret but I don't like talking about it and yet..."

"Sometimes you want to talk about it?"

"Yeah."

"When I came here, I wouldn't talk to anyone about my parents. I'd get angry and even violent if someone asked about them. It hurt just to think about them, but part of me really wanted to talk about them. Tyler is the one who got me to talk. I felt so much better when I finally opened up to him. It didn't bring my parents back, but sharing the pain made it feel less painful."

"You're brave. I came this close to jumping you," Brayden said, holding his fingers about a quarter-inch apart.

"Yeah, I know. You looked ready to pummel me."

"You really got in my face."

"We're a lot alike. I knew that's what it would take to get you to talk."

"Why did you want me to talk? We barely know each other and we haven't exactly been buddies."

"I don't like to see anyone suffer. I know what it's like. Things are much better for me than they were, but I carry pain with me that will never go away. No matter what I do my parents are still going to be dead. It hurts. It hurts a lot. Sometimes, I don't feel like I can stand it. When I saw you crying... well, guys like you and me don't cry easily. I knew something horrible had happened to you, and I also knew you were alone with it. I wouldn't wish that on someone I hated."

"You're a nice guy."

"You start spreading that around and you'll be picking up your teeth off the floor."

"Your dirty little secret is safe with me."

"I'm nice, sometimes, but I'm also selfish and I can be a real jerk and I'd be lying if I said I'm sorry about that."

Brayden stared into the distance.

"What was Stuart like?" I asked.

Brayden looked at me, momentarily surprised that I knew he was thinking about his dead boyfriend. I could read it in his eyes. It was the same way I'm sure I looked when I was thinking about my parents.

"He was beautiful, and I don't mean just physically. The first time I saw him... wow; that blond hair and those eyes...and his body. Damn! I wanted him so bad. He looked into my eyes and we connected. Just like that. In that moment everything changed. It wasn't just lust anymore. I fell in love with him, right then and right there. It was like... it was like we were made for each other. I know that sounds like a cliché, but that was exactly it. As I got to know him better, it became more and more apparent that he was as beautiful inside as outside. He was so strong. He was never afraid to stand up for someone who was getting picked on. He was all guy, but he cared about everyone around him. When we played soccer, he was an animal. Guys on other teams were scared of him because he was so fearless and ferocious. I remember one game... he got in this other guy's face and they got in a fistfight right there on the field. I had to help pull him off the other guy because he had him down and was ground pounding him. After that game, we were walking home and he stooped down on the sidewalk. I had no idea what he was doing, but then I saw this little earthworm in his hand. He picked up it off the concrete and put it in the grass. He looked at me and said, "The concrete sucks all the moisture from their bodies. They die if they stay on a sidewalk too long." He'd just been kicked out of a game for kicking someone's ass and there he was rescuing an earthworm."

Brayden actually laughed for moment, but then he looked at me and tears filled his eyes. He wiped them away quickly.

"He's not really gone, you know. He's inside you. When you spent time together, he became a part of you. He'll always be with you," I said.

"Sometimes I feel like he is with me."

"That's because he is. I can feel my mom and dad like that. Sometimes, I can feel them so strongly I expect them to appear. I can't see them but I know they are there."

"So, you think there's a life after death?"

"I'm sure of it. I don't know how it works or what happens, but it's real. I don't believe any religious bullshit. I'm not even sure I believe in a god, but there's something there. How could there not be? I think that whatever is there is something we can't understand, so I don't even try. I just know that it's there. I really believe I'll be with my parents again someday and you'll be with Stuart too."

"I wish I believed like that, but I don't know what I believe."

"I'll believe it for you."

Brayden smiled again. He was very good-looking when he was brooding, but when he smiled... Wow. Stuart wasn't the only one in their relationship who was beautiful.

"Caspian!" a waiter called out.

I waved my hand and soon our Sriracha scrambles were before us. I buttered my toast and sprinkled it with the brown, unprocessed sugar I could find only at the Bakehouse. I took a bite and nearly moaned. Mom would have loved the Bakehouse toast. She couldn't be here, so I was going to enjoy it for her.

Brayden and I didn't talk much while we ate, but I think he liked eating with me. I was a loner, but I liked to be with others too. I remembered my days of sitting alone in the cafeteria during my self-imposed exile. I projected a defiant air, but I'd been lonely and felt a little self-conscious too.

We talked more after we'd finished eating. We stayed away from the serious topics and instead talked about teachers we liked and didn't like, which jocks we thought were probably homos, and what was the coolest car.

"Hey, um, why don't you start sitting with me at lunch? I know from experience that sitting alone sucks and the gang I sit with is really cool, with the possible exception of Dylan."

"I don't know if I want to sit near him. He'll be leering at me and trying to grope me."

"If he touches you, smack the crap out of him. I find that the threat of violence is usually enough to keep him at bay."

"I don't know..."

"Come on, you surely aren't scared of Dylan."

"Screw you! I'm not afraid of *him* or anyone!"

"So sit with us."

"Maybe."

"Well, if you do, I promise you don't have to sit by Dylan. I'd offer to hold him while you punch him if he got on your nerves, but I'm sure you can handle him by himself."

"Yeah, but he sure went after that Cory kid. He fights like a girl, but he was all over Cory."

"I pictured him as a cat with all that kicking and scratching. I would probably have gotten my ass kicked if Dylan hadn't helped me with Cory. That dude is strong."

"He's also about twice your size."

"That's why us little guys have to stick together," I said.

"Who are you calling little?"

"Well... you aren't blond..."

"I've got plenty where it counts, smartass, not that you'll be seeing it."

"Saving it for Dylan?"

"Screw you."

"No, thanks. *I* have a boyfriend." My face paled. "Damn! I'm sorry! I didn't mean..."

"Relax. I know what you meant. Stuart would have thought that was funny."

I smiled.

"See? I told you. He's still with you."

# Chapter 8

"Well, hello. Look who is heading in our direction. Mmm," Dylan said.

I looked up. Brayden was heading our way. I grinned. On the walk back from the Bakehouse, I'd worked to convince Brayden to join our table. All the effort had paid off.

"Don't start coming onto him or I will kick your ass, Dylan," I said in my most menacing tone. Dylan paled slightly. He knew I meant business.

"Hey, Brayden," I called out when he was near. "Sit by me."

Brayden hesitated slightly. I could see him fighting with himself. His instinct was to isolate himself, but he knew he couldn't go on being alone forever. He also knew his dead boyfriend would not want him to be alone. Brayden sat down next to me.

"Guys, this is Brayden, former enemy, then ally, then enemy, and now friend. He's the one who took on Cory and Justin when they were trying to bash Dylan. Brayden, you've met Tyler and Dylan, but that's Caleb, Tyreece, and Jesse. You'll have to forgive Jesse. He usually has his nose stuck in a magazine. He isn't rude. He's just obsessed with fashion."

"Hey," Brayden said.

Dylan gazed at Brayden dreamily. I was willing to bet he was picturing him naked. It was a good thing Dylan didn't know Brayden was gay or he'd have been on him even more. Then again, maybe not: Dylan never let a little thing like sexual orientation stop him when he was after a guy.

Brayden didn't talk much. He wasn't unfriendly, but he was in his usual sullen mood. I noticed several girls giving him the same look Dylan did. Girls loved the brooding type, but tough luck for them. Brayden wasn't interested in girls.

The guys kept up an easy conversation and didn't talk about anything that would leave Brayden feeling like an outsider. Every group has inside jokes and shared experiences that make no sense to someone new. I was a recent addition myself, but even my short time with the guys had made me one of them. Brayden didn't have that yet. At least, he wasn't still sitting alone.

"Dude, stop leering at me," Brayden snarled after a few minutes. No one had to ask whom he was talking to.

"But you're soooo hot," Dylan said.

"Just because I jumped in to save you from those jerks doesn't mean I won't kick your ass myself. I'm not interested so back off."

Brayden was one scary dude. Dylan, of course, was unaffected.

"You're so confident and strong."

"Dylan, shut up," I said. "He's not interested. Do you know what 'not interested' means?"

"That's like playing hard to get, right?" Dylan asked.

I banged my head on the table. When I raised my head, Dylan was staring at me.

"What?" he asked innocently.

I growled in frustration.

"You drive me crazy!" I said.

"Well, my offer of a three-way still stands," Dylan said, looking like a dog hoping to be invited for a walk.

"NO!" Tyler and I said together.

I could swear I saw Brayden smile for a moment.

"Most of us have decided to find Dylan amusing," Jesse said, actually putting down his magazine. "I think of him as the puppy I never had."

Jesse petted Dylan's hair. I thought Dylan was going to do his dog impression, but he was too busy swooning with pleasure. Jesse had actually touched him.

"I think of him as a pain-in-the-ass!" I said.

"I don't usually top, but I can give it a try," Dylan said eagerly.

"That's not what I meant!"

This time I was sure of it. Brayden smiled. Dylan had that effect on people. He was hard not to like and believe me I had tried.

Near the end of lunch, I looked at Tyler and motioned toward Dylan with my eyes. My boyfriend got the message easily. When the bell rang and everyone stood, I walked along with Brayden.

"I'll walk along with you to class," I said.

Dylan moved in, but Tyler cut him off.

"Hey, Dylan. Which boy do you think is cuter in *Big Time Rush*?" Tyler asked. He knew exactly how to distract Dylan.

"They're all soooo hot, but I have a thing for James! He's so sexy! Did you see that episode where he showed his abs? I wanna lick him all over!"

I winked at Tyler. Brayden and I made our escape.

"Dylan is actually harmless," I said. "He was always drooling over me before Tyler and I started dating. I threatened to beat his face in now and then and that helped keep him in line. He still drools over me, but he won't make a move because I'm with Tyler."

"Is that dude like… not too bright? He seems kind of dim."

I laughed.

"Actually, Dylan is smart. It's just that he lives in his own little gay world where straight means that a guy is only willing to receive head and not give it. I believe he really thinks that guys only hook up with girls to make babies."

"So, he's insane."

"A little."

"I want to kick his ass, but… he's so damned funny."

"That's Dylan. I've wanted to bash his head into the table more times than I can count, but he's disarming. Every time I'm ready to pound him he acts goofy or says something so clueless he makes me laugh."

"So, is that Jesse kid gay?"

"No."

"No?"

"I was sure he was gay when I met him too, but he's not."

"Are you sure? He's got to be a homo."

"I'm sure. According to Tyler, Dylan has done his best to get into Jesse's pants and he's failed. If Dylan can't seduce him, no one can."

We arrived at our creative writing class and dropped into our seats, which were next to each other. I leaned over and spoke quietly.

"You know every girl in this room wants you," I said.

Brayden's only response was to raise one eyebrow. Yeah, he knew, but like me, he didn't care. At least the girls didn't chase me as much anymore. Coming out and having a boyfriend did tend to cut down on female interest, although for some it merely made me a challenge. They could forget it. I was not available. Even if I was single, I wasn't up for sex with girls. Yuck!

When class ended, Brayden and I went our separate ways. I hoped he'd continue to sit at our table at lunch. I didn't know what he was going through and yet I had a good idea. Losing someone you love hurts. Brayden had the extra burden of wondering if his boyfriend would still be alive if only he done things a little differently. He couldn't help but wonder. As horrible as my experience was, I think Brayden had it much harder. I wanted to help him. I just wasn't sure how.

***

"I can't believe Brayden sat with us!"

I pulled my head out of my locker. Dylan was hopping up and down with excitement.

"I invited him."

"When? Have you been hanging out with him? Do you know where he lives? Did he say anything about me?"

Dylan asked his questions so fast it was like one continuous question.

"I ran into him and spent a little time with him yesterday. I don't know where he lives and if I did, I wouldn't tell you because you'd get yourself in trouble for stalking him. He said he thinks you're annoying and he's going to punch you in the face if you keep bothering him."

"He really talked about me?"

"Dylan! Did you just hear what I said? He doesn't like you. He doesn't want you leering at him or pawing him. If you don't leave him alone, he will kick your ass and when he does I'm not going to stop him. I would think the time he went after you would be hint enough that he's not interested."

"Yeah, but then he saved me! Just like you did!"

Dylan hugged me before I had a chance to duck.

"Get off me!"

"Dylan! Off my boyfriend!" Tyler yelled as he walked up.

"I couldn't help myself. He encouraged me."

"Encouraged you?" Tyler asked. "How? By not knocking your teeth out?"

Dylan laughed.

"Awww!" he said, moving toward me again.

"Back!" I said, pointing.

"So, why were you hugging Dylan? Are you two having a secret affair?" Tyler asked.

"That is not even funny."

"Come on, Caspian. We don't have to hide it anymore," Dylan said, trying to put his arm over my shoulder. I shoved him off.

"Go away!" I said.

Dylan just giggled.

"You're so sexy when you're angry."

He actually tried to hug me again.

"Dyyyy-laan," I growled in warning.

"Shouldn't the jocks be getting *naked* right about now so they can put on their *uniforms* for practice?" Tyler said.

Dylan took off like a shot.

"You shouldn't have said that. He's going to get himself killed."

"He'll be fine. He hooks up with half the jocks on the down low anyway. The worst they'll do is toss him out, which they've probably done several times before."

"That boy is... different," I said.

"I just hope he doesn't end up with some sexually transmitted disease."

I nodded, but I didn't even want to think about that.

# Chapter 9

I slept in Saturday morning until 11, and then Tyler came over after lunch. We finished up our homework and made out on my bed. When Percy left, we wasted no time in getting naked. We were all over each other just like before. I was so worked up I couldn't wait to fuck Tyler again, but when I went for a condom, he stopped me.

"I want to try top this time," he said.

I hadn't anticipated that.

"Um...I thought you were a bottom," I said, confused.

"I think I am, mostly, but how will I know if I don't try?"

"Uh, I don't know. I..."

"You don't want to?"

"It's just... I'd feel... It would make me feel like a girl."

Tyler frowned. I knew I'd said the wrong thing.

"Do you think of me as a girl because I let you top me?"

"No, I... I just..."

"Fine," Tyler said. I could tell by the tone of his voice he was pissed off.

We lay back on my bed, not speaking for several moments. I really didn't think of Tyler as a girl because he'd bottomed for me. Tyler was more sensitive and less aggressive than me, but he was still all guy. He wasn't flamboyant like Dylan. So, why did I have this stupid idea in my head that bottoming would make me feel like a girl?

I turned my head to look at Tyler. His anger had turned to sadness. Damn. The last thing I wanted to do was hurt him.

"Um... does it hurt a lot?" I asked.

"It hurts at first, but then it hurts less and feels good. Even the pain becomes a part of it and turns to pleasure."

"How can pain become pleasure?"

"It's hard to explain. When you were in me and it hurt, I felt... like I was giving you something. I was enduring the pain to make you feel very, very good. I guess there's a submissive side to it too. I was submitting to you, letting you dominate me and yet you weren't really dominating me. We were making each other feel good."

"Oh," I said.

The pain didn't frighten me much. I didn't enjoy pain, but I could take it. I was sure Dylan bottomed a lot and if he could take the pain, I surely could. It was the other part that bothered me. I didn't want to feel as if I was submitting to someone. But, this was Tyler. It's not like we were rivals and I was surrendering. I wanted to make him feel good. I was being selfish. Tyler had given it up for me so why couldn't I do the same for him? So what if I was submitting to him? Surely I had the courage to be vulnerable. Surely I was brave enough to risk feeling... girlish... if it even came to that. I wasn't a coward. That thought made up my mind for me. I reached over, grabbed the condom and some lube, and handed them to Tyler.

"Fuck me," I said.

A smile slowly spread across Tyler's face. I'm sure he knew a good deal of what I'd been thinking. He knew I was doing this for him. I hoped I didn't dislike it too much. At least it would be a new experience, another sexual first, and I'd know if I liked it or not. I didn't expect to like it. I didn't want... I realized something. I didn't want to like it. Was that the real reason I was hesitant? That was just stupid. So what if I liked it? I was the same Caspian Perseus no matter what I liked to do in bed.

Tyler was ready. He pulled my legs up over his shoulders just as I had his. I was uncomfortable, not physically uncomfortable, but the very position made me feel like a girl.

*Man up, Caspian. Stop being stupid.*

Tyler pushed inside me and I cried out in pain. I couldn't help it. My ass was on fire. Tyler held perfectly still, just as I had. I didn't tell him to pull it out although that's exactly what I wanted to tell him. I could do this. Dammit! If Dylan could do this, I could!

I nodded for Tyler to go in deeper. The pain hit me again, but it wasn't so bad this time. I was ready for it. Tyler kept inching himself in, and the pain decreased. In a few more moments, he was all the way in. An expression of ecstasy crossed his features.

Tyler slowly pulled out and pushed in again. He was right. The pain diminished and even what pain remained began to feel good. The sensation of Tyler inside me felt weird and I wanted him to stop, but yet there was a sexual pleasure to it I didn't want to end.

I was determined to see this to the end, not only for Tyler, but for me. I was going to experience bottoming from beginning to end. Then, I'd know if it was for me or not. At the moment I was thinking "not," but we weren't finished.

Tyler went faster and harder. Sweat trickled down his lean torso and he breathed harder and harder. I began to moan and that surprised me, but I gave into the pleasure. I wanted Tyler to stop and yet part of me didn't.

It hurt. The pain didn't become pleasure for me. It kind of mixed in with the pleasure, but it was still pain. Tyler looked totally hot above me, but I willed him to finish. I gritted my teeth. I wanted him to stop, but I wasn't going to ask. I couldn't live with myself if I couldn't do what Dylan probably did with ease.

It was hottest near the end. I still wanted Tyler to stop, but watching him was hot. He was totally consumed with fucking me. His muscles tensed and flexed and his expression was one of pure pleasure. I felt him throb inside me and Tyler cried out in ecstasy.

Tyler collapsed on top of me. His heart pounded against my chest and he was all sweaty. Mercifully, he pulled out of me. He rolled off me and we lay there on our backs with Tyler panting. My boyfriend was a stud, but I didn't like bottoming. It felt kind of good, but the whole idea of it was uncomfortable and it hurt! I was probably going to be sore for days. I'd tried bottoming and it was not for me.

Tyler leaned up on one elbow and gazed at me. We smiled at each other. Tyler kept looking at me.

"You're not a bottom, are you?"

I slowly shook my head, hoping he wouldn't be too disappointed.

"I guess it's a good thing I am then."

"I'll... I'll bottom for you sometimes if you want," I said. Speaking the words was a great sacrifice because the truth was that once was more than enough.

"No. You wanted me to stop, didn't you?"

I nodded.

"Thanks for doing it for me. I wanted to give topping a try, but... it's not my thing. It was hot, but it didn't feel quite right. From now on, you're the top."

Tyler kissed me on the lips, then grinned as he noticed my aroused state. He leaned over and took me into his mouth. I moaned and in only a few moments cried out with pleasure as Tyler took me over the edge.

We slipped into the shower together and did a little making out as the hot water pounded down upon us. I wondered if some heteros didn't bash gays simply because they were jealous. It was much easier for us gay boys to get together. Poor straight boys had to plead and beg and take girls on expensive dates to get even a little action, but boys like Tyler and me could just go at it whenever we were alone. Then again, before I met Tyler, I wasn't getting any. I was isolated and alone so maybe gay boys didn't have it so easy after all.

We dried off and dressed. Tyler wanted to go for a walk and I didn't hate the idea so I agreed. We stepped outside and walked aimlessly around the neighborhood.

"Are you okay?" Tyler asked.

"I'm a little sore, but I'm fine."

"How do you *feel*?"

I looked at Tyler with a question in my eyes.

"I mean, how do you feel emotionally? Are you okay with what we did?"

"I'm fine. I'm sorry about what I said about the bottom being a girl. That was just stupid. I didn't think of you as a girl when I was on top. I was thinking how incredibly sexy you were and how hot you looked." I grinned.

"So, no regrets?"

I stopped for a moment and looked at Tyler. He was obviously concerned.

"I'm fine, Tyler, really. I don't want to do it again, but I'm glad I tried it. Now, I know it's not for me. I was a little curious about it. You were really into bottoming for me and Dylan bends over for guys *all* the time, so there had to be something enjoyable about it. It felt good part of the time and was kind of hot. It's not for me, but I think I understand now why some guys are into it. I'm just glad *you* like it." I grinned.

"Oh, I like it a lot."

We walked all over downtown. We passed by Bub's Hamburgers & Ice Cream, the Scholar's Inn Bakehouse, Howard's Bookstore, the Trojan Horse, and Opie Taylor's, among other places. After strolling around the square we headed for campus.

We followed the path beside Dunn Meadow and stopped for a moment at the spot where I first kissed Tyler.

"That was probably the most unusual first kiss *ever*," Tyler said, teasing me. He was thinking about our first kiss too.

I had kissed Tyler at the end of a fistfight. I had him down on his back and was all ready to slug him in the face when I lost control and did what I'd been denying I wanted to do. I darted in and kissed Tyler on the lips.

"Boys with issues make life an adventure and I had lots of issues. I still do," I said.

"True, but now you're dealing with your problems."

"Thanks to you. If it wasn't for you and Percy..."

Tyler just smiled and we walked on. We walked all over campus, visiting familiar sites. We strolled through Dunn's Woods, stopped at the Rose Well House, and then left campus through the Sample Gates. I felt like I was walking through a big movie set where the story of my life was being filmed.

By the time we returned home, my legs and feet were tired. Percy was back and he was in a very good mood. Tyler eyed him suspiciously.

"He's too happy. I think he's up to something," Tyler said.

"I still think they're planning on sending us both away to boarding school."

"Daniel and I are taking you to DeAngelo's at six. You'll find out then," Percy said.

"You don't want to wait a moment longer. You want to tell us now," Tyler said, staring into Percy's eyes.

"You're not a Jedi, Tyler. Give it up."

"It was worth a shot."

"You're such a geek," I said, then smiled.

***

Six p.m. rolled around quickly. I was curious about whatever Percy and Daniel wanted to discuss with Tyler and me, but it was probably something stupid, like a trip to some boring historic site that I didn't want to see. Percy was into all that old crap, but I liked living life, not looking at leftovers from previous lives. Tyler was more curious than me. He sensed something bigger than a trip was up. I hoped so. Percy made me go with him to tour the Wiley House in town. B-o-r-i-n-g!

Percy, Tyler, and I climbed into the Prius, and Percy drove the short distance to Tyler's place to pick up Daniel. Both Percy and Daniel were dressed up really nice in button-down shirts and khaki pants. Tyler had convinced me to put on a blue polo shirt instead of my usual black. I'd dumped my eyeliner a couple of days before. The spiked wristbands and collar were staying, at least until I got tired of them too. I didn't tell Tyler, but I kind of liked the blue shirt. Percy bought it for me, but I'd never worn it before. Tyler looked very sharp in his pale yellow polo and jeans, but then Tyler always looked good.

DeAngelo's was an upscale Italian place in Eastland Plaza, which was just across from College Mall. The atmosphere was elegant but not snooty. Still, I would rather have eaten at the China Buffet a couple of doors down.

Percy motioned for Tyler and me slide into the booth first, probably to keep us from escaping. Percy sat by me and Daniel sat by his son. Our waiter soon arrived and took our drink orders. We spent the next couple of minutes browsing menus.

By the time the waiter had returned, Tyler and I had decided to share a B-Town Biggie Calzone. Percy said they were *really* big so neither of us figured we could handle one alone. We ordered ours with pepperoni, extra mozzarella, and spicy Asiago cheese. Daniel ordered Creole Seafood Cannelloni and Percy ordered Roasted Chicken and Artichoke Ravioli.

"Okay, we're here and we've ordered. Start talking," Tyler said.

I grinned. Tyler was amusing when he got pushy.

Percy took Daniel's hand across the table.

"Your father and I are committing to each other," Percy said.

"You mean you're getting married? Yes!" Tyler said.

"We're not getting officially married, which is illegal in Indiana."

"Which is total bullshit!" I said, then quieted down.

"You could go to Iowa where you can get married," Tyler said.

"True, but neither of us feel a marriage is necessary. Neither of us are much on ceremonies, and weddings tend to be boring affairs."

"Thank God!" I said, then quieted down again when everyone looked at me. "What?"

"We don't need a piece of paper that says we're together. This is it, right here and right now, we are officially a couple, now and forever," Daniel said.

"But there has to be a ceremony! This is big! It's huge! My dad is getting married! Well, the same as married," Tyler said.

"Better than married," Percy said, smiling at Daniel.

I didn't quite get that and I don't think Tyler did either, but there was obviously some deep meaning hidden in Percy's words.

"We have to invite Grandmother and Grandfather and your parents too, Percy. I can arrange everything. Caspian will help me, I'm sure." Tyler looked at me and he could tell I wasn't thrilled with the idea. "I'm sure Dylan will help too. We'll get a cake and..."

Daniel held up his hand. It was a good thing because I think Tyler would have gone on and on forever. I smiled just watching him. I don't think I'd seen him so excited before.

"What do you think?" Daniel asked Percy.

"Can we keep it small and simple with just a few friends and family members?" Percy asked, looking at Tyler.

"We will keep it very small," Tyler promised. "Just a cake and some lights and decorations and a little, short ceremony. I just want everyone to be there for this. It's important."

"You'll hound me until I say 'yes' won't you," Percy said. It was not a question.

"Mercilessly," Tyler said.

"Okay then, but keep it small, less than a dozen people if at all possible, and nothing fancy. I do not wear ties, *ever*."

Daniel laughed.

"This is going to be sooooo cool," Tyler said. "I can't wait to start planning!"

Tyler hugged his dad and would have hugged Percy if he could have reached him.

"We can have the ceremony in that gazebo out back, but it will have to be painted. I'll decorate it with clear lights and..."

"It's November, Tyler," Daniel said.

"We will use the double-parlor! We'll put up a big, white Christmas tree and decorate it with clear lights. We can put more lights around the fireplace and…"

Percy, Daniel, and I ate fresh-baked bread with olive oil and Parmesan cheese while Tyler spewed out ideas for the commitment ceremony. I had to fight not to laugh because he'd ask us about an idea and move on to another before anyone had a chance to open his mouth. The boy was out of control.

The waiter sat a huge calzone between Tyler and me. It was the first calzone I'd ever seen. It looked like a pizza folded over and it smelled delicious.

Tyler kept talking while we ate although not as much. Some of the rest of us had a chance to speak. My mind was spinning. Percy was getting married? I knew my uncle and Tyler's dad were really close, but… married or the same as married anyway? It was a bit much to take in all at once.

After we were all well-stuffed, Percy drove us back home and we all sat at the kitchen table.

"We have a few more things to discuss with you," Percy said.

"Here it comes. Boarding school," I said.

"As tempting as that idea is, no," Percy said.

"Percy and I have been looking at houses," Daniel said.

"Houses?" Tyler asked. "You mean, move?"

"This will be *our* home," Daniel said, indicating all four of us. "We need a place that can belong to all of us."

"Why do we have to move? I don't want to move. I've lived there since I was five. Our house is plenty big enough. Why can't the house we live in now be *our* house?"

"That is a possibility we discussed."

"I really don't want to move, Dad."

"We haven't had much luck finding a place so far," Percy said.

"So stop looking. You and Caspian can move in with us. It will be *our* home."

"What do you think?" Percy asked me.

"Well, uh… this is all happening so fast, but I guess so. Our house is too small for four."

"You won't mind moving?" Percy asked. I could tell he was concerned.

"No. I won't mind *if* you hire movers."

Daniel and Percy looked at each other and smiled.

"You can have the room next to mine! This will be soooo cool!" Tyler said, smiling at me.

Daniel looked at Percy.

"So, what do you think?" Daniel asked.

"What do *you* think?" Percy asked.

"I like the idea. I wasn't entirely happy about moving. So, tell me what you think."

"I wasn't looking forward to more house-hunting, and I had my doubts about Tyler wanting to move so why not?"

"When can you move in?" Tyler asked, totally excited again.

"We'll discuss that," Percy said.

"I guess that solves the house problem. We do have some other matters to discuss," Daniel said.

"Like?" Tyler asked.

"Daniel and I will be having some legal work done so that we'll have advantages and rights similar to those we would have if we were married."

"Like what?" Tyler asked.

"We will arrange it so that if one of us is in the hospital, the other will be admitted as family. There will be wills, of course, and various other arrangements, and there is one that concerns both of you."

Tyler and I looked at Percy. I had no idea what he was talking about.

"How would you feel if we both adopted you, Caspian?" Daniel asked me.

I was speechless.

"I would adopt you, too, Tyler, but you're eighteen so you can't be adopted. I already think of you as my son," Percy said.

Tyler was up and out of his seat hugging Percy in a flash. I just sat there. Tears began to roll down my cheeks. Daniel cared enough about me to adopt me?

"This is so incredible! We get to have two dads!" Tyler said.

Suddenly, everyone was looking at me.

"What do you say, Caspian?" Daniel asked.

I nodded through my tears. I still couldn't speak.

Percy hugged me to him, then Tyler hugged me, then Daniel got up and hugged me too. Percy was my guardian and I knew he loved me, but suddenly I felt like I had a family again. I didn't realize until the moment just how much that meant to me.

We sat back down and talked for a bit more, then Tyler and I went to my room while Percy and Daniel kept talking. They probably had a lot to figure out, although I think they'd mostly planned it all out before telling Tyler and me what was going on.

Tyler gave me a hug and then a quick kiss as we entered my room.

"Are you going to be okay with moving?" Tyler asked, sitting down on my bed.

"I've only lived here with Percy for a couple of months. I think of this as home, but I'm not especially attached to it. There is nothing left of my home in California. I would have been upset if we moved from there, but..."

Tyler nodded.

"Your new room will bigger than this one and has a cool view of the side yard and you can see into the bedroom window of the house next door."

"So?"

"Brice Parker lives next door. He works out shirtless in his bedroom and he often runs around in his room naked."

"You Peeking Tom!"

"Hey, if he didn't want anyone to see, he'd close the curtains."

I laughed.

"Does Dylan know about the view?"

"No way! I'd never get him out of there. He'd either want to stay in my room or move in to what will now be your bedroom."

"Well, he's not moving in with me!"

"Living together will be so cool," Tyler said.

"You don't feel weird about Percy and me moving in?"

"Are you kidding? I've wanted Dad and Percy to get together like this from almost the moment I met Percy. Now you... there was a time I was not at all happy you had entered the picture, but now I love it!"

Tyler hugged me and kissed me on the lips. Our kiss was lingering. We pulled apart and smiled. I gazed into Tyler's eyes.

"I didn't know your dad cared enough about me to adopt me. I knew he liked me, but..."

"He cares about you a lot, Caspian. He wants us to be a family."

I smiled again.

"I'm glad I quit wearing the eyeliner or I'd have black streaks down my face. Having a family again makes me think about Mom and Dad."

"You've had a family all along, Caspian. You've always had Percy. Now, you'll have a bigger family!"

"I always thought it would be cool to have a brother," I said.

"Me too."

Tyler hugged me close. I felt safe and content as I hadn't since the night Mom and Dad died.

# Chapter 10

"Are you sure I'm not going to be a third wheel?" Brayden asked as he walked with Tyler and me to the parking lot at the end of the school day.

"Of course not," Tyler said.

"We can invite Dylan and make it a double-date," I said, grinning.

"That's not even funny," Brayden said.

"I thought it was," I said.

Brayden rolled his eyes.

We climbed in Tyler's car and joined the line waiting to get out of the parking lot. Sadye walked past and nodded at us. I guess Dylan told her how we'd saved his ass. It sometimes took five or ten minutes to get out of the lot, since everyone was leaving, except for the jocks who had practice, members of clubs, and the drama queers.

"So, where is this place we're going to again?" Brayden asked.

"Bub's Burgers. It has some of the best burgers in town. If you can eat a lot, they have one that weighs a pound *after* it's cooked. If you eat the whole thing, you get your picture on the wall."

"I bet I can eat one," Brayden said.

"I bet you can't," I said.

"What do you want to bet?"

"If you eat the whole thing, I'll pay for it. If you don't... you have to kiss Dylan on the lips—with tongue."

Brayden looked momentarily frightened, so I started flapping my arms like a chicken and clucking.

"Okay, you are on," he said.

"Dylan is going to owe me after this," I said.

"No, you're going to owe me whatever it costs for the burger."

Tyler drove us downtown and parked in front of Bub's. We went inside and were soon escorted to a booth. The walls were covered with photos of those who had consumed an entire one-pound burger. I was betting Brayden couldn't do it. I know I couldn't!

Tyler and I ordered a "Big Ugly", the one-pound burger, with cheddar cheese, bacon, lettuce, and tomato. We also ordered Cokes and sweet potato fries with marshmallow dipping sauce. Brayden ordered a "Big Ugly" with Swiss cheese and onion. He skipped fries, which was wise, but ordered a Coke.

"You shouldn't have ordered onion," I said.

"Why not?"

"Dylan might not like your breath when you're making out with him later, *with tongue*," I said.

"It's not gonna happen. I'm going to enjoy my *free* burger and then my picture will be up on the wall with all the others."

Brayden smiled. It was good to see him smile. It was good that he was out with us. Brayden needed to live again.

We talked about school. Tyler filled Brayden in on Caleb, Tyreece, and Jesse. I did Dylan a big favor by suggesting non-violent ways to keep him at bay.

Our burgers arrived soon and I laughed at Brayden as his eyes widened. His burger, like ours, covered an entire plate. Braden looked up at me and a determined look crossed his face. He took a bite.

"Delicious. I may need to order another," he said.

"Ha! If you ate two 'Big Ugly' burgers, *I'd* make out with Dylan."

I knew I was safe. I didn't think anyone could eat two.

Tyler cut our burger in half and we shared. Half of a "Big Ugly" was enough for me although Tyler actually could eat a whole one by himself. His photo was on the wall several times.

The burger was fantastic, as were the fries. Dipping fries in marshmallow sauce might seem weird, but it's perfect for sweet potato fries. I had been skeptical the first time I tried them, but I had been won over.

Brayden finished off half his burger with no problem, but then he began to slow down. I offered him fries a couple of times just to be a nuisance. Brayden watched as Tyler fed me a fry. Tyler and I both laughed when marshmallow sauce ran down my chin. Brayden looked thoughtful and sad.

"Stuart would have loved this place," he said.

"I bet you miss him a lot," Tyler said. With Brayden's permission, I had told Tyler what happened to Stuart.

"So much it hurts," Brayden said.

"Do you think he could have finished a 'Big Ugly?'" Tyler asked.

I tensed. I was afraid Tyler was making a big mistake by asking about Brayden's dead boyfriend, but I was wrong. Brayden actually smiled for a moment with the memory of the boy he loved.

"He could have eaten one of these with ease. He could really pack it away and yet he didn't have an ounce of fat on him. He had the most beautiful body and he was so... wonderful."

Brayden looked across the booth at Tyler and I sitting together.

"You guys are very lucky to have each other."

"We know," Tyler said.

"We need to find you someone," I said.

"I don't know. It's... I'd feel like I was cheating on Stuart."

"What would he have to say about that?" I asked.

Brayden thought for a moment.

"He'd tell me not to be stupid. He'd tell me that he was dead, not me, and that I need to get on with my life."

"Maybe you should listen to him."

"Maybe."

"We'll have to give this some thought," Tyler said.

Brayden shot us a glare.

"If either of you suggests Dylan, you're dead meat."

Tyler and I laughed, but Brayden sighed. He gazed out the window for a moment.

"God, I wish Stuart was here."

I reached across the table and took Brayden's hand.

"He is. He's not here in the way you wish he could be, but he is here. He's a part of you and always will be."

"He's right, you know. Everyone we meet becomes a part of us. We are who we are because of those around us," Tyler said. "Stuart is a part of you. Now that you've told us about him, he's a part of all of us."

"I think maybe it's even more than that," I said. "I don't claim to know about the afterlife, but I think we're all joined together. I think we're all part of each other. I think Stuart really is here with us right now, just like my parents are here. They're not just here because I remember them. They are here because their spirit or soul or whatever was truly them is always with me. Stuart is with you just the same. He always will be."

Tyler looked at me amazed when I stopped speaking. I wasn't quite sure where that came from myself. I just felt it inside me. I don't think I could have said it even an hour before because that's not what I felt or believed then. It just appeared within me, which made me sure it was right.

Brayden looked at me with a slight smile on his lips.

"You really believe that. Don't you?"

"Yes."

"Sometimes... a lot of the time... I can feel Stuart with me. Sometimes, he's like a little voice whispering in my mind. Sometimes, he's an almost physical force. When I'm especially down and miss him the most, I feel like he's right there with me."

"He is," I said quietly.

Brayden kept gazing at me.

"You're not at all what I expected," he said.

"You're not what I expected either. Just what *did* you expect?"

"The day I met you, I thought you'd be a smartass, self-centered, uncaring, and maybe even a bit of a bully. I keep having to change my opinion of you."

"Oh, I am a smartass and sometimes I'm self-centered, but isn't everyone self-centered now and then?"

"Jesse is most of the time," Tyler said and grinned. "If you ever need to distract him, put a mirror in front of his face. He won't be able to look away."

Brayden grinned at Tyler for a moment, but then looked back at me. I realized I was still holding his hand. I released it and pulled my hand back across the table.

"So, giving up on your burger? Should I call Dylan and tell him to pucker up?"

"Not on your life."

Brayden bit into his burger with a mischievous glint in his eyes. I had a feeling he'd finish that burger even if it made him hurl.

I was getting near the end of my half of the "Big Ugly" and felt close to hurling myself. Tyler gave no sign of being full. I swear he could eat anything!

Brayden was coming to life, but a veil of sadness clung to him. Thoughts of the boy he loved were never far from his mind. He'd been so sad for so long that the least pleasant event was joyous by comparison, but happiness reminded him of Stuart, which reminded Brayden of his loss and made him sad again. The loss of Stuart was a weight around his neck, constantly pulling him down. I understood only too well. I knew the sharp sting of loss. Sometimes, I missed my parents so much that... I looked up when I felt eyes on me. Both Tyler and Brayden gazed at me with concern. Tyler reached out and wiped away the tear I hadn't even realized had run down my cheek.

"What's wrong?" Tyler asked.

"You were thinking about your parents just now, weren't you?" Brayden asked.

"Yeah, but I'm okay now. It's just... hard sometimes."

Brayden nodded. He knew. He understood in a way even Tyler didn't. Tyler's mom had died when he was a baby. He couldn't even remember her. Maybe in a way that was worse, but probably not. I valued my memories of my parents, but they also brought me pain. The memories were a reminder of what I had lost.

Brayden reached across the table and took my hand, just as I had taken his before. He held my hand firmly and looked into my eyes.

"We can get through this together," he said.

I nodded, then Brayden released my hand. I gazed at Tyler. He was worried about me. I could tell. I hated making him worry. I wanted to hide my pain so Tyler would never see it, but I knew that was a mistake. If I hid my pain, it would grow. I'd tried keeping it to myself and it had been the biggest mistake of my life. I gave Tyler a little smile to let him know I was okay.

We ate, talked, and even laughed a little without any more emotional scenes. The sadness and pain was there, like an underground river flowing just below us, but the three of us had a good time. Tyler and I finished our shared burger and fries, and I watched as more and more of Brayden's "Big Ugly" disappeared.

"Wouldn't you like a shake to go with that?" I asked.

"You're afraid I'm going to win. Be afraid. Be *very* afraid."

I liked Brayden. He had a devilish sense of humor.

I lost the bet. Brayden finished off his entire "Big Ugly." Brayden motioned for Tyler and me to get on either side of him when the waiter came to take his picture. When the waiter showed the photo to us moments later we looked like three best buddies out on the town. Brayden was smiling in the picture. He was living again.

We asked for one check. Tyler handed me some cash to pay for his part and I took care of the rest. Brayden grinned. He loved that I'd lost the bet.

"Dylan would be so disappointed if he knew he had a shot at making out with you," I said.

"We can tell him if you like, just to torment him," Brayden said.

"You're a little bit evil. I like that," Tyler said.

We left Bub's and climbed back into Tyler's car. We dropped Brayden off at his house and then headed back to my place.

"You don't mind that Brayden and I held hands, do you?" I asked.

"I might be just a little jealous, but no, I don't mind. I'm glad you met him. I think you're good for him and I think he'll be good for you. He understands what you're going through in a way I can't."

"*You* have been very good for me too. Just ask Percy!"

"We should get Brayden to hang out with us more. Of course, I want time alone with you too," Tyler said.

"Mmm, I want some time alone with you right now."

We arrived at my place just then. Percy's blue Prius was in the drive.

"We'll get our chance," Tyler said. "Until then..."

I scooted over and pulled Tyler toward me. Our lips met and we kissed deeply. We sat there and made out for a good five minutes.

"Now, I not only want to be alone with you. I *NEED* it!" I said.

Tyler laughed.

"I know the feeling, but I have to get home and I'm sure Dad will be there. We'll just have to watch and wait for our chance."

Tyler's eyes sparkled mischievously, holding a promise of what was soon to come. Our next naked encounter couldn't come soon enough for me.

\*\*\*

Brayden sat with us at lunch again the next day. Dylan spent most of lunch checking Brayden out, but he didn't try anything. I think he behaved because there was a very built wrestler sitting at a nearby table who was wearing a tank top. The dude was ripped, and Dylan's gaze kept flowing in his direction.

I had an easy lunch. Between Brayden and the hunky wrestler, Dylan didn't have much time to leer at me. He hadn't been quite as much of a pain since Tyler and I began dating, but he still checked me out and sometimes couldn't keep his hands to himself. The boy was a male nymphomaniac.

Tyler was busy after school, but he still ran Brayden and me to our homes to pick up our skateboards and pads and then back to the skate park near the school. Having a boyfriend old enough to drive was a huge advantage! We kissed when he dropped me off. I wanted to keep right on kissing him, but I couldn't always have what I wanted.

"I can come pick you up later," Tyler said.

"No. I'll call Percy. He will come get us. I know you're busy. Thanks for taking us to get our stuff. I wish you could join us."

"I'm always happy to do things for my favorite boyfriend. I'll join you another time."

I smiled as Tyler drove away and then what he'd said hit me.

"Hey!"

I couldn't be sure, but I thought I saw Tyler laughing as he drove away.

It was cool out, but we were dressed warmly in hoodies. Brayden and I strapped on our pads, carried our skateboards to the skating area, and took off. The park had some cool ramps.

Tyler and I skated there a lot. That was yet another cool thing about Tyler. He was a skater.

We skated mostly in silence. There were a couple of younger kids there, but the park wasn't busy. Brayden had some awesome moves and I have to admit I was showing off a little. I grew up in California, and I'd spent a good part of my life on a skateboard. I'd even put in quite a bit of time surfing. I sure wouldn't be surfing in Indiana, but I could still put my skating skills to good use.

Brayden and I began skating in concert. We just flowed into it without trying. We crisscrossed and jumped, parting and coming back together as if we were performing a synchronized routine. Our movements were symmetrical. The younger boys stopped to watch us. Brayden and I smiled at each other. There was a connection between us just then. We were in synch. I think that's the moment we became friends. It was as if we were a part of each other. We didn't have to think about what we were doing. We just skated and our movements came together in a skater's dance.

We skated for a good two hours. I didn't want to stop, but I was exhausted! Brayden and I carried our skateboards over to a bench and sat down. I pulled out my phone and called Percy. He said he'd be there in ten minutes.

"I'm starving!" Brayden said.

"Me too. I'll see if I can con my uncle into taking us out to eat."

"You're devious. I like you better and better. You remind me of Stuart in some ways."

"Yeah?"

"He had the same devilish, mischievous thing going that you do. He had a touch of bad ass in him too. He was easy to get along with, but if someone made him mad, watch out!"

I laughed.

"I never thought he'd be the kind to kill himself," Brayden said.

I immediately stopped laughing. Just like that, Brayden turned from happy to sad.

"I think anyone can be driven to suicide. I've thought about it. I think most people think about it at some point."

"I almost killed myself too. I'm the one who found him and when I saw what he'd done…"

Deep sadness and pain came on Brayden swiftly. Pain was like that sometimes. It wasn't there and then it was. Brayden began to sob. I scooted over to him and wrapped my arm around him. The younger kids had already left, so there was no one to see Brayden cry.

"He was hanging there, in the middle of the locker room. His face was blue... his eyes stared into space. It was so unreal that I couldn't accept it. I knew what I was seeing, but... it just couldn't be real, but it was real. I looked up in Stuart's eyes. They were dead. He wasn't there anymore. Whatever was Stuart was gone."

I almost couldn't imagine the horror of what Brayden had experienced. I'd been through something traumatic, but Brayden found his boyfriend's dead body. How did he even sleep at night?

"I climbed up on the chair he had stood upon to hang himself. I grabbed him and hugged him to me and bawled my eyes out. I couldn't believe he'd done it. Things were hard leading up to his death, very hard, for both of us. I'd thought of killing myself, but I never dreamed... Stuart was the strong one. I'm strong, but no one was as strong as him.

"There was a note lying on a nearby bench. It was a note to me. Stuart told me in his note that he loved me and he was sorry for taking his own life, but he couldn't endure the torment a moment more. He couldn't take all the hatred and abuse. He asked me to forgive him and said he would love me forever. I slipped the note into my pocket before I screamed for help. Maybe I shouldn't have, but it was my note. He wrote it for me and it was the last bit of contact I'd ever have with him."

"I understand."

"I did something that night I really wish I hadn't done. I missed Stuart so much. I wanted him back so badly. Then, all that pain turned to anger. I was furious with him for leaving me behind. I took the only photo I had of the two of us together and ripped it to pieces. As soon as I did it, I realized what I'd done. It was as if I'd lost him all over again. It was such a stupid thing to do."

"It wasn't stupid. You were in pain. I think being angry in that situation is completely understandable."

"I wish I hadn't done it. Now, I have no photo of Stuart and me together."

Brayden looked into my eyes.

"I'm sorry. I keep laying all this heavy shit on you."

"Don't be sorry. I'd laid down some pretty heavy shit myself. I think we were meant to meet. We need each other."

Brayden nodded. He could feel it too.

Brayden stood, walked over to the drinking fountain, and washed away the evidence of his tears in its chilly water. He returned to the bench and gazed into my eyes.

"Thanks for being here for me, Caspian. Thanks for sharing your time with Tyler with me too. Thanks for getting in my face and not backing down the day you found me in the stadium."

"Getting in people's faces is what I do."

I smiled and Brayden smiled back for a moment. Percy arrived just then. We climbed in his Prius.

"This is Brayden. He's a friend from school. Brayden, this is my uncle, Percy. Just humor him if he tries to act cool."

"Nice to meet you, Brayden," Percy said as if he didn't hear the "cool" remark.

"It's nice to meet you."

"So... since you're my favorite uncle..."

"I'm your only uncle. What do you want?"

Brayden laughed at Percy's accusing tone.

"Will you take us out to eat? We are starved!"

"I will do even better than that. I have some errands to run, so I'll drop you off somewhere, and then come back for you. That way you won't have to eat with me."

"Whew! That was a close one!" I said.

"Just for that I'll leave you at McDonald's."

"No! Please! Anything but that!"

I liked McDonald's sundaes and it was a good place to get a soft drink, but their burgers... not so great.

"I'll have pity on you, this time. So, what do you guys feel like eating?"

"How about pizza?" I asked Brayden.

"Sounds good to me."

"Then I suggest Mother Bear's. It has some of the best pizza in town," Percy said.

"I've never been there," I said.

"You'll love it. It's popular with the IU crowd. It's right across from campus on 3rd Street."

A few minutes later, Percy dropped us off behind Mother Bear's, after handing me a couple of twenties.

"I'll call when I'm on my way back. I'll meet you back right here."

"Thanks."

"Your uncle is pretty cool," Brayden said as Percy drove away.

"Don't let him hear you say that. You'll ruin all the effort I've put into making him think he's uncool. He's a writer, so he's a little odd, but he's not bad."

Actually, I liked Percy a lot. I loved him, but I wasn't going to say that out loud. Talk about uncool.

Mother Bear's was filled with high-backed, wooden booths. The walls, tables, and backs of the booths were covered in graffiti. We sat down in a booth and I was surprised to see "Tyler Perseus 1989" written on the wall. That was my uncle's real name, but most everyone knows him by one of his pennames, Percy DeForest Spock. Tyler, my boyfriend, was named after him. It's a long and involved story.

"What do you like on pizza?" I asked.

"Pepperoni for sure and onions are good."

"I can live with that. Green peppers? Sausage?"

"Sure. I'm so hungry I could eat a pizza box, so I'll go for anything."

When the waitress came, we ordered a large, deep dish, pepperoni, onion, green pepper, and sausage pizza with two Cokes.

"I eat out a lot more since I've met you. I'll buy next time," Brayden said.

"Okay, but my uncle is paying this time and you won the bet at Bub's so I actually haven't paid yet. Man, I didn't think you could finish off a 'Big Ugly!'"

"So you just wanted to make me kiss Dylan? Did you have a deal worked out with him?"

"No, but I probably would have told him that if he gave me fifty bucks I'd convince you to make out with him."

"For fifty bucks I might!"

"Whore."

"Pimp."

"I like a guy I can trade insults with," I said.

"You can always insult Dylan."

"It's impossible. If I called him a whore, he'd take it as a compliment. If I called him a slut, he'd start bragging about all the straight boys he's seduced. Insults do not take with that boy."

Brayden smiled.

"I could use some making out. I haven't had sex since... since Stuart. I'm not even sure I want to. Maybe I couldn't even do it."

"It's like riding a bicycle," I said.

"If you think sex is like riding a bicycle, then you must be doing it wrong."

"I *meant* that it's something you don't forget how to do. It's instinct."

"Then why didn't you say so?"

I growled in frustration and a satisfied smirk appeared on Brayden's face, but as so often happened, his expression immediately turned to sadness.

"Did you two have sex a lot?" I asked.

"All the time. If we had two minutes alone, we were all over each other and if we had more time... Damn!"

I laughed.

"We hooked up in a restroom stall at school once. I topped him while guys were going in and out of the restroom."

"Weren't you scared of getting caught?"

"Yeah, but that was part of the excitement. We only did it once because it was so risky, but we got it on at school a few different times. We did it in the woods, a car, and a dugout on the baseball field. We did it all over the place."

"You make Tyler and me sound tame."

"Well, your boyfriend is more... low key than Stuart. I'm not putting Tyler down. I just mean that he seems very calm and kind of quiet."

"He's neither when he gets worked up. He can get wild."

"I'm sure, but Stuart was extra-wild. He was very adventurous about everything and especially about sex. He said we should live each day as if it was our last, because we never knew..."

Brayden's voice trailed off and his sadness returned.

"I'm sorry. I shouldn't be asking you questions about Stuart."

"No. It's okay, really. I want to talk about him. After he died, everyone was afraid to talk about him. They wouldn't even mention his name around me. It was as if he'd never existed at all. I know my parents and the few friends I had left were trying not to bring up painful memories, but it felt like he meant nothing to them. It was as if he was so unimportant he was forgotten the moment he died. I know that's not how it was, but that's what it felt like. Some boys at school were extremely cruel to me after he died. They'd say the nastiest things about Stuart, but in a way that was better than not hearing his name at all. At least they acknowledged his existence."

"If I ever say anything I shouldn't or anything that makes you feel bad, just tell me. I am blond, you know."

"Sure, use your blond hair as an excuse."

"Hey, if I have to listen to all the stupid blond jokes, then I have a right to use being blond as an excuse."

"Stuart used to get so sick of blond jokes. His hair was so light blond it was almost white. I've always loved blonds."

"We are pretty special."

"Please. Don't make me nauseous. We'll be eating soon."

I stuck out my tongue.

Brayden looked at me across the table.

"Thanks for inviting me to sit with your friends at lunch. Thanks for getting me out to do things again. Since Stuart died, I've kept to myself. I didn't want to get close to anyone because losing him hurt so much, but... it's not very much fun sitting alone in my room or eating lunch alone while everyone else is talking and laughing."

"If you get to know others, you will get hurt, but I think if you keep to yourself it hurts even more," I said. "I walked down that path. I tried to shut everyone out. My anger kept me going for a while, but I was so lonely. Tyler tired to pull me into his group of friends, but I was a jerk. They all thought I was an asshole and they were right. Tyler even tried to attack me once at lunch."

"Your boyfriend tried to attack you?"

"This was before we were dating. It was before I let anyone know I was gay. I was pretending to be a homophobe and doing such a good job I made Tyler almost hate me."

"How did you guys go from that to dating?"

"It's a long story, but Tyler is the kind of guy that cares about everyone. I made him cease to care about me for a while, but I began to lose control and let the real me show through. We had sort of a love/hate thing going for a while, not exactly, but that's as close as I can come to describing it. He finally got me to open up and things got a lot better after that. My uncle helped a lot too. I tried to drive him away, but no matter what I did he wouldn't let go."

"So Tyler got in your face like you got in mine?"

"More or less."

"And now you guys are dating."

"And doing it!"

"Don't talk about doing it. Sometimes, I think I'm gonna explode."

"You mean you don't want to hear about how I pulled his legs up over my shoulders and..."

"Shut up!"

"He was so tight. He was a virgin before I..."

"I'm not listening," Brayden said, holding his hands over his ears and humming.

I stopped talking until Brayden removed his hands from his ears.

"Tyler gives the best head."

My timing was unfortunate. Our waitress arrived with our pizza just then and heard my comment. I gave Brayden the evil eye as he laughed his ass off. The waitress merely grinned.

"You're a jerk," I said when Brayden stopped laughing.

"Like you wouldn't have laughed at me if I'd gotten caught saying that."

"You'd better not be saying it. Tyler is *my* boyfriend."

"You know what I mean."

"Yes, but that has nothing to do with it," I said, crossing my arms and glaring at Brayden.

"Quit pretending you're mad and have some pizza. You're paying for it, after all."

I took a bite of pizza. It was incredible. Percy was right, not that I was going to admit it.

We ate and talked. Brayden's mood shifted back and forth. He would be having a good time one moment and then a look of deep sadness would cross his features. I knew exactly what he was experiencing. Grief could hit suddenly and be triggered by just about anything. If I was walking in the mall and heard a woman's voice that sounded like my mom's, a wave of pain and sadness could engulf me. Sometimes, when I was having fun, I'd suddenly feel guilty because I had escaped from the fire that killed my parents. Once in a while, Percy's laugh or sneeze or the way he talked reminded me of my dad, and I had to fight back the tears. Sadness could come a moment behind happiness and could flow back into happiness just as quickly. Brayden was riding an emotional roller coaster. Anyone who didn't know better might think he was going to be fine, but I knew the path ahead of him was difficult. I was traveling the same path only I was further along.

Brayden and I had demolished nearly the entire pizza when my cell phone rang. It was Percy. I spoke with him briefly and then disconnected.

"That was Percy. He's coming to pick us up."

"Good timing. I might pop if I ate another slice."

"Have another slice then. This I have to see."

"You are an evil, evil boy, Caspian."

"Thank you."

I paid the check, and Brayden and I walked outside. Soon, Percy drove up and we climbed in. Percy took Brayden home and then we drove back to our place. I called Tyler on the way.

"So, how was your date?" Tyler asked.

"I should have made it a date after that 'favorite boyfriend' crack," I said. "We had a good time skate-boarding and then Percy took us to Mother Bear's."

"Poor Percy," Tyler said.

"No, we didn't have to endure Percy's horrible jokes. You're right, that is a fate worse than death. He dropped us off," I said, looking at Percy.

"I can hear Tyler's side of the conversation," Percy said.

I stuck my tongue out at my uncle and Tyler laughed. He could obviously hear Percy as well.

"How did it go with Brayden?" Tyler asked.

"We talked a lot. I got him to laugh some, but… he's having a hard time dealing with what happened."

"Who wouldn't?"

"Yeah. At least he went skateboarding with me and had some fun. We talked about Stuart. He's glad he has someone to talk to about what he's going through."

"We'll keep including him in our plans when we can," Tyler said.

"That's what he needs most, to be included, so he doesn't just brood. I'm going to go. We're almost home and you know how nosy Percy is. We can have a *private* conversation later," I said, looking at Percy and shooting him a smart-aleck grin.

Percy smiled at me when we got home.

"What?" I asked.

"I think it's very kind and compassionate of you to help Brayden through his troubles," Percy said.

"Whatever," I said because I didn't know what else to say. Percy didn't buy my act. He could always see through me. He smiled again and mussed my hair.

"Hey! Watch the hair, man!"

Percy laughed and we went inside.

# Chapter 11

"I have the decorating scheme all worked out," Tyler said as I climbed into his car the next morning.

"For what?"

"The wedding!"

I suddenly wished Brayden were with us. Tyler hadn't mentioned the ceremony once when he was with us and it was a welcome break.

"Since Dad and Percy haven't set a date yet, it's probably going to be around Christmas when we have the commitment ceremony. I want to do a Christmas theme, but not the traditional red and green. I want to use white and blue. We will have a big white Christmas tree with lots of clear and blue lights. We can all wear white!"

"I don't want to wear white," I said.

"Well, you can't wear black. You'll look handsome in white."

"I don't want to argue, so let's talk about that later."

"Okay. I'm thinking a white wedding cake with silver. I want it to have the look of sparkling snow."

I pretended to be interested. I was happy that Percy and Daniel were hooking up and that we were all becoming a family, but weddings had to be the most boring thing *ever*. I'm talking total snooze fest.

Tyler was still talking about his plans when we reached school. He kept talking as we walked inside. I wanted to tell him to shut up, but he was so happy I couldn't ruin it for him. Instead, I just nodded a lot and kept myself from rolling my eyes. Getting away from Tyler and into my classes was actually a relief.

After the last morning class, Tyler and I met at my locker to walk down to lunch together. I steeled myself for yet more wedding talk, but mercifully Tyler talked about his eagerness for the holidays instead. My relief was short lived. We had not even set our trays down on the table before Tyler made an announcement.

"Dad and Percy are getting married!" he said.

Tyreece smiled and clapped Tyler on the back. He knew how much this meant to him.

"That's great, man," Caleb said.

"Can I help plan the wedding?" Dylan asked, as excited and eager as Tyler had been since he convinced Percy and Daniel to have a ceremony.

"Yes, I will definitely need your help. I have tons of ideas."

Brayden and I shared a look of disinterest and then Brayden smiled. He could tell I did not care about the ceremony. I was happy for Percy and Daniel, but ceremonies were boring and sickeningly sentimental.

"I have a theme planned out, white and blue and silver. I think Dad, Percy, Caspian, and I should all wear white."

"I'm not wearing white," I said.

Jesse looked up. The conversation had wandered into fashion and that always captured Jesse's interest.

"You'd look really good in white," Jesse said.

"No."

"I'll work on Caspian. It will be my contribution," Jesse said.

"If you come near me with white, I will kill you," I said.

"We'll look at some options," Jesse said. I eyed him suspiciously. I didn't trust him. His "options" would probably be shades of off-white. It wasn't gonna happen. I wasn't going to dress up to look like I should be standing on the top of a wedding cake.

"You're all invited, of course," Tyler said. "It's going to be a very small affair, but I want all of you to be here, including you, Brayden. We haven't known each other long, but I consider you a friend."

Brayden smiled just a little. He was no more thrilled about a wedding invitation that I was, but the invitation meant he was considered one of the gang.

Tyler and Dylan chatted away. Dylan eagerly listened to Tyler's plans and offered suggestions of his own. He was so into the wedding plans he didn't even notice when Brice Parker walked by in a tank top. I noticed. I couldn't wait to watch him work out shirtless. I wondered if he really did run around naked in his room or if Tyler was only trying to get my hopes up.

"Oh! Guess what else!" Tyler said. "Dad is going to adopt Caspian."

"So, you guys are going to be step-brothers?" Brayden asked, looking at us strangely.

"Yeah!" Tyler said.

"You're going to be step-brothers and you're dating," Brayden said slowly.

"Whoa!" Dylan said. "You'll be dating your brother! Incest! Taboo is sooo hot!"

"Well, we're not... genetically related. We'll be adopted brothers, but we're not biological brothers. It's..."

Tyler was flustered. We were both so excited that we were going to be family that we hadn't thought about the fact that we were also boyfriends.

"Hey, if this was Tennessee it would be perfectly acceptable," Jesse said. "I think they have to marry their cousin or sister or brother down there. It's the law."

"It is not," Tyreece said.

"You two are on the cutting edge!" Dylan said. "A guy dating a guy isn't that big of a deal anymore, but incest..."

"Would you stop using that word?" Tyler asked. "It sounds so... disgusting."

"Well, you are the one doing it with your brother," Caleb said.

Caleb laughed for a moment but quickly stopped. Tyler looked extremely uncomfortable. I felt a little uneasy myself. I didn't much care what others thought, but I wasn't looking forward to all the keeping-it-in-the-family cracks that were sure to come from every direction.

"Sorry," Caleb said. "You know how I feel about you, Tyler, and I even like Caspian a little."

I scratched the side of my head with my middle finger.

"I think it's great you two are going to be adopted brothers. It may make things a little awkward, but you knew this was a possibility, right?" Caleb said.

"I always hoped Dad and Percy would get together, but I never thought about the adoption. I just thought Caspian and I might be living in the same house."

I knew everything was going too well. I'd expected something like this. Well, not like this exactly, but I'd been waiting on something to mess up my life. I frowned.

"Hey, things will work out," Caleb said. "Your dad and Percy are hooking up. It's exactly what you wanted."

"Yeah," Tyler said, smiling.

"I know just what to get them for a wedding present. Me!" Dylan said.

"NO!" Tyler said.

"Come on, a sexy teen boy is the perfect gift for a gay couple!" Dylan argued.

"That is wrong on so many levels," I said.

"Don't you mean it's a perfect gift for you, Dylan?" Jesse asked.

"That too! Percy and Daniel are soooo hot!"

"Stop thinking about it. It's not going to happen," Tyler said.

"Dude!" Tyreece said, staring at Dylan. "I can't think of a more inappropriate present. That's just sick."

"How is it inappropriate?" Dylan asked.

I rolled my eyes. He really was clueless.

"You want to give guys who have just committed to each other a night with an under-age boy?" Tyreece asked incredulously.

"It does sound kind of bad when you put it that way," Dylan admitted.

"Kind of?" Caleb asked. "Kind of???"

"It's not going to happen," Tyler repeated. "Percy and my dad do not think of you that way. You're just a kid to them."

"I'm not a kid!"

"You sure act like one," Brayden said.

"Let me put an end to this," I said. "Dylan, if you make any move on my uncle or Tyler's dad, I will personally beat the crap of you."

Dylan looked frightened. He could tell by the expression on my face and the tone of my voice that I meant business.

"You guys are no fun at all!" Dylan crossed his arms and pouted.

"Am I dreaming this? This can't be real," Brayden said.

"You'll get used to it," Tyreece said.

"You guys are weird, but you're not boring," Brayden said.

"Boring is the worst offense ever, after poor grooming and bad fashion choices," Jesse said.

Brayden and I both rolled our eyes.

"If you want entertainment, Brayden, we can mess up Jesse's hair," Caleb said.

"Don't you dare! You touch my hair and I'll loosen the bolts on your wheels."

Caleb laughed.

"Excuse me! We're planning a wedding here!" Dylan said.

"No, you and Tyler are planning a wedding, not us," I said.

"You don't want to be part of planning your uncle's wedding?" Tyler asked.

Wow, Tyler was finally getting it.

"Think about it, Tyler. Would you want to go to any wedding that *I* helped plan?" I asked.

"I see your point." Tyler grinned.

"I'm helping to make it a nice ceremony by not planning it. I'll help move furniture around or something, but I'm not into all this wedding stuff."

"I think Caspian is secretly straight," Caleb said. "Come on, admit it. You're a heterosexual, aren't you?"

"Those are fighting words," I said. Caleb grinned.

"Oh, he's definitely not straight," Tyler said.

"Shut up, Tyler," I warned.

Dylan looked back and forth between us, gazing at each of us carefully. I felt like a specimen under a microscope.

"Dude! You bottomed, didn't you?" Dylan said, staring at me with a huge grin on his face. "You took it up the butt!"

My mouth dropped open in shock. It was the surest way of letting everyone know Dylan was right, but I simply couldn't believe he had figured it out.

"Caspian on the bottom. I never thought *that* would happen," Caleb said.

"Topped by your brother no less," Dylan said.

"Would you shut up about that? Besides, we aren't brothers... *yet*," I said.

"I thought you were walking a little funny," Tyreece said.

"If you're trying to embarrass me, it's not going to work. Yeah, I took it in the ass. So what? I'm secure enough in my masculinity not to fear experimenting. Besides, there is nothing wrong with being a bottom." I didn't mention my doubts or hesitation to try bottoming, and Tyler was cool enough not to mention them either.

"Good answer," Tyreece said. "You know I'm just teasing you and no one will ever accuse you of not being masculine."

"If they do, I'll knock their teeth out."

"If all gay boys were as scary as you, there would be no bashers," Jesse said, laughing.

"There's nothing wrong with having a feminine side," Dylan said.

"No, there isn't, if that's you, but it's not me," I said.

Everyone looked at me. I think they were surprised by my words.

"What? I think everyone should be who and what they are. I know I put on an act when I first moved here, but you also know I had my reasons. That mistake taught me that no one should try to be what they aren't or even pretend to be what they aren't. I don't like being called feminine because I'm not. Dylan has a feminine side and as *annoying* as I find him, I admire him for his courage in being himself."

"Thank you," Dylan said. "Let me give you a big kiss for that!"

Dylan began to stand up.

"Come near me and you die!"

"I'm not picking up much of a feminine vibe from Caspian," Tyreece said.

"Unless it's a vibe from a female serial killer," Caleb added.

"I would never kill cereal!"

"Serial, not cereal. You blonds are soooo dumb," Caleb said.

"Hey!" Dylan and I said together.

"I'm proud of you for being secure enough in your masculinity to be a dumb blond," Tyreece said. I growled at him.

"All right. Leave my boyfriend alone," Tyler said. "Quit bothering Dylan too. We have important plans to make."

I turned my attention to my meatball sub and potato wedges and tried to tune Tyler and Dylan out. At the end of lunch, Tyler took off with Dylan, abandoning me. Brayden and I dumped our trays and headed to our lockers together.

"I think your boyfriend has a new boyfriend," Brayden said.

"I'm glad Dylan is into all the wedding-crap."

"I don't really get the whole two-guys-getting-married thing myself."

"They're not getting married. It's a commitment ceremony. Daniel and Percy didn't even want a ceremony. That was Tyler's idea."

"I still don't get it. I can understand dating, but the commitment thing is so old-fashioned. It's almost like they're trying to be straight."

"No. They just want to be together so they want to make a commitment. They were willing to just tell Tyler and me they were a couple, move in together, draw up some legal papers, and leave it at that. I wish they would have, but Tyler had to turn it into an event."

"You sound pissed off."

"I'm not pissed off. Well, maybe a little. The whole thing just seems like a big waste of time and Tyler wants me to wear white!"

"I heard."

"I'm not wearing white!"

"I heard that too."

"Tyler will probably keep hounding me about it. Sometimes, he makes me so mad."

"Stuart made me mad sometimes. I wish he was here so I could be mad at him right now."

I looked at Brayden. I thought he was slipping into sadness, but the expression on his face told me he was making a point.

"So you're saying I should shut up and enjoy what I have?" I asked.

"Yes. Besides, you'll look sexy in white."

"I'm not wearing white!"

"Sure, you aren't." Brayden made a sound like a whip cracking.

"I am not whipped!"

"Of course you're not."

I gave Brayden the evil eye and growled. He laughed.

"Jerk."

At the end of the school day, I discovered my boyfriend was ditching me to spend time with Dylan. They were going to check out bakeries and cake designs. Tyler invited me to come along, but the last thing I wanted to do was look at pictures of wedding cakes. My only interest in cake was eating it.

Tyler dropped me at home. I did my homework and then called Brayden and asked him over to play Xbox. I loved playing Fight Night, Super Street Fighter, and UFC Undisputed, but Tyler wasn't into fight games. Brayden was all over UFC Undisputed. We battled it out for a couple of hours before Percy interrupted us and offered to order sandwiches from Jimmy John's.

We stopped long enough to eat when the delivery guy dropped off our sandwiches. Brayden and I sat with Percy at the kitchen table. My Vito sub was great. It was an Italian sub with salami and tons of other stuff. I'd been so wrapped up in our game I hadn't even realized I was hungry, but I devoured the whole thing as well as lots of Cool Ranch Doritos. I think Brayden liked Percy. They talked cars while we ate.

As soon as we'd eaten, Brayden and I headed back to my bedroom to beat the crap out of each other—in the game, that is. I was thrilled to have someone to play my kind of games with and Brayden was totally into trying to kick my butt.

We played until our thumbs ached and our fingers became numb, then we lay back on my bed and stared at the ceiling.

"I haven't played a game like that since... Stuart died."

"Did you guys play a lot of video games?"

"Oh, yeah. We had running battles. Sometimes, we made it interesting."

"How?"

"We made bets."

"For money?" I asked, a little confused. That didn't seem so interesting.

"No. We were both mostly tops so..."

I laughed.

"The loser had it take it up the butt," I said.

"Exactly. How did you like your experimentation?"

"Not so much.  It was hot in a way and I liked doing it for Tyler, but… it's not my thing.  It felt really weird mostly.  It hurt too, but that's not what I disliked about it most.  It felt uncomfortable and I just felt like I was playing the wrong role, you know?"

"I understand.  That's the way it was with us.  So, is Tyler also a top or…"

"He's mostly a bottom although we've only gone all the way twice."

"You're lucky then.  Stuart and I took turns, except when we bet, then it was winner takes all and believe me we played hard to win.  Neither of us was into being on bottom, but there was something hot about it because we were doing it for each other.  Being on top feels soooo good!"

"I know.  Mmm."

I could smell Brayden's cologne, Aeropostale, I think.  It smelled really good.  We turned on our sides and looked into each other's eyes.  Brayden was very handsome and definitely masculine.

"You know what else I like to do besides play video games?" Brayden asked.

"What?"

My breath came a little faster.  I was afraid he might lean over and kiss me.  I was even more afraid that I'd let him.  I was worked up, if you know what I mean, so if we kissed…

"I like to wrestle!"

Brayden pounced on me.  I giggled with surprise and relief.  Giggling made me weak and allowed Brayden to get on top, but I squirmed from beneath him and we struggled to subdue each other into submission.

Brayden was tough.  We were well-matched.  If either of us knew any actual wrestling moves, we would've had an advantage, but I wasn't into organized sports and Brayden had been a soccer player, not a wrestler.  Brayden was strong, but he struggled to get me under control.  Just when one of us seemed to be getting the upper hand, the balance of power shifted.

Wrestling with Brayden aroused me.  I didn't want him to know, but I couldn't hide it for long.  The evidence poked into him.  Brayden was breathing harder, but that didn't mean anything.  I was too but that wasn't because I was turned on. Then, I felt it—the obvious evidence that Brayden was aroused too.

The danger came moments later. Our faces came within inches of each other and we gazed into each other's eyes. I felt a powerful compulsion to kiss him. I even began to lean in, but then I got control of myself and broke away.

"Let's call it a draw!" I said.

I slid to a sitting position. I couldn't stand up. I guess it didn't matter if I did or not. Brayden knew what was going on in my pants.

"I should probably get going. It's getting late," Brayden said.

"Want me to get Percy to drive you?"

"Nah. I don't live that far. I need to cool off anyway."

That's as close as either of us came to acknowledging that something had almost happened between us.

"I'll see you at school tomorrow. Maybe we won't have to listen to wedding plans at lunch," I said.

"Let's hope not! Thanks for... everything."

"Thanks for coming over. I can never get Tyler to play the games I like and Percy... well, forget that."

When Brayden departed, I sat down at my desk and rolled a pencil between my fingers. Brayden was *really* hot. If I wasn't with Tyler and if Percy hadn't been in the house... I was going to have to be careful. Something had almost happened between us, something that would have made me feel far guiltier than I did at the moment. I couldn't let anything like that happen, but I wanted to be friends with Brayden. He needed someone and I could share things with Brayden I couldn't with anyone else. The tragedies that had derailed our lives were different, but we understood each other in a way no one who hadn't had their life ripped apart could. We also just plain had a lot in common. I was tired of playing video games by myself.

I wandered into the living room. Percy was drinking a cup of hot tea. He was *always* drinking a cup of hot tea.

"Did you guys manage to kill everyone?" Percy asked.

"We were mainly playing UFC."

Percy looked at me blankly.

"It's a fight game."

"There are so many games now. I can't begin to keep them straight."

"Ha! Like you ever played video games."

"I spent hundreds of hours playing *Warcraft*."

"*World of Warcraft*? Really?"

"This was before *World of Warcraft*, but more or less the same game. I played with computer opponents."

"Figures you'd only play *old* games."

"Who you calling old, punk?"

"You!"

Percy laughed.

"*Warcraft* isn't that old. Way back, I played a text game called *Zork*."

"A text game?"

"This was before computer graphics were sophisticated."

"So, like in the 1950s?"

"I'm not that old, Caspian."

"Of course, you're not," I said in my most insincere tone.

"I do remember the first video game."

"You lived in a cave and ran from dinosaurs then, right?"

"I know where you sleep, Caspian."

"Yeah, yeah. I'm terrified. So what was the first video game?"

"It was called *Pong*. It was basically ping-pong played on a TV. There were two controllers and they moved a small rectangle up and down. The object was to hit the ball back to the other player."

"I'm familiar with ping-pong. That's it? That's all it did? What was the second video game called? *Watching Paint Dry*?"

"Laugh if you want, but everyone thought it was cool."

"I guess there wasn't much entertainment back then."

"Not as much as there is now."

"Thanks for the ancient history lesson. I'll make use of it next year when I have to take World History."

"You are such a smart alec."

"Yeah!" I laughed.

"So what do you think about us moving in with Daniel and Tyler?" Percy asked.

"It will be cool. Daniel can't possibly be as boring as you."

"You're just full of compliments tonight."

"Aww, you're okay, for an old guy. It's cool you found someone to date who makes you happy at your age."

Percy gazed at me, trying to figure out if he'd been insulted or not.

"Tyler was driving me nuts today with his plans for the ceremony. On the way to school, he talked so much about his plans it was all I could do not to tell him to shut up. I was rescued at lunch when Dylan jumped into the planning. I thought Tyler and Dylan were going to wet themselves with excitement. They went out after school to look at cakes. Tyler wants me to wear white, which I am NOT going to do. I don't get being so into planning something like that."

"You and Tyler have different interests. You're very different kinds of boys."

"Yeah."

I looked sideways at Percy, debating if I wanted to talk to him about what was running through my mind.

"Tyler and I have been dating," I said.

"I know that."

"Well, we, uh... we got pretty serious at least as far as sex."

"I'm not too surprised by that, Caspian."

"We went all the way."

Percy looked at me, but I couldn't read him.

"I hope you used protection."

"Yeah."

"I'm glad to hear that."

"It's just that... well, the guys were teasing us at lunch. I don't mind so much, but I think Tyler does and I feel kind of weird about Tyler and me... together."

"Because you're going to be family?"

"Uh... yeah!"

"I think that would be awkward."

"Do you think it's wrong of us to be together?"

"I'm not entirely comfortable with the two of you dating, but it's not wrong. I'm more concerned about the age difference. Three years is a big difference at your age. I also think your relationship will become increasingly difficult when we move in with Daniel and Tyler."

"Yeah and... I like Brayden," I admitted.

Percy didn't answer for a moment. I could tell he was thinking.

"I can see why you like him. The two of you have a lot in common."

"I feel guilty liking him. Tonight we almost kissed."

"I think it's natural for you to be drawn to someone who is so much like you. I don't think you have to feel guilty for that. I'm sure Tyler feels attracted to other guys too."

"Are you? Attracted to other guys, I mean?"

"Yes."

"You're about to be the same as married and you're attracted to other guys besides Daniel?"

"Yes. I don't think humans are meant to be monogamous. It's natural to be attracted to others."

"Why do you want to commit to Daniel when you believe that?"

"I want to be with him. I want to know we will be there for each other and for Tyler and for you. I also want Daniel to know how strongly I feel about him."

"Couldn't you have all that without the commitment?"

"To a certain extent, yes, but there are times when one wants to take those extra steps, to truly make a commitment. It's also something I just want, that Daniel and I both want. Our lives have been connected since we were teens. We want to strengthen that bond."

"I guess I can understand although I don't think that much of committing to someone."

"At your age, you shouldn't be thinking about commitment too strongly. Now is your time to explore and to meet new people. It's your time to figure out what and who you want."

"I've been spending some time with Brayden. He's really cool. He's been through some stuff a lot like me. His boyfriend killed himself."

Percy suddenly looked very sad.

"That must be very difficult for him."

"Yes. We talk about it, and we talk about Mom and Dad too. He's experiencing now what I did. I want to help him."

"I'm proud of you."

"Talking helps me too. He understands. I know you and Tyler try, but you don't really know what it's like to experience what I did. Brayden doesn't either, but he comes a lot closer."

"I'm glad you've found someone who understands. You know I'm always here for you, but my comprehension only goes so far."

"Yeah, that's something I really like about Brayden. We don't talk about his boyfriend or my parents much, but sometimes we do and there's always...."

"A connection there."

"Yeah. That's it. I really like spending time with him, but I still like Tyler. It's just that now when I think about being with Tyler, it feels... awkward."

"Have you talked to Tyler about this?"

"No."

"Maybe you should."

"I don't want to hurt him and I'm not even sure about how I feel. Tyler has helped me a lot."

"It's best to be honest about how you feel, even if doing so will hurt someone. It may well prevent you from hurting him even more later. Take some time and figure out how you feel about Tyler and about Brayden. The situation between Tyler and you is getting more complicated, and I'm sorry about that. He will be going away to school this fall too. Even if he attends IU, he may not live at home and even if he does, he will still be entering a new world."

"So, you're saying we're doomed?"

"No. I don't think it's very likely the two of you will continue dating while Tyler is in college. I don't think it's a good idea either. You both need to explore who you are. You need to get to know different people and date different guys. The two of you may come back together someday when that three-year age difference doesn't mean so much. After a few years, the difference won't mean anything at all. Look at Daniel and me. We dated when we were teens. We lost touch, but now we're back together again twenty years later."

"You guys are soooo old!"

"Only to you."

"Keep telling yourself that."

I looked down at my feet for a few moments.

"Why does this have to be so hard?"

"I don't have the answer to that, but don't worry too much. I know Tyler. He will be a little hurt that you're interested in someone else, but he'll probably be a little relieved as well."

"Why?"

"He knows his life will be changing soon. I think he'll be glad that you have someone."

"Well, I'm not talking about dating Brayden. I mean... maybe, but just being friends and hanging out and then maybe... sex."

"Getting to know someone and figuring out where things are going is a lot of the fun."

"If you say so."

"I do."

"You're not mad that Tyler and I went all the way, are you?"

"I would prefer that you hadn't, but I am glad you used protection and that your first time was with Tyler."

"It sounds like you are glad we did it," I teased.

"The parent in me thinks you are too young. The teenager in me understands completely."

"How old were you when you first went all the way?"

"I don't really want to talk about that."

"Oh, I see. You're just saying that because you don't remember. You lost your virginity back in the olden times."

I ducked as Percy pretended he was going to smack me.

"You won't tell Tyler what we talked about, will you?" I asked.

"Of course not."

"I didn't think so. I just wanted to make sure. I want to think about all this."

"I think that's a wise idea."

"Thanks, Percy."

"Any time."

I got up and hugged Percy tight. He wrapped his arms around me and hugged me back just as hard. I missed my parents, but I was glad Percy was in my life.

# Chapter 12

"Could I... um... have some money?" I asked Percy. My uncle was pretty free with cash, as long as he didn't think I was spending it on something stupid.

"Let me guess. You saw a shirt at Abercrombie & Fitch you just have to have."

"That's not funny. Just because I'm wearing a few different colors now does not make me a cookie-cutter-preppy-wannabe."

Percy laughed. He often thought he was funny. He was usually wrong.

"There's a movie I want to see. I'm going to ask Tyler to go with me. Oh, and can you drive us?"

"What movie?"

It was the question I was dreading. You're probably thinking it was because I wanted to see an R-rated movie, but that's not it. I seriously doubt Percy would care. He says that no R-rated movie could possibly be as bad as the evening news. I had a far greater reason for dreading the question.

"Well... uh... *Star Trek*."

"*Star Trek*?" Percy said, arching one eyebrow. There was a hint of glee in his tone. "Aren't you the boy who is always making fun of me for what you call my *Star Trek* obsession?"

"Grrr! This is why I didn't want you to know! The preview looked cool, okay? It's supposed to be a *Star Trek* movie for those who aren't into *Star Trek*."

Percy dug into his wallet and handed me some cash.

"I'll be happy to drive you. I think you'll like it."

"You've already seen it?"

"Of course. Would someone with the last name Spock miss out on a *Star Trek* movie? Daniel and I went a couple of nights ago."

"That was a stupid question. Of course you've seen it. I'm surprised you don't watch it *every* night."

"I could go with you," Percy said, and then laughed evilly.

"That's not funny. Do you want to totally destroy my reputation?"

"I've thought about it, but no."

I gave Percy the evil eye but smiled slightly, totally ruining the effect.

"Thanks for the money."

"You're welcome."

I began to leave the room.

"Caspian?"

"Yeah?"

"If you want to borrow some of my *Star Trek* novels to read, I'll be happy to loan them to you."

I growled and hurried out of the room. Percy was going to have way too much fun teasing me about this.

I called Tyler.

"Tyler's cellphone. He's busy right now. Can I take a message?"

"Dylan?"

"Yeah. Caspian?"

"Yes. What are you doing with Tyler's phone?"

"I mugged him."

"No, really."

"We're at the Steak 'n Shake planning a menu for the ceremony and sharing a banana split. Tyler's in the restroom."

I released a frustrated sigh.

"You aren't mad at me, are you? We're just planning the wedding. I promise."

"No. No. I'm not mad at you. It's just that Tyler spends all his time planning that stupid ceremony."

"Uh, well... he's back. Here he is."

I heard Dylan tell Tyler it was me on the phone.

"Hey, Caspian. What up?" Tyler asked.

Tyler was so cheerful and friendly my anger disappeared.

"You want to go to a movie with me tomorrow night?"

"Oh, I can't. I'd like to, but between homework and planning the wedding..."

"How about the night after?"

"Um... I'm going to be really busy during the evenings this week. What movie anyway?"

"Never mind. Go back to having fun planning your wedding."

I hug up without saying "goodbye" or giving Tyler a chance to speak. I shouldn't have, but I was tired of hearing about nothing but that stupid ceremony. I didn't even want to go to it!

I took a few moments to calm myself, then called Brayden.

"Hey, you want to go see a movie with me tomorrow night?"

"What movie?" Brayden asked.

"I want to see *Star Trek*."

"Yeah, cool. I want to see that. I'm buying this time."

"I can pay. I got some money from Percy."

"No. This time I'm paying. You pay too often."

I sighed.

"What?"

"I was just thinking I wouldn't have had to endure the torment of asking for money to go see a *Star Trek* movie if I'd know you'd pay."

"Why is that such a big deal?"

"Percy loves *Star Trek,* and I have been known to give him a hard time about it."

"Which means you torment him mercilessly."

"Yeah."

"I get it. I bet that was torture."

"The worst part is it gives him ammunition. I'll never hear the end of it."

"I feel for you, buddy. Why aren't you going with your boyfriend?"

"I asked him. He's busy planning that stupid wedding."

"Oh, so I'm your second choice," Brayden said, pretending to be upset.

"Well, he is hotter than you."

"Ha! You are just blinded by sex. I'm *way* hotter than your boyfriend."

Actually, Brayden was hotter, but I wasn't going to comment on that.

"He's too busy for me anyway. He spends all his time with Dylan now."

"Do I detect a bit of jealousy?"

"Maybe just a little. Tyler wouldn't *do* anything with Dylan, but it would be nice if my boyfriend had time to go to a movie with me."

"Well, even though I'm your *second* choice, I'll make sure you have a good time."

"How long will you be tormenting me with the 'second choice' thing?"

"Probably just until the movie starts."

"I guess I'll have to live with that."

Brayden and I talked for almost another hour. We started talking about video games and that led into computers, which led into why I never chatted online. Brayden gave me his Yahoo Messenger name. I had a Yahoo Email account but had never used Messenger. I promised to download it and talk to Brayden online sometime soon.

I hit my homework after getting off the phone, then turned on my computer. I used my computer for games, checking out skating, music, and the occasional porn site (okay, way more than occasional) but didn't get much into email and hadn't chatted online before. I guess I hadn't bothered because I talked daily to everyone I knew at school.

Anything involving a computer came to me easily and downloading and installing Yahoo Messenger required no effort at all. I tried to come up with a cool screen-name like skaterboy or hotgoth, but all the names I tried were taken. I finally just used my name and threw in some seemingly random numbers. At least my name, Caspian Perseus, was cool. Perseus was a rare last name and I had never met another Caspian.

I signed on and added Brayden's screen name to my list. I liked seeing Brayden's screen name on my Messenger. He wasn't with me, but yet seeing his name made me feel like he was in my room.

Brayden: Hey.

Me: Do u chat on here a lot?

Brayden: Yeah, but only 2 ppl I don't know, until now.

Me: People u don't know?

Brayden: It was easier talking 2 ppl I didn't know after Stuart died. My friends and family acted weird around me. Most tried very hard not 2 mention Stuart and others tried 2 b supportive. I didn't want 2 talk about him at all for a long time. I didn't talk about him until that day u and I got into it at Armstrong Stadium. By talking 2 people I didn't know, I didn't have 2 worry about them bringing up Stuart.

Me: Isn't it scary talking 2 strangers?

Brayden: No. It's not like I was going 2 meet any of them. A couple of guys wanted 2 meet me, but I didn't want 2 make friends or hook up. I wanted 2 b left alone, but I was lonely too. That's why I got into chatting on here. I could talk about whatever I wanted and it helped me forget that Stuart was gone, at least for a while.

Me: I'm going 2 give the guys my screen name tomorrow, except maybe Dylan. LOL. I bet most of them r on here.

Brayden: Probably. I think I'm ready to give them my screen name 2, not that any of them have asked for it.

Me: I think they don't want 2 push and you're not exactly easy to approach.

Brayden: LOL. Yeah, I haven't exactly encouraged ne1 2 b my friend, except you :)

Me: That's because I'm special.

Brayden: Keep telling yourself that, C.

Me: U should let the guys in. I know it's hard, but life is easier with friends.

Brayden: I know. It's just scary 2 take the risk.

Me: Because ur afraid if u let yourself start 2 like someone you'll lose them too, right?

Brayden: Yes.

Me: That's what scared me, but the risk is worth it. Spending time with the guys keeps me from dwelling on what happened. It doesn't make the pain go away, but there is less pain because I'm doing other things besides brooding on that night.

Brayden: Part of me wants 2 follow ur advice. Part of me wants 2 withdraw and go back 2 sitting alone.

Me: Don't do that. Trust me. I used 2 b u. I was brave enough 2 take the risk. Surely u are 2.

Brayden: Using psychology on me now?

Me: I'm just taking advantage of ur competitive edge. Of course, if u want to admit that I'm stronger and braver than you...

Brayden: Never!

Me: LOL. That's what I thought. Let the guys in. I'm not saying u have to date anyone. Just allow urself 2 have some friends. You already have 1. Well, make that 2. Tyler likes u a lot as well.

Brayden: Thanks.

Me: U know what I don't like about talking online?

Brayden: What?

Me: All this typing!

Brayden: LOL.

Me: I also can't tell if u r sticking ur tongue out at me.

Brayden: That's what an emoticon is 4.

Me: A what?

Brayden: Like the smiley face I sent earlier :)

Me: Oh!

Brayden: U blonds sure r dumb.

Me: U r only brave enough 2 say it because u r safe from a butt-kicking.

Brayden: I'll say it 2 ur face tomorrow and I'll still b safe from a butt-kicking.

Me: Blow me.

Brayden: Ur bf would get jealous.

Me: LOL.

Brayden: Hey, I gtg, but ttyl, k?

Me: What's ttyl?

Brayden: Talk to you later.

Me: Oh!

Brayden: Goodnight, dumb blond.

Brayden signed off before I had a chance to come back at him, but I'd get him tomorrow.

*** 

Chatting online can get addictive. I soon had the screen names of all my friends and chatted with them in the evenings and night. I left Yahoo Messenger on whenever I was on my computer.

I mostly talked with Brayden. He was online more than the others, but the main reason I talked to him the most was that we had the most in common. Tyler was my boyfriend, but he was more intellectual than me. Caleb was a jock, Dylan was mostly interested in shopping, and Jesse was obsessed with fashion and personal care products. Tyreece and I chatted some, but it was Brayden that I really connected with.

I discovered something else about chatting online; it was easier than face-to-face communication. I don't mean it was physically easier. I wasn't a big fan of typing. I mean it was easier to talk about personal feelings. Brayden and I had already talked about some deeply personal events in our lives, but I could say things chatting to him that I couldn't in person. Maybe it was because I didn't have to look into his eyes. Part of it was that I didn't have to speak right away. I could think about what I wanted to say and get it just right before I typed it out. There were often long pauses between messages because Brayden and I were often doing other things while chatting. I might go off to use the restroom or to get a drink and then answer Brayden's message when I returned.

Brayden and I had long chats about his boyfriend and my parents. We told stories about them and talked about how much we missed them and how much we'd like to have just one more hour with them. We talked about the guilt we experienced for surviving.

Brayden: I sometimes feel like a coward 4 not killing myself when I found Stuart dead. Sometimes, I feel like I should have taken him down, put the rope back in place, and hanged myself with the same noose.

Me: I've been wondering about something. You found Stuart in the locker room, right?

Brayden: Yeah.

Me: What were u doing there? U had both quit the soccer team, right?

Brayden: Yes. The reason I was there is kind of weird, but I'm almost sure Stuart hung himself in the locker room as a statement. It was his way of telling his former friends and teammates how much they'd hurt him.

Me: Did they get the message?

Brayden: Yeah, loud and clear, especially later when I screamed at them that they'd killed Stuart.

Me: U did that?

Brayden: I went kind of crazy for a while after I found Stuart dead. I'm not the least bit sorry I told those bastards what I thought about them. U should have seen them. Some of their faces went so pale when I went off on them they were as white as a ghost.

Me: U still haven't told me why u were in the locker room.

Brayden: Don't tell anyone else this, but I was pulled there. I had this strong feeling that I had 2 go there. I ignored it at first, but the feeling was overpowering. I had to go. I didn't know why I felt a compulsion 2 go 2 the locker room, but then I found him. If I'd had any guts, I would've killed myself right then and there. I was a coward.

Me: Hey, none of that. You had the guts 2 live. You didn't take the easy way out. U r the opposite of a coward.

Brayden: I don't know. I don't think of Stuart as a coward 4 losing hope and ending his life. He just became overwhelmed and didn't see ne other way out.

Me: Yeah, I didn't mean 2 say Stuart was a coward.

Brayden: I always thought of him as the strong 1. I'm strong, but Stuart was something else. They still got him. All the bullies and haters made his life so hard he couldn't take it anymore. What I don't understand is how I could find the strength to keep going when he couldn't.

Me: U r different people. There was something in u that kept u going and I doubt there is ne way 2 know what it was that kept u from giving up.

Brayden: It was the hardest 2 keep going right after Stuart killed himself. I felt like I had no reason 2 live. I even wondered if he wanted me 2 follow him. Maybe he wanted us 2 b together in death. I thought about killing myself. I thought about it a lot, but I kept thinking that there was no way to undo it if it was a mistake. I figured I could always kill myself later if that's what I decided 2 do, but I couldn't un-kill myself. Time passed and I kept thinking about blowing my brains out or chugging a bottle of pills, but I thought about it less and less. I was never sure if I should do it or not, so I kept putting it off until tomorrow or next week. I kept thinking that I'd think about it later. After a while I grew numb. I stopped feeling much of anything. The pain wasn't gone, but it wasn't really there either so I figured the time for doing myself in had passed. If I was going to do it, I should have done it as soon as I found Stuart dead.

Me: I'm glad u didn't kill yourself. I would never have met u and we would never have been able to play video games together :)

Brayden: I miss him so much, Caspian. I know why he did it, but I wonder why he couldn't hold on 4 me. He had 2 know how much his death would hurt me but he did it anyway. Sometimes, I still hate him 4 it and then I feel so guilty for hating him. I miss him so much. I just want him back.

I didn't have to see or hear Brayden to know that he was crying.

Me: I want my parents back 2, but I know they aren't coming back, ever. My only options r 2 off myself or keep going. I'm going to keep going. If I can keep going, so can you.

There was no answer for a few minutes. I began to get worried. I didn't think Brayden would kill himself, but what if I was wrong? What if he was doing it as I sat there waiting for a message that would never come?

Brayden: I'll keep going. It's 2 late 2 give up now. I've already been through so much.

I released a breath I didn't even know I'd been holding.

Me: We aren't the only ones with problems, u know. Think about Caleb. He was a football star and now he will never walk again. What must that be like? I don't think I could stand being stuck in a wheelchair 4 the rest of my life, but what must it be like for him?

Brayden: Yeah.

Me: Tyler can't even remember his mom. She died when he was so young he can't even picture her face. What about Dylan? With his girly voice and those flailing hands, he might as well b wearing a target.

Brayden: True, but Jesse and Tyreece don't look like they have problems.

Me: I'm sure they do. Their problems just aren't as obvious although I'm sure being black isn't a picnic. There r still a lot of prejudiced, stupid people out there.

Brayden: U mean Christians and Republicans?

Me: Well, not exactly, but I guess those groups have more than their share of stupid, prejudiced people.

Brayden: Christians are hypocrites. They are evil. They killed Stuart as surely as if they'd shot him dead.

I didn't know what to say to that. I thought about typing something about stereotypes and how he shouldn't lump a whole group together as if they were all the same, but I didn't think he would appreciate that argument. I couldn't exactly say he was wrong either. The worst of the haters were always devout churchgoers or Republicans. I was glad Percy never tried to make me go to church. He didn't go either. Was it because of the haters?

Brayden: Sorry. I'm getting a little intense.

Me: Just a little, but it's ok.

Brayden: While we're talking about Tyreece, is he really as big as I've heard?

Me: How should I know and didn't we talk about this before?

Brayden: Well, Tyler says u r easy, so I figured u'd seen it.

Me: Ha. Ha. Jerk. I'm only easy 4 Tyler.

Brayden: Ohhhhhh!

A lot of our talks went like that. We would get into something serious, then lighten the mood up by saying something stupid or making fun of each other. Brayden and I still talked at school, but our real talks took place online and on the phone too.

# Chapter 13

Christmas was coming up fast! I had lived my life in California and Christmas decorations there had always looked somewhat out of place. There was a big difference between the palm trees decorated with lights and all the Christmas specials with real Christmas trees, sleigh rides and snow. I had never actually seen real snow, not in person. Percy said it often didn't snow in Bloomington until January, but he also said it could snow as early as Thanksgiving, which had already come and gone. I couldn't wait to see real snow!

Then, it happened. I woke up on the morning of Saturday, December 12$^{th}$ to see something fluffy and white gathered against the windowpanes. At first, I was confused and felt like I was dreaming, but then I realized what I was seeing. It was snow!

I opened up the window and grabbed a handful. It was freezing cold, which made perfect sense, and it was powdery. It began to melt and compact in my hands. I scooped up some more and made my very first snowball. It wasn't very big, but I smiled with glee. I closed the window, slipped on my boxer-briefs, and stealthily went in search of Percy. I found him in the kitchen.

"Hey, Percy," I said.

He turned and I nailed him with the snowball.

"You know you'll pay for that later," Percy threatened, but I knew he wasn't mad. I laughed.

"Bring it on! I have to get outside! I can't believe it's snowing!"

I hurried towards the kitchen door.

"Uh, Caspian?"

"What?" I asked.

"You might want to put on some clothes. It's about thirty degrees outside. I know you're from California, but you see it only snows when it's cold and I think you'll be a little chilly in your boxer briefs."

"I knew that!"

"Of course you did."

"Oh, shut up."

Percy laughed.

I hurried to my room. I really had been about to run outside in my underwear, not because I was stupid, but because I was so excited about the snow I just wasn't thinking. As soon as I dressed, I reached for my phone, but then I remembered Tyler was spending the day with Dylan making final preparations for the wedding. I hoped they were the final preparations! The commitment ceremony was in one week and Tyler had been planning it forever! I sent Brayden a quick text instead. He was downtown so we arranged to meet at the Sample Gates in half an hour.

I could have asked Percy to drive me, but I wanted to walk. I was about to leave when Percy stepped into my room. He looked me up and down.

"Wear your toboggan, scarf, and gloves."

"What's a toboggan? Isn't that some kind of sled?"

"Well, it is a kind of sled, but in this part of the Midwest and in the South it's also a knitted cap."

"Oh! That red cap that looks like someone's mother knitted it. It will mess up my hair."

Percy gave me a look that said "Just wear it" so I dug it out of the dresser drawer along with the unused matching red scarf and lined leather gloves.

"Happy now?" I asked, pulling it all on.

"Delighted. Have fun."

"Always."

I stepped outside into the falling snow. I raised my face to the cloudy sky and a snowflake landed on my nose. It quickly melted. I laughed, then looked back toward the house to see if Percy was watching. I thought I saw a curtain move, so I hurried on. I wasn't sure how long it would take me to walk down to campus.

The snow fell all around me as I walked down the sidewalks. It made no sound but gave me the same comfy and cozy feeling I had when walking under an umbrella in the rain. I slipped but regained my balance before my butt had a chance to hit the pavement. I made a mental note: snow is slick. A Midwest winter was hard on a California boy!

Bloomington looked so different covered in white. The snow was everywhere: on yards, rooftops, cars, the side walk, and the trees. It kept falling, big fluffy flakes all cold and fragile. The little crystals melted when they touched my bare skin. I was already glad I'd worn the toboggan, scarf, and gloves. It hadn't been this cold before! Only the day before the temperature was in the mid-40s. I felt like I was walking inside a big freezer then and now it was a lot colder!

The blocks slipped by as I looked all around me. As I hit downtown, I noticed Christmas decorations which had been up since November. There were wreaths and bows and lights on street lamps. There were Christmas trees in shop windows and lights everywhere. With the snow falling down, I felt like I was inside a Christmas card or maybe a Christmas snow globe. I'd had one when I was a kid. Santa, reindeer, and plastic snow swirled around when I shook the globe. Yeah, walking downtown was like a being inside a snow globe, only better because the snow was real.

I walked down Kirkwood Avenue and could see the Sample Gates ahead. A huge wreath with red bows and Christmas bulbs was hung on each gate. The snow covered everything, including Brayden who stood wearing his own toboggan and scarf, only his were dark green.

"I can't believe it's snowing!" I said as I stepped up to him.

Brayden laughed.

"You act like you've never seen snow before."

"I haven't!"

"Ever?"

I shook my head.

"I'm from California."

"It snows in California."

"Not in the part of California where I lived!"

"Your eyes are sparkling," Brayden said.

"Sparkling?"

"Yeah. You know how someone's eyes sparkle when they're *really* excited? You look like that now and it's as if you're glowing, lit up from the inside."

"I'll tell you something if you promise not to tell *anyone* else," I said.

"I promise. What?"

"I got so excited when I saw it snowing, I almost ran outside in my boxer briefs."

Brayden laughed for a few moments, then stopped. He gazed at me and smiled.

"Thanks, Caspian."

"For what?"

"For making me laugh. I've laughed a lot since we began hanging out. I didn't laugh before I met you, not since Stuart died."

I smiled back. I did a lot of smiling when I was with Brayden.

"Come on. Let's walk through Dunn's Woods," I said, taking Brayden by the hand and not letting go.

We walked through the forest. The leaves were gone, but the tree trunks were beautiful in the falling snow. We followed the snow covered brick paths that wandered through the woods. We walked in silence. We didn't need to talk just then. It was enough to just be together.

We came upon the Rose Well House. Percy had shown it to me before. He said it was his favorite spot on campus. It was a beautiful little gazebo-like structure made of limestone. There were stained glass panels in the roof.

"This is really cool," Brayden said, sitting on one of the benches inside.

"Yeah, my uncle said part of *Breaking Away* was filmed here."

"What's that?"

"A movie about the Little 500. It was filmed in Bloomington. Beware. If you go near Percy, he will make you watch it."

"Next question. What's the Little 500? A race with go carts?"

"That would be cool, but no. It's a bike race. It's a huge deal here."

The snow fell down all around the well house. The wind got up at bit and we were trapped in a mini blizzard. Everything was white for a few moments.

"You know what?" Brayden said after a bit.

"What?"

"My ass is freezing!"

Brayden stood up. I hadn't sat on the cold stone, but I was chilled too.

"Let's go get something hot to drink. I know just the place. Percy took me there."

We walked toward the Indiana Memorial Union, called the IMU for short. It was the student union for IU, and there were lots of places to eat inside. We entered and walked down a hallway. We passed the Starbucks because I had somewhere better in mind. We walked through the South Lounge with its blazing fireplace, then down yet more hallways. We took the stairs down one level and there was our destination; Sugar and Spice.

We each ordered a hot chocolate but decided to share a chocolate chip cookie because they were so big. Once we had our stuff, we headed back upstairs to the South Lounge and sat in a leather loveseat before the fire. The warmth was as delicious as the hot chocolate and cookie.

Brayden sat close to me. I resisted the urge to put my arm around him. I didn't want to cross the line between friends and more than friends. I did have a boyfriend, after all, and I loved him very much.

We sipped our hot chocolate and ate our cookie. There was a Christmas tree nearby as well as wreaths with red bows and evergreen swag decorated with mistletoe and holly berries.

"It's so… Christmassy in Bloomington," I said.

"Well, it is December and Christmas is coming soon so why should that surprise you?"

"It's just so different from California."

"Don't tell me you didn't have Christmas there."

"Oh, we did. We decorated and had a tree, but it didn't seem like Christmas because it was 80 degrees outside and palm trees were swaying in the breeze."

"Sounds like paradise."

"Not at Christmas. This is Christmas."

"It probably didn't snow in Bethlehem either."

"Well, Percy says most of the Christmas story is wrong. Jesus wasn't born on December the 25th and wasn't born in Bethlehem."

"Was Percy there? I know he's old, but I didn't know he was *that* old."

"Ha Ha. No, he said the church usurped an old winter holiday and said Jesus was born then. The whole "Mary and Joseph going to Bethlehem to be counted for taxes" is wrong too."

"How does Percy know that?"

"He knows a lot about history. He said that at that time and in that part of the world any kind of count or census was conducted where people lived, not where they had come from. It's just like today. If there were a census, I wouldn't have to go back to California. Percy said that no one would force a pregnant woman that far along to make such a journey either. It just wasn't done."

"That does make a lot of sense."

"Percy said the church claimed Jesus was born in Bethlehem because there was a prophecy that said the Messiah would be born there. They were trying to make Jesus sound more important. Percy says that Messiah doesn't even mean what most people think. It actually means "war lord." The Messiah was expected to lead the people in battle to conquer their foes."

"That doesn't sound like Jesus. So, does your uncle believe in Jesus at all?"

"Oh, yeah. He says he most definitely lived although he wasn't born on Christmas, wasn't born in Bethlehem, and wasn't a carpenter."

"No?"

"He couldn't have been. There were no trees as we know them in that part of the world. There were only what we would call shrubs. Even olive trees aren't big or straight enough to make things with. Furniture made of wood would have been very rare and expensive. Someone would have had to have been rich to be a carpenter."

"So the whole "performing miracles and healing people" thing isn't true either?"

"Percy said those parts are true."

"Really?"

"He said there is evidence that Jesus could heal people, something about electromagnetic fields or something. There are some people who can manipulate such fields, and lots of people went to Jesus to be healed."

"That's weird. Your uncle thinks the more believable stuff didn't happen, but that the hard-to-believe stuff did."

"He knows a lot about it. He studies all kinds of history and archaeology."

Brayden laughed.

"What?"

"No one would believe the two of us are sitting in front of a fire discussing Jesus."

"True, so let's not tell them."

"Deal."

"Okay. I'm warm. Let's go get cold again," I said.

"You love the snow, don't you?"

"Yeah!"

"You are as excited as Dylan is about... everything."

"Don't make me kick your butt."

"I only said you're as excited as him, not that you're like him."

"We will save the fight for later then."

The nearest exit wasn't far from the lounge, so we were back out in the falling snow in moments. We walked around the end of the IMU, past the old Dunn cemetery. Even the tombstones looked Christmassy all covered with snow.

We walked back down the other side of the IMU and were soon on the path that led beside Dunn Meadow. In the fall the meadow was green and well-built, shirtless college boys lounged there in the sun. Now, a blanket of white covered the meadow, and only a handful of college boys played in the snow.

The Jordan River, which was no more than a large stream, flowed nosily on the other side of the path. Brayden and I talked, walked, and caught snowflakes on our tongues. Suddenly, out of nowhere, a snowball hit Brayden in the head. It exploded and showered me with snow. Both of us darted off the path and grabbed up some snow. In moments we were firing back at our attackers. A furious snowball fight erupted. It was Brayden and me against four older, bigger college guys.

I'd never been in a snowball fight, of course. It's hard to have one without snow. One thing I learned fast is that getting hit in the face with a snowball hurt! I didn't mind the pain, especially when I clobbered the guy who got me in the side of the head. There was no cover without retreating to the trees so we were all sitting ducks.

We battled it out, but we were outnumbered. After a few minutes of getting pounded, Brayden and I looked at each other and made a silent decision. We turned from our attackers, lowered our pants, mooned them, and then ran like hell. Unfortunately, Brayden took one on the butt before he got his pants all the way back up, and the college boys howled with laughter. We ran about a block and then walked. I smiled at Brayden gleefully.

"What?"

"I can't wait to tell the guys you took it in the butt from a college boy."

"That sounds like something else entirely."

"Exactly."

"Don't tell them that! Dylan will get too excited. Besides, you're the bottom."

"Once! I tried it once! At least I didn't take it from a college boy I don't even know."

"I took a snowball to the butt. You took something quite different."

Brayden grabbed his jeans and tried moving them from side to side.

"Problem?"

"I've got snow in my crack."

"So, can I tell the guys you have a crack problem too?"

"Oh! You did not just say that! That's so pathetic! Boo!"

I laughed.

"I'm getting hungry," Brayden said.

"Let's eat somewhere. Oh! We can sit at the counter in the Bakehouse and watch the falling snow."

"You and your snow. You'd sleep with it if it didn't melt."

"At least I didn't take it in the butt."

"Ouch."

"Oh. I think Tyler said he might be free for a late lunch. You don't mind if I invite him, do you?"

"He *is* your boyfriend."

I whipped out my cell phone and called Tyler. He was just wrapping things up with Dylan and was hungry too. He agreed to meet us at the Bakehouse. As soon as I pushed the button to disconnect, I had a horrible thought.

"What?" Brayden asked, reading my apprehensive expression.

"Tyler said he was just finishing things up when Dylan. What if he brings him?"

"If he does, you sit by him."

"You know you like him," I said, half teasing, half serious.

"I like him at a distance. He's just too much. He's too over-the-top."

"He has his calm moments."

"Yeah, but what about the other 59 minutes in the hour?"

Brayden and I both laughed.

"I like Dylan," I said. "You just have to keep him in line. Threats of violence usually work."

"Would you really follow up on your threats?"

"Yes, and Dylan knows it. When I draw the line, he knows not to cross."

"I'll give that a try. Dylan does have some good qualities, but don't tell him I said that."

When we arrived at the Bakehouse a few minutes later, Tyler was just coming in the other door—alone. We all went up to the counter and placed our orders. I ordered a Bakehouse breakfast, which comes with two eggs, toast, home fries, and bacon. Tyler ordered a three egg white cheddar omelet, which comes with toast. Brayden ordered biscuits & gravy with bacon and toast.

I'd planned to sit at the counter so we could watch the snow, but there were no available spots. We found a booth and Brayden slid in beside me.

"What have you guys been doing?" Tyler asked.

"We robbed a bank earlier," Brayden said.

"Then we stole a Corvette and did some drag racing. I stole the car for you, but unfortunately, I totaled it."

"I told you not to take that corner so fast," Brayden said. "Unfortunately, all the cash from the bank job was in the back seat when the car went up in flames."

"We did foil that terrorist plot. Little did we know when we stole the car that there was a bomb in the trunk. They had planned to blow up Subway! Even though I prefer Jimmy Johns, I'm glad we saved Subway from being blown to bits," I said.

Tyler just looked at us.

"Are you two finished?"

"Fine," Brayden said. "We won't tell you about saving the kids from the orphanage fire."

"Bloomington doesn't have an orphanage," Tyler said.

"Well, not anymore! It just burned down!" I said.

"What did you *really* do?"

"We took a walk in the snow, bought hot chocolate and a cookie at Sugar & Spice, got in a snowball fight with some college boys, and then mooned them," I said.

"Now that I believe."

"Yeah, and Brayden..."

I closed my mouth. I'd forgotten I wasn't supposed to talk about him taking it in the butt with a snowball.

"Go on, you can tell him, but don't tell anyone else," Brayden said.

"Brayden didn't get his pants up fast enough and got hit with a snowball, right in the crack! He took one up the butt."

Tyler laughed.

"I wish I hadn't agreed not to tell anyone," Tyler said.

"How is your butt now?" I asked Brayden.

"Warmer."

I could see out the windows and the snow still fell steadily outside. I was glad to be in the warmth of the Bakehouse. The interior smelled of freshly baked bread, hamburgers, and hot coffee.

Our food soon arrived and that cut down on the conversation considerably, but we still talked.

"Jesse and I found you something to wear for the commitment ceremony," Tyler said.

I froze.

"It's not white, is it?"

"Fight. Fight," Brayden said.

"No and it's not formal either. Percy and Dad forbid me to make the ceremony formal. You will be wearing a light blue dress shirt with slacks and no, the slacks are not white."

"No tie, right? How light of blue are we talking?"

"Percy absolutely refuses to wear a tie *ever* so you don't have to wear one either. Percy told me long ago that if anything requires a tie he does not go. The blue isn't too light. You'll like it."

"I guess I can live with light blue."

"You two are starting to sound like Jesse," Brayden said.

"That's just cruel," I said.

Brayden laughed. I loved to see him laugh. I took his hand, squeezed it, and grinned at him. My smile faded as I realized what I was doing. Tyler looked down at our joined hands. I pulled my hand guilty away. Tyler didn't say anything and I couldn't read his expression, but I was very afraid I'd hurt him.

*Oh crap.*

Brayden didn't seem to catch on that anything had happened. He told us a story about a little restaurant where he and Stuart used to eat. There was sadness in his voice, but there was happiness that came from the memories too. It was like that for me when I remembered the good times with Mom and Dad. The grief and sadness were there, but when I remembered my parents, they were with me again.

Tyler drove us home when we finished eating. He dropped Brayden off first. I watched Tyler and waited for him to say something about what had happened in the Bakehouse. I didn't know what to expect. He might explode or worse, he might cry. He stopped the car and shut off the engine in front of Percy's house. Tyler turned to look at me but didn't say anything.

"Want to come in?" I asked.

There was another pause, but then Tyler smiled.

"Yeah."

We climbed out of the car and walked up the snow-covered sidewalk. The house was quiet when we entered. There was a note on the kitchen table saying that Percy was out running errands. Tyler and I walked into my room where we pulled off our winter clothing. I loved the snow, but it felt good to get out from under all those extra clothes.

I waited for Tyler to say something about what had happened in The Bakehouse, but instead he pulled me to him and hugged me close. We just held each other for several moments, then pulled back and looked into each other's eyes. Tyler leaned in and kissed me. Our kissed deepened and our tongues entwined. Our hands began to roam, but then we both pulled back. We stood there looking into each other's eyes. I felt so sad at that moment I thought I might cry.

"You like Brayden a lot, don't you?" Tyler asked.

"I haven't cheated on you," I said.

"I didn't say you did."

There was an awkward pause.

"It's okay that you like him."

Tyler's expression didn't match his words. He looked like he might cry.

"When I held his hand... I didn't mean... I just wanted him to know I was there. I was so happy that he could talk about Stuart like that. I didn't mean to hurt you."

"It... hurt a little, but you were just being there for a friend."

"We haven't done anything else. I promise. I wouldn't cheat on you. Well, I did once, but..."

"Shh," Tyler said, placing his finger on my lips. "That's in the past and I understand. I believe you. I'm not accusing you of anything, but we need to talk about *us*, Caspian."

I didn't say anything. I didn't want to have this talk. My heart began to beat faster. I was anxious and even a little afraid.

"You felt it just now, didn't you?" Tyler asked. "There's something we're both feeling."

My lower lip began to tremble and tears rimmed my eyes. Tyler had tears in his eyes too.

"It doesn't feel right anymore," I whispered.

Tyler nodded.

"It's because we're about to become family, isn't it?" I asked.

"Yeah. I love you, Caspian, but being together feels weird now. It doesn't feel right."

I'd been feeling it too. Feeling it, but not wanting to say.

"I feel differently about you now. I love you as much as ever and I think even more, but I love you differently. You know what I mean, right? I think you're feeling it too."

"Yeah. Like family," I said.

Tyler nodded.

"When we were together... when we had sex... it was hot." Tyler grinned and so did I. "I'm sure you've noticed we haven't done anything recently. I know I've been busy and I've been spending a lot of time with Dylan, but I haven't tried to initiate anything with you because I feel... I don't want to say odd, but... it just doesn't feel quite right."

I nodded.

"That's why I haven't tried anything, even though I've been mad horny."

Tyler laughed for a moment but then grew still and looked sad.

"Just now, I kissed you because I wanted to make sure and... I am. It doesn't feel right anymore, does it?"

I shook my head. Tyler was saying what I felt but didn't want to say. I didn't want to lose him.

"We're breaking up. Aren't we?" I said. Tears rimmed my eyes.

"Don't think of it as breaking up, Caspian. Think of it as becoming brothers. I love you. It's just that that love has changed. If anything, it's stronger. I care about you so much. I love being with you. You mean more to me than I can say. I've always wanted a brother, and I'm really happy that it's going to be you."

Tyler began crying then. I pulled him close and held him in my arms. I could feel his body shuddering with sobs.

"This could be better than being boyfriends," I said quietly.

"It will be better."

We hugged each other close and Tyler stopped crying.

"I never had a brother before," I said. I leaned back and looked at Tyler. "I'll have a big brother now."

"I'll have a little brother who can save me if bullies come after me," Tyler said.

I laughed.

"Are you okay with this?" Tyler asked.

"Yeah. I mean... I don't like things changing between us, but things have already changed, haven't they? I was feeling what you were, but I didn't want to say because I was afraid of losing you."

"You'll never lose me."

"I know," I said and hugged Tyler tighter.

"The guys are going to be so disappointed," Tyler said.

"Why?" I asked, leaning back again and then releasing my former boyfriend.

"Because this will ruin all their incest jokes."

"Well, we did have sex. They will still get to point that out."

"And they will," Tyler said.

"Without question."

"I wonder how everyone else will react?" Tyler asked. "Everyone knows we were dating and they probably assume we had sex."

"Which we have," I said. "Who cares what they think? There is nothing wrong with what we did. I don't care what anyone thinks and neither should you. If anyone gives you trouble, I will kick their ass!"

Tyler smiled, then laughed, hugged me again, and then kissed my forehead. I kissed him on the cheek and grinned.

"Are you okay?" Tyler asked.

"Yeah. I can't say I won't be sad, but I'm happy too, you know?"

"I know."

We heard the front door open and close. Percy was home.

"I should get going. I'll see you at school if not before."

"Yeah, and we'll talk online before that!"

"Yes, and very soon we'll be living under the same roof. I'll see you later, Caspian. I love you."

"I love you too."

I stayed in my room as Tyler departed. I heard him talking to Percy for a few moments and then he was gone. Part of me felt like crying, but mostly, I was happy. Tyler was right. This wasn't breaking up. We were becoming brothers.

# Chapter 14

I woke up Sunday morning feeling different. I lay there wondering why as I stared at the ceiling, and then it hit me. Tyler and I weren't boyfriends anymore. A wave of sadness hit me but then passed, turned into happiness, and became sadness again. I wondered if everyone was kind of messed up or if it was just me.

I almost felt guilty for not feeling worse. The breakup seemed too easy. There wasn't much of a buildup to it. Tyler and I both began feeling weird about our sexual relationship. As soon as we discussed those feelings, we ended it. I felt as if the end of our relationship should have been more... I don't know... dramatic?

*Great, now I'm turning into Dylan. Perish the thought!*

I guess I shouldn't expect real life to be like a movie. Sometimes even significant events like breaking up with a boyfriend weren't that dramatic. The act of breaking up was simple, but the feelings both Tyler and I felt were intense. I knew breaking up would have been much, much harder if other emotions weren't involved. The pain was dulled by the thought that Tyler was about to become my family. He was going to be my brother. Part of my family had been ripped away from me, but now I was actually gaining a brother. There was Daniel to think about too. I was going to have two dads! Neither Percy nor Daniel could ever take the place of my dad. I knew they wouldn't try, but to know they were there, to know they cared that much about me... words just can't express how wonderful that made me feel.

Losing Tyler as my boyfriend was hard, but before the pain of that loss could properly form, it was replaced by knowledge that all I'd really lost was sex. Tyler still loved me. We could still hug. We could still kiss although our tongues had to stay out of kissing from now on. I didn't mind that. Making out with Tyler now would seem... odd. All that was truly valuable in my relationship with Tyler was still there. When all was said and done, I'd lost very little and gained so very much.

I showered, dressed, and walked into the kitchen. A wonderful smell greeted me, and then I beheld a sight that shocked me more than anything I'd ever seen before. Percy was cooking!

"Has the world gone mad? You're fixing breakfast!"

Percy turned, looked at me, and laughed.

"I've fixed breakfast before."

"Toasting Pop Tarts or bagels or microwaving donuts doesn't count. What are you cooking?"

"French toast."

I gazed around the kitchen. I closed my eyes tightly, then opened them again.

"What are you doing?" Percy asked.

"I thought I might be dreaming."

"Very funny."

"I'm serious! This is so bizarre it's dream-like."

"It's not that bizarre."

"Oh yes, it is. Your idea of cooking is microwaving the leftovers from the restaurant we visited the night before. Look at that pile of French toast! There is enough for twelve people there."

"Most of this will be frozen so we can eat it later. Preparing French toast makes a mess so I make a big batch and then don't make it again for months. You're timing is perfect. This is the last skillet-full. Set the table and we'll have breakfast."

"Okay. I need to talk to you anyway."

"About what?"

"Tyler and I broke up last night."

Percy stopped flipping French toast and looked at me.

"Are you okay?"

"Mostly."

As I sat out plates, napkins, and forks on the antique oak kitchen table, I gave Percy the short version of the talk I'd had with Tyler the night before.

"I feel sad about breaking up. I feel like I've lost something. I also feel excited and happy because Tyler and I are going to be brothers. I keep going back and forth from sad to happy and from lonely to excited."

"That's exactly what I'd expect you to feel right now," Percy said as he heaped my plate with French toast.

"It is?"

"You have lost and gained something very important at the same time. It might be easier if you think of it this way: imagine someone else as the boyfriend you broke up with last night. You would be sad and upset about that, right?"

"Yeah."

"Okay, so you're sad and upset about breaking up with your boyfriend, but you're also excited because Tyler will soon be your brother. You feel the loss of breaking up and the happiness of gaining a brother. One emotion isn't going to wipe out the other. You're going to feel them both. It's a little more confusing for you since the boyfriend you lost and the brother you're gaining are the same person, but it's also a better situation because if you think about it you've lost very little and gained a great deal. You still have the love and friendship. Things have changed, but not as much as you think."

"Yeah, that's kind of what I was thinking. Maybe I'm not as messed up as I think?"

"Well, you are blond."

"Shut up!" I laughed. "Whoa! This is the best French toast ever! You bought this somewhere and just pretended to make it. This came from the Bakehouse, didn't it?"

"No."

"Daniel came over, made French toast, and left again before I got up?"

"No."

"You *really* made this?"

"Yes."

"Wow! I think this French toast is better than sex."

I could almost feel my face go pale. I'd said a little too much. I wouldn't have cared if I was talking to anyone else, but then again Percy already knew Tyler and I had gone all the way. Percy laughed.

"I'll tell you what, Caspian. Until you're thirty-two, whenever you think about having sex, you can just have some of my French toast instead."

"How many times do I have to tell you? You shouldn't try to be funny, Percy."

"Go to your room!"

"You're not good at pretending to be mad either."

"So, all I'm good for is making French toast, huh?"

"Well, that and driving me places and doing the laundry."

I grinned slightly.

"Shut up and eat your French toast. Here, try some powdered sugar on it. It makes it even better."

Percy and I talked as we ate, mostly about our upcoming move, which was going to be a little after Christmas. He was hiring a mover and I was thankful for that. Otherwise Tyler and I would have experienced the torment of carrying heavy furniture. It would be bad enough as it was.

"We never did buy you new bedroom furniture. Do you have time to go shopping today?"

"Yeah, I have time, but I've kind of grown accustomed to my furniture. I was thinking that maybe I could get a DVD player and a bigger TV..."

"Okay," Percy said.

"Yeah?"

"Sure. If you don't want new furniture, we'll spend the money on a DVD player and a TV. The TV you have is a little small."

"Thanks, Percy."

We finished breakfast then Percy drove me to Best Buy. I picked out a cool Blu-ray DVD player that also did online streaming for Netflix, Pandora, and Facebook. Percy actually let me get a 47" TV, which is as big as the one in our living room. Christmas had come early for me!

"Of course, you realize you're only getting socks and underwear for Christmas," Percy said as if he could read my mind.

"Noooooooooooo!" I said.

"I'm kidding. I would never be that cruel. Clothes are the worst Christmas present ever for anyone under twenty although fruitcake is almost as bad. Hmm..."

"Don't even think about it."

One of the college boys who worked in Best Buy was eyeing Percy. They shared a smile, which I thought was odd since Percy was about to do the commitment thing with Daniel and didn't strike me as the cheating type. When we were outside the store loading my stuff into the Prius, my curiosity got the best of me.

"What was up with you and that guy in there? He was definitely checking you out. You're taken, remember?"

"You noticed that, did you?"

"I'm not blind."

"He's someone from my past."

"Couldn't be very far back. How old is he? Nineteen?"

"He's twenty or so now."

"How do you know him?"

"I don't think I should be discussing this with my fifteen-year-old nephew."

"No way! You hooked up with him? That's disgusting!"

Percy and I climbed in the Prius.

"Why is that disgusting?"

"You're old!"

"I'm not that old. I'm thirty-eight."

"You could be his dad!"

"I'm positive I'm not his father, Caspian," Percy said with a slight grin.

"I can't believe it! My uncle is a chicken hawk."

"He was nineteen when we hooked up, Caspian."

"Eww. Eww. I don't want to hear more."

"You asked."

"Does Daniel know you've hooked up with college boys?"

"Of course."

"Hooking up with a boy half your age! That's so perverted!"

Percy laughed.

"Some young guys are into older guys. You've dated an older man yourself."

"Tyler is three years older."

"At your age, three years is a big difference."

"Don't try to change the subject. I can't believe it. My uncle is a cradle-robber."

"Well, if it makes you feel any better, I'm devoted to Daniel. There will be no more college boys."

"Well, I hope not. How embarrassing. If my friends found out…"

"They would be impressed that I could seduce a college jock although he did the seducing if I remember right."

"Eww. Eww. I'm not listening anymore!"

I covered my ears and hummed, but I could still hear Percy laughing. In a very few minutes, we were back home.

"You are an evil, evil man," I said.

"Thank you. I take after my nephew. I'll help you carry in your TV and set it in place, but you get to hook it up."

"That's okay. *Old* people aren't good with electronics anyway."

"Keep it up and I'll sic the AARP on you."

"What's that?"

"It's a gang of old people who take out young punks like you."

I eyed Percy. I was almost positive he was putting me on, but I wasn't entirely sure.

We carried my stuff in and I got everything set up just fine, except I couldn't make any of the streaming stuff work. I messed around with it for a while trying to figure it out. The last thing I wanted to do is ask Percy for help after I'd made the "old people aren't good at electronics" comment. When I was out of options, I walked into the living room.

"Um... I need some help. I can't get YouTube or Netflix or any of the streaming stuff to work."

I waited, but no smart remarks were forthcoming. Percy didn't so much as grin. I think that was worse than him giving me a hard time. I knew it was coming. I wished he could just get it over with.

Percy checked things out for under a minute and then held up the DSL cable.

"It works better if you plug this in."

I wanted to hide under the bed. Could I have made a stupider mistake? Still, Percy didn't taunt me. He just patted me on the back and left the room. Then, I heard it. He was laughing. I turned a bit red. I was glad Percy wasn't there to see it. He would have enjoyed it way too much.

YouTube was so cool on a 47" screen! I couldn't wait to show Tyler and Brayden! I smiled when I thought of Tyler and Brayden together. Tyler was as much a part of my life as always and Brayden... now I didn't have to be so careful around him. If we both got excited wrestling again, maybe I'd make a move.

I didn't want to start anything up with Brayden too fast. That might hurt Tyler. I didn't even know if Brayden would be interested in being more than friends. He might mess around a little, but the death of his boyfriend still brought him pain. I doubted he was ready for another. I'm not sure I was ready for a boyfriend either. Tyler was my first. It was good with him, but I didn't know if I was ready to have another. It was too soon. I didn't know if I wanted to tie myself down to just one guy, either. As much as I loved Tyler, I'd been tempted by other guys. It almost seemed like there were more guys to be tempted by once Tyler and I started dating. Freedom was a good thing. Dylan would probably be after me, but I could fend him off by threatening to punch him.

I messed around with YouTube for a good hour, then set up Netflix. Percy had an account I could use. I added some more stuff to the queue but didn't watch anything yet.

I looked outside. It was snowing again. The snow called to me. I thought about calling Tyler, but then remembered he and Dylan were having yet another planning session. I called Brayden instead and soon I was out the door and walking through the winter wonderland to his house. I'm sure everyone else in Bloomington took it for granted, but the snow fascinated me. Sometimes, like now, it floated gently down. Other times, it dive bombed like an eagle plunging after a rabbit. I appreciated snow in a way few others could. Snow was a miracle.

I tried to catch snowflakes on my tongue as I neared Brayden's house. The Peanuts gang did that in *A Charlie Brown Christmas*, except for Lucy who said they weren't ripe yet. I agreed with Linus. They seemed ripe to me.

"You're just fascinated with snow, aren't you?"

I lowered my head. Brayden had come out to meet me.

"You would be too if you hadn't seen it before yesterday."

"What else fascinates you? Have ever seen a microwave oven? It heats things in seconds—like magic. We also have something in Indiana we call fire."

"You are such a smart ass. Knock it off. That's *my* job."

"I've been a smart ass since the moment I could talk so I'm not stopping now."

"So like you've been a smart ass for what ... three, maybe four years?"

Brayden flipped me off with a smile.

"So, what do you want to do?"

"We could moon some more college boys."

"Let's not. It took forever to get my butt warm again."

"Oh yeah, the regrettable crack incident."

"You don't know cold until you've had snow up the butt."

"That would be good for a greeting card. Hey, let's build a snowman."

"I bet you don't even know how," Brayden said.

"Sure, I do. I've seen it on TV. Besides, I have you to show me and I've got an idea."

I leaned over and whispered in Brayden's ear, even though there was no one to hear.

We walked back the way I'd come. The snow was falling more heavily now and faster too. It was hurtling down all around and on us. The top of Brayden's toboggan was covered in white and it took only a very few minutes to get back home.

I really didn't know much about building a snowman. All I'd seen on TV was kids rolling a big snowball, but I wasn't quite sure how it got to that point. Brayden grabbed up some snow and packed it into a ball. At first I thought he was going to attack me, so I quickly made a snowball too. *That* I could do.

Brayden didn't pelt me. He dropped the ball on the ground and began to roll it. His snowball grew larger and larger. I began rolling mine but had some trouble making it round. It was almost wheel-shaped before I caught on that I had to turn the ball as I rolled it. Soon, Brayden's snowball was too big for him to move alone, so I abandoned mine for a while and helped with his. There was sure no danger that he'd pelt me with his snowball. It was more than three feet tall!

We rolled the first snowball into position and then worked on mine. We made it big but not so big we couldn't lift it. We struggled to get it into place, but we managed it. The last snowball was easy since it didn't have to be nearly as big. We lifted the head into position.

"Stay here, I'll sneak in and get what we need. I'll be right back," I said.

Percy was in the kitchen, oblivious to the fact that I'd come back home with Brayden. I took off my shoes, crept around in my socks, grabbed what I needed, put my shoes back on, and rejoined Braden outside. My mission was a success. I returned with Percy's old-fashioned black cap, my mirrored sunglasses, and an old black coat. Together, Brayden and I dressed up the menacing-looking snowman that stared directly into Percy's office window.

We laughed evilly as we walked around to the front of the house and entered through the front door.

Percy came out of the kitchen as we pulled off our coats, scarves, and gloves.

"Hey, guys. I didn't hear you come in. I was just heading out for a bit. You can ignore the note I left on the kitchen table, Caspian," said Percy as he pulled on his coat.

"Consider it ignored. Don't hurry back!"

"I'm not gone yet, Caspian. I can stay if you like," Percy said, mischievously.

"Let me get the door for you!" I said.

Percy laughed as he departed. Brayden and I had the place to ourselves. I shivered. I was still chilled from being outside for so long.

"You California boys are lightweights," Brayden said. "You can't take the cold."

"Where I come from, sixty is cold!"

"Well, welcome to Indiana. You haven't seen anything yet. Just wait until the temperature hits zero."

I shivered again.

"Don't even say that!"

"Be afraid. Be very afraid. Sometimes, the temperature goes below zero."

"Now you're just making things up."

"Nope. Below zero temperatures are rare in southern Indiana, but it does get that cold here."

"Hey! What makes you an expert on Indiana? You haven't lived here as long as I have!"

"True, but my grandparents only live a hundred miles from here and we visit them at Christmas so I know a lot more than you, California boy."

I stuck out my tongue.

"Hot chocolate is a good cure for cold," Brayden said. "Let's make some. You do know how to make hot chocolate, right?"

"How should I know how to make hot chocolate? I'm from California! If Californians want hot chocolate, which we usually don't, we go to Starbucks."

Brayden rolled his eyes.

"Do I have to do everything? First, you can't make a snowball and now I discover you can't make hot chocolate."

"I made a great snowball!"

"Yeah, *after* you copied me. Before you learned from the master, you looked like you were trying to invent the wheel. Lead me to the kitchen."

I glared at Brayden moment and twitched my eye as if I had a nervous tick. It made him laugh.

I pulled Brayden into the kitchen and rummaged through the old cupboards that passed for cabinets. All of Percy's furniture was *old* and it wasn't because he was poor. He just liked old stuff, but then he was a bit odd. I found a box of Swiss Miss cocoa and opened it up. There were individual packets inside.

"Now what?" I asked.

"We pour it in a cup and it magically makes hot chocolate."

"Are you *always* a smart ass?"

"I'm just trying to keep up with you, Caspian."

"That is a tough job."

"Next, we heat water in a tea kettle. You do know how to do that, right?"

Actually, I'd never done it before, but I'd seen Percy do it countless times. He was *always* making hot tea and I mean always. I put water in the tea kettle, turned on a burner on the stove, and put the kettle on.

"Wow, you do know how. You're almost a gourmet chef."

"Hey, I have a cooking handicap. I live with Percy."

"He doesn't cook?"

"He did make French toast this morning, but that was the first time I ever actually saw him cook anything."

"That's sad."

"Yeah, well. He's a writer. They're really weird, at least Percy is and he says all writers are kind of strange."

"He seemed normal enough."

"That's because you haven't spent much time with him. He's actually pretty cool, but I never let him know I think so."

Brayden laughed again. Every time he laughed, I smiled.

I managed to pour almost-boiling water into a couple of mugs without spilling anything or scalding myself. We stirred up the hot cocoa mix and a chocolaty scent arose with the steam.

I waited until Brayden tried his before I tried mine. I'd heard about people burning their tongue on hot chocolate so I figured Brayden could be my guinea pig. The hot chocolate was delicious.

"This is better than Starbucks," I said.

"Perhaps you're a natural cocoa-ista."

"I think the way I stirred was key."

"I never thought you'd be this goofy," Brayden said.

"I'm not goofy. I'm a bad ass!"

"Yeah, well. I'm not going to argue with you because you are a bad ass and it takes one to know one, but you're also goofy."

"I can live with that."

We drank our hot chocolate at the table and I began to warm up nicely. I was trying not to notice how sexy Brayden looked. It seemed inappropriate since Tyler and I had just broken up. Then again, I had noticed Brayden's handsome features and sexy body before Tyler and I had quit dating so maybe it wasn't bad after all.

"Tyler and I broke up," I announced abruptly.

"Really?"

"Yeah. Yesterday."

"Are you okay?"

"Yeah, I am. I'm kind of sad, but it was a mutual decision. Dating was beginning to feel weird."

"Because you're about to become adopted brothers?"

"Yeah."

"That would be pretty weird but also kind of hot."

"Really?"

"Come on, haven't you ever thought about brothers doing it, especially twin brothers? I'd do it with twins in a heartbeat."

I laughed.

"Okay, I'll admit I have the twin fantasy too. I guess we're both perverts."

"Ha! I bet most of the guys at school have fantasies about doing it with twins although most probably fantasize about girls."

"Now that is perverted."

"I can see where you're coming from, Caspian. I think I'd feel kind of strange dating my brother."

"Yeah. I love Tyler. We're even closer than we were before, but now he feels..."

"Like a brother?"

"Yeah. He's still hot and I still get excited thinking about what we did with each other, but...well, last night we kissed. We tried to get into it, but it felt weird. We both knew then that sex doesn't belong in our relationship anymore."

"I'm sorry."

"I don't think I am. I mean, doing it with Tyler was hot and I mean blow-your-mind hot, but he's going to be family now. He's going to be my brother. I never thought about it before, but now that it's happening I feel like it's what I've always wanted."

"You know everyone at school will still give you a hard time."

"Yes, but I don't care so much about that. I don't like people getting into my business, but they can say and think what they want."

"A lot of them will think the two of you are still doing it together."

"They'll probably get off on thinking that too, even though they won't admit it."

"I'm sure Dylan will."

"I'm sure he already has. I am going to miss sex with Tyler."

"He was that good, huh?"

"Oh, yeah!"

"I may have to try him out then."

"What?"

"Well, Tyler is hot in a studious kind of way."

"Hey, that's my brother you're talking about!"

"Yeah, and your brother is hot and you know it better than anyone."

Brayden and I smiled at each other. I liked the ease we'd developed with each other.

"Are you going to have your own room or will you share with Tyler?" Brayden asked.

"I'll have my own room."

"Cool. It might be hard for you two to resist each other otherwise."

"I don't know about that."

"Come on, you are both guys. You know what guys are like."

"True."

When we finished our hot chocolate, I led Brayden to my room.

"When did you get the big TV?"

"Yesterday. Percy bought me a Blu-ray player too. Wait until you see how Xbox looks on the big screen."

We began playing. At some point, Percy came home, but I only nodded when he stuck his head in the door and greeted us. I did keep watch in case he went into his office. After a few minutes, he did. Brayden and I paused our game and listened. Our wait wasn't long. A loud "whoa!" came from Percy's office. We quickly returned to our game and acted innocent when Percy looked into my room again.

"Very funny, guys."

"I don't know what you're talking about," I said.

"Sure, you don't."

Brayden and I grinned as Percy left the room.

# Chapter 15

I walked into the living room wearing the clothes Tyler had selected for Percy and Daniel's commitment ceremony. Now I knew why he didn't send them until the last minute.

"I will kill him on sight," I said.

"Tyler?" Percy asked.

"Yes! I told him I wasn't wearing white!"

"You look very nice in that dress-shirt and it's pale blue, not white."

"It's so pale it's almost white and the slacks *are* white! He lied to me! I'm going to hang him with these slacks. I'm going to string him up and watch his face turn purple."

"That doesn't sound like brotherly love to me."

"He will die slowly and painfully," I said, staring into the distance. "Maybe I'll film it for YouTube. It might go viral."

"I don't believe murder is allowed on YouTube. Hey, your hair is different."

"Yeah. I want to grow it longer. Spikes can only go so high without some serious product use, so spiking my hair is out."

"You look very handsome, although I liked your spiked hair."

"Really?"

"Yes. It was very... you. It looked good."

My uncle liked spiked hair? Maybe he wasn't stuck in the past as much as I thought.

"Thanks."

"Caspian, I know you'd probably rather not go to this ceremony at all, but it's very important to Tyler. Thank you for going through this for him."

"I'm still going to kill him."

"Do it after the ceremony, will you?"

"I'll have some cake first."

Dammit! Percy was eroding my fury.

"How do you feel about today?" I asked.

"Daniel and I hadn't planned on a ceremony, but I think not having a ceremony would have been a mistake. There are friends coming that I haven't seen since high school. Your grandparents are coming. I didn't know so many people would care. Daniel and I don't need a ceremony to show how much we love each other, but being surrounded by so many people we care about, and who care about us, means a lot to both of us. I'm very glad you're going to be there, Caspian. I love you."

Percy hugged me.

"I love you, too."

"Wearing those clothes isn't so bad, is it?"

"Yes."

"I owe you one then."

"I owe Tyler one," I said, punching my fist into the palm of my hand.

Percy laughed.

"You're already beginning to act like brothers."

I grinned. I walked over to the mirror to check myself out. I hadn't worn my black-eyeliner for a while now. My hair was too long to be properly spiked although I'd managed until only the day before. It took forever to get my hair just right yesterday morning, so even if the ceremony wasn't today I wouldn't have spiked my hair. The only way to get my hair to stand straight up now would be to use glue. I had taken off my collar and wristbands, but that was for today only. They clashed with the clothes Tyler had sent over. I was thinking about switching to a hemp necklace. I was getting kind of tired of the Goth look. It didn't seem me anymore. Besides, I wanted something new.

I gazed at my reflection. I looked pretty good, but the boy looking back at me looked like someone else. The shirt wasn't so bad, but I didn't go in for light colors. I had only recently begun wearing colors other than black. The white slacks were definitely too much. This was the one and only time I was going to wear them. At least I could put them to good use when I lynched Tyler.

"Are you ready?" Percy asked.

"Are *you*?"

"Yes, I am."

Percy almost looked like he might cry, but I knew he was happy. He was very lucky to have found someone he not only loved but liked so much he wanted to spend his life with him. I didn't know if that kind of commitment would be for me. Dating Tyler had been great, but even then I'd felt confined. I wanted and needed freedom, but maybe old people like Percy and Daniel were ready to settle down. They were past doing wild things. Then again, Percy had hooked up with college boys before Daniel came back into his life. I still couldn't believe that! Eww! It was kind of gross, but at the same time I was impressed. *My* uncle could land hunky college boys like the one in Best Buy? Now that was an accomplishment.

We walked out to the Prius and climbed in. I reached down and turned on my seat warmer. It was the best part of the car! My butt and back began to feel nice and toasty warm. I looked over at Percy. He was dressed all in white, except for the black pea coat he'd put on to come outside. He looked good in a dress shirt, but then he was the intellectual-writer type.

We drove the short distance to Tyler's house. There were cars everywhere and we had to park a couple of blocks away. The ceremony was due to start in about thirty minutes so we still had plenty of time. The ceremony could hardly start without Percy.

Dylan ambushed me the moment I stepped in the front door.

"You've got to see this! It's beautiful!" Dylan said pulling me into the living room where friends and family mingled. An instrumental version of *Winter Wonderland* played in the background.

"Whoa," I said.

Clear Christmas lights radiated out from a crystal chandelier in the center of room and outlined every window and doorway. At one end of the room was a huge white Christmas tree covered with white roses and lit with clear and blue Christmas lights. It glowed like the northern lights. Icicles hung from every branch and an angel with golden hair sat at the top.

"We spent hours on the lights alone and you wouldn't believe how long we spent putting thousands of icicles on one at a time," Dylan said.

"It's beautiful."

"I knew you'd like it!"

"You're looking very handsome, Caspian," Jesse said, looking like a model in a cream cable knit sweater.

"Were these clothes your doing?" I asked, wondering if I needed to schedule a double lynching. In my astonishment over the decorations, I'd almost forgotten my fury over being dressed like a wedding cake.

"I'd like to take all the credit, but Tyler and Dylan helped pick your outfit."

A triple lynching was obviously in order.

"Dylan," I said turning upon him and growling.

"Please don't kill me!" Dylan begged, giving me his best puppy dog eyes. "We did the best we could. You don't know what this means to Tyler. He wanted everything white so bad, and Jesse and I knew you hated the idea of wearing all white so we picked out the shirt and..."

"Oh, just forget it. I can't stay angry at you when you look so pathetic."

"I hear that's the way he gets dates," Jesse said.

"Ha! My incredible talents get me all the dates I want," Dylan said.

"If you call hookups dates," I said.

Dylan grinned.

I looked around but couldn't see Brayden. He was probably too smart to show up. I did spot Tyreece and Caleb and then...

"Grandmother!" I said, rushing over to where my grandparents stood with Percy.

I gave her a big hug, and she hugged me back. I hadn't seen my grandparents in two years. They lived in Florida, which was a long way from California and even Indiana.

"You've grown so much!" Grandmother said. "You're so handsome, Caspian. You were such a cute little boy, but now you're becoming a very good-looking young man."

"Try not to embarrass the boy," Grandfather said. "How are you, Caspian?"

I gave grandfather a hug next. When I looked back at grandmother, she had tears in her eyes.

"You look so much like your father," she said.

I felt really bad for my grandparents then. I'd lost my parents, and they had lost their son.

"We're very proud of you, Percy," Grandfather said. "You've obviously done a great job with Caspian."

"It wasn't easy!" I said, laughing.

"Go to your room," Percy said, teasing me.

"I think I will! I want to check it out!"

I turned and hurried up the stairs. Tyler saw me leaving and followed me. I passed Tyler's room and found the one I knew would be mine. It had two large windows looking out over the side yard to the house next door where Brice Parker lived. Soon enough I would discover if Brice really did run around his bedroom naked or if Tyler was just putting me on. I hoped he ran around naked. Brice was hot!

The large room had been emptied of furniture and my own would soon be moved in. The walls were freshly painted white. Like Percy's house, this was an old home but larger. The woodwork was kind of cool. It was dark, heavy, and masculine. I was sure Percy liked the house. He liked anything old.

"Think it will do?" Tyler asked.

"It's bigger than my current room and the view is nicer."

"Wait until you see Brice."

I laughed.

"You're not too mad about the clothes, are you?"

"I feel ridiculous, but I might forgive you. I had planned on lynching you with these pants, but I'm more inclined to a short beating now."

"I guess I deserve it, but I want everything to be as close to perfect as possible."

"Just remember you owe me, and you owe me big!"

"Deal."

"The living room looks like a winter wonderland," I said.

"That's what Dylan and I were going for." Tyler gazed at me and smiled.

"You succeeded."

"I can't believe our dads are about to get married," Tyler said. A look of remorse crossed his face. "I'm sorry. I didn't mean... I guess I just think of Percy as your dad."

"It's okay, Tyler. He's the closest thing I have to a dad now, and I know my dad would want me to think of Percy as my father too."

Tyler smiled.

"Soon, you'll have two dads and a brother."

"I can't wait," I said.

"You mean it?"

"Of course, I mean it."

Tyler hugged me tightly, then kissed me on the cheek.

"I think your party is a success so far," I said.

"Everyone I invited came, even my grandparents," Tyler said.

"Where do they live anyway?"

"Florida."

"Mine too. What is it with old people and Florida?"

"I think it's mandatory. Once you turn sixty, you have to move to Florida."

"I guess I should appreciate Percy while he is still around then. He'll have to move down south in a couple of years."

"He's not that old, Caspian."

"I know, but I like to pretend I think he is."

"You're just a bit evil."

"It's part of my charm."

"Come on. Let's go downstairs. It's almost time to begin."

Brayden was talking with Caleb and Tyreece when I walked downstairs with Tyler. He was dressed up but had obviously chosen his own clothing. He wore a black dress shirt and black pants. It made him look very handsome, but then Brayden was always handsome.

"Nice outfit," Brayden said as I approached.

"Don't remind me. I'm pretending I'm not wearing clothes that blind everyone who looks in my direction."

"Well, the shirt isn't white, but what's with the pants?"

"Tyler, Jesse, and Dylan are what's with my pants and they will pay. Oh, they will pay! I've decided not to murder them, but violence is imminent." That wasn't true, of course, but appearances were important.

"So a beat down is the entertainment?"

"Good idea!"

Dylan came near. I shot him a dirty look and growled at him. He hurried along.

"The place does look nice," Brayden said.

"What about that cake?" Tyreece said. "Now that is what I call a cake!"

At one end of the room was an enormous cake that looked just like the house we were standing in. The cake had to be a good three feet tall and was nearly as wide. I had no idea such a cake could even be made. It sat on an even larger sheet cake with white icing and coconut snow. Decorated Christmas trees stood in the yard. There was a sidewalk and even a picket fence and all of it was edible! People were taking pictures of it. It looked too good to eat, but I had no doubt it would soon be consumed. I had to fight the urge to take a bite out of the roof. That would have paid Tyler back for my outfit, but I couldn't do that to my soon-to-be-brother.

"Dad? Percy?" called out Tyler.

Tyler looked extremely handsome dressed all in white. It was too much white and yet it wasn't. He fit perfectly with the setting.

Percy and Daniel stepped up to the cake, and everyone gathered around in a big half circle. Tyler came and stood by me and held my hand. I reached out and took Brayden's hand as he stood at my other side. I smiled when I felt him squeeze. The light coming from above made Percy and Daniel look as if they were standing in bright moonlight. They looked very handsome and very good together. "Christmas Time is Here" began to play in the background.

"Thank you all for coming. Percy and I don't feel we need a ceremony to confirm that we love each other and want to be together, but my son... our son... Tyler had other ideas. Very soon, Percy, Tyler, Caspian, and I will live in this home as a family and we're very glad to share this moment with you."

Daniel then looked at Percy, who spoke next.

"You can all relax. There won't be a boring ceremony that you've all heard a dozen times before. This is it."

Several of the guests, including me, laughed. I gazed at Tyler for a moment. He was grinning, and tears ran down his cheeks. I squeezed his hand and felt him squeeze back.

"We haven't seen some on you in years, not since our high school days. It's fitting you are here now because you were there the first time Daniel and I dated. It's been a very long engagement. There are others here we see seldom and more that we see daily and we're very pleased that you all came this day to be with us on this wonderful occasion."

Percy turned and looked at Daniel.

"I've waited my whole life for you. I thought I'd lost you long ago, but now you're back and you're not getting away. So this is it, we'll be together from this day and there is no escape."

"I love you," Daniel said.

"I love you too."

Daniel leaned in and kissed Percy, then everyone clapped and cheered.

"Now that's my idea of a wedding," Brayden said. He looked over at my brother. "Good job, Tyler."

Tyler was crying too much to answer, but he nodded. I led him over to Daniel and Percy and we shared a group hug.

After the thankfully brief and nowhere-near-as-boring-as-I-expected ceremony, I met a lot of people I didn't know. Percy and Daniel introduced Tyler and me to their old school friends: Jonah, Lizzie, Shane, and Thor. Yeah, that's right, Thor. I'd never met anyone with that name before, but I didn't mention it because the dude was built. He had a menacing look and I was kind of scared of him, not that I'd admit it.

Percy and Daniel spent a lot of time talking with their old school friends. I learned that Percy hadn't seen them since he graduated and that Daniel had lost touch with them for years but had finally reestablished contact.

Finally, the moment everyone had been waiting on arrived. It was time to cut the cake. Percy and Daniel cut it together and began handing out slices. I was forced to scoop vanilla ice cream with Tyler. Both Percy and Daniel believed in child labor. Finally, everyone was served and I got a piece of cake with ice cream myself. For those who wanted seconds, it was strictly self-service because I was off the job.

Tyler, our friends, and I gathered in one corner. We talked and ate cake and ice cream, then talked more and ate more cake and ice cream. Instrumental Christmas music played in the background and the gathering seemed as much Christmas party as wedding.

"So, when do you two officially become brothers?" Jesse asked.

"It will probably be a few weeks yet. Dad says it takes time for the paperwork," Tyler said. "We figure we're officially brothers as of today."

"You should have kept dating. Doing it with your brother would be sooo hot!" Dylan said.

"Keep it down, Dylan!" Caleb said. "There are old people present. They aren't as cool as us."

"Percy and Daniel may be older, but they are cool *and* hot!" Dylan said. "I still think I would have been the perfect wedding present."

"I'm warning you, Dylan," I said, clinching my fists.

"Okay! Okay! I'll wait until their first anniversary to make a move."

"You already made a move at Tyler's birthday party," Caleb said, laughing.

"I still can't believe you did that," Tyler said.

"I go after what I want," Dylan said.

"I think we all know that already," Jesse said.

Dylan grinned.

"Speaking of going after what I want, now that Tyler and Caspian aren't dating…" Dylan began.

"No," Tyler said. "That would be too weird. I can't think of you like that."

"Fine, you'll do it with your brother but not me."

"Quiet, will you!" Tyler said. "We weren't brothers when we did it."

"In my fantasies you were," Dylan said. "I guess that leaves Caspian."

"Do you really think we could get along, Dylan? I threaten to rearrange your face at least once a week."

"Yeah, but just think of the sex—angry sex, make up sex…"

"Do not go on," Jesse said.

"Besides, I'm not talking about dating. I just want sex."

"I think we should carve that on your tombstone," Tyreece suggested.

"It's not gonna happen, Dylan," I said.

Dylan looked around.

"Why aren't there any cute boys at this party? Except for all of you, I mean."

"Because Percy and Daniel are old, so their friends are old," I said.

"They aren't old, merely older," Tyler said.

"And Percy and Daniel are hot!" Dylan said.

"Eat some cake," Tyreece said and stuffed a piece in Dylan's mouth.

"I think Tyler and Dylan should become professional wedding planners. I have to admit this is the best wedding ever," I said.

"You're admitting you like it?" Brayden asked with a raised eyebrow.

"I'd rather be battling it out in some video game, but as ceremonies go, this one wasn't bad. No crappy music, no preacher droning on and on, no stuffy formality with the possible exception of my outfit, no cheesy games, and no boring repetition of the same old crap."

"Thanks!" Tyler and Dylan said.

"You know what? I think Tyler and Dylan would make a cute couple," I said.

Tyler glared at me, and I grinned back.

"Me too, but not exclusive!" Dylan said.

"Yeah, if Dylan went exclusive, how would the football team get by?" Jesse said.

"Or the soccer team," Tyreece said.

"Or the baseball team, the swim team, the wrestling team..." Caleb said then trailed off as the list became too long.

Dylan only grinned in response. I'm sure he took it all as a compliment.

The party went on for a long time. People stood around, talked, and ate while Christmas music played in the background. It probably sounds pretty boring, but it was actually fun. I was a little sorry we didn't get to throw rice or birdseed at Percy and Daniel, but only because I would have pelted them good!

Dylan spent a lot of time checking out Thor. I have to admit that for an older guy he was hot. He must have really been something when he was in high school! Dylan didn't try anything with him. I think he was too afraid.

Percy and Daniel spent most of their time talking with their old high school friends. I wondered what it felt like to talk to someone you hadn't seen for twenty years. They must all look so different from the way they did way back then. I had a hard time picturing Percy as a high school boy. Daniel was easier because Tyler looked like Daniel did back then, at least that's what everyone said.

Percy and Daniel didn't spend all their time with their old friends. They got around to everyone. Tyler and I joined our grandparents for a while. Grandmother couldn't keep from hugging me, but then I noticed Tyler getting the same treatment from his grandmother. I guess they were all soon to become *our* grandparents. Tyler smiled at me as our grandparents discovered they only lived about three miles from each other. What were the odds of that? They had once both lived in Bloomington and now they lived hundreds of miles away but only a few miles apart.

I escaped from my grandparents and joined Brayden on a couch. He seemed to content to listen to the music and watch Dylan drool over Thor.

"Dylan is entertaining, isn't he?" I said.

"Entertaining, but annoying."

"True. Hmm. I have to pay Dylan, Jesse, and Tyler back for making me dress like this, but a beating lacks imagination. Don't you think?"

"How about one of the classics? Tie them to an ant hill and cover them with honey."

"Dylan would probably enjoy it."

"How about stretching them on a rack?"

"I'm too lazy to build one and Dylan would enjoy that too."

"Fill their lockers with Vaseline?"

"Dylan would see that as a gift."

"Yeah, he probably does use a lot of Vaseline. Hmm, this is harder than I thought."

"Revenge is exhausting. I don't think I'll plan anything. I'll just wait for a spontaneous opportunity."

"Yeah, don't put too much effort into it because then it becomes a punishment for you. You could just trip Dylan as he's walking past a guy he wants to impress. You'll be living with Tyler, so there will be hundreds of opportunities for payback. My motto is: never put off until tomorrow what you can put off until next week."

"Exactly!"

"What about Jesse?"

"Jesse will be easy to punish. I'll just mess up his hair."

Dylan walked up and grinned at us.

"What?" Brayden asked.

"You guys are sitting awfully close together. Is there something you want to tell me?"

"Even if there was something to tell, we wouldn't tell you because you'd enjoy it and you deserve to be punished for picking out my clothes," I said.

"Are you still going on about that?" Dylan said.

"Still? I'm wearing the clothes now!"

"Well, if you want to take them off, I won't mind."

"Dylan," I growled.

Dylan dropped down beside me and grinned.

"I'll be happy to make it up to you. I'll do *anything* you want."

I hate to admit this, but I was getting a little turned on.

"No, Dylan."

"Come on, you aren't dating Tyler anymore so..."

"Dylan..."

"Back off, Dylan. He's mine," Brayden said.

Dylan looked back and forth between us and grinned.

"Ha! I knew it! If you ever want a third..."

"Go away, Dylan," Brayden said.

Dylan smiled at us again, giggled, and left.

"That should keep him off both of us for a while," Brayden said.

"True, but you know he'll talk."

"Do you care?"

"No."

"Me either."

Brayden and I looked at each other and laughed, but then he looked so sad my heart went out to him. He gazed over at Percy and Daniel and tears rimmed his eyes.

"Are you okay?" I asked.

"I'm being stupid. You remind me of Stuart sometimes. Telling Dylan we're a couple made me really miss Stuart. Then, I thought about how Stuart and I will never get to spend our lives together. We'll never have a commitment celebration like this one."

I scooted even closer and put my arm around Brayden's shoulders.

"You're not being stupid."

"Yeah, I am. I'm mourning an entire future when I have no idea how things would've worked out with Stuart. I sit here and picture this fantasy that isn't even really me and then get upset about it. That's stupid."

"Sometimes I get mad at people for things I imagined they did. Some stupid scene will play out in my mind and I'll be furious over something that's all in my head."

Brayden smiled at my stupidity for a moment but then grew sad again.

"I miss him so much, but I'm tired of missing him. I feel like nothing will ever be okay. Since I've met you, I feel better, but losing Stuart keeps coming back at me. I feel like I'm going to be sad for the rest of my life."

"Yeah. I see Tyler with his dad and it makes me happy, but then it makes me sad because my dad is gone. I was watching Percy with his parents earlier and thinking how it's not fair that he still has his parents and mine are gone. I'm just fifteen. Parents shouldn't die when you're a kid."

Tears welled up in my eyes and one spilled out and rolled down my cheek. I quickly wiped it away.

"Damn. I'm sorry, Caspian. I should have just kept my mouth shut. Now I've upset you too."

"No. You shouldn't keep it to yourself. We talked about that, remember? I went down that road and it's a mistake. Yeah, you drew the pain out of me, but it would've come out sooner or later and sooner is better. Don't ever hold back on me. Tell me exactly what you're feeling. I'm not going to hold back with you. When I'm hurting because I miss my Mom and Dad, I'm going to tell you because you understand better than anyone else."

I squeezed Brayden's shoulder. Dylan picked that moment to look in our direction and he smiled slyly.

"We need to talk to each other about this stuff. If we talk to others about it, we might damage our reps as the biggest bad asses at North High School, next to Sadye of course. *That* girl is scary. I could *never* get my nipples pierced."

Brayden laughed.

"I'm tough. I will get through this. I always get through everything, but I never imagined that I'd have to handle Stuart killing himself. This is so much bigger than anything that has come before and this time he's not here to help me." Brayden turned and looked into my eyes. "I'm glad you're here. I need you."

"I need you, too."

Brayden gazed into my eyes almost as if he wanted to kiss me. I wondered if we could be more than friends.

# Chapter 16

Percy's house was more crowded than usual as Christmas neared. My grandparents were staying until the day after Christmas. Percy was glad to spend time with them. He called his parents a couple of times a week, but he rarely saw them. I saw them even less, although they had never missed a birthday or Christmas. I always received a card in the mail with money or gift cards inside.

Percy gave up his bedroom and slept on a cot in his office. I offered him my bedroom, but he said there was no reason for us both to be moved out of our rooms. It was perfect. I didn't have to give up my room, but I got credit for being thoughtful.

This was to be my first Christmas without Mom and Dad. During the last couple of days, I'd been thinking about all the Christmases before. When I was a kid, I mostly thought of what I was going to get, but even then Christmas was a lot more to me that presents. Christmas was decorating the tree with Mom and Dad, catching the scent of Mom's sugar cookies wafting on the air, and listening to Christmas music. One of my favorite parts of Christmas was getting up on Christmas morning to find my stocking magically stuffed with goodies. It wasn't so much the candy and little wrapped presents that were special as it was the fact that all that stuff just appeared during the night. Even after I figured out Mom and Dad filled my stocking, there was still something magical about it.

I really missed Mom and Dad. I missed shopping for their Christmas presents. I usually put it off until the last thing because I could never figure out what to get them. I was down to the wire again. Our Christmas was to be on Christmas Eve and I still needed presents for Percy, Daniel, Tyler, and my grandparents. I wanted to get something for Brayden too. I liked being under pressure this year because it helped make things seem normal. I didn't have my parents to buy gifts for, but I had others. The last minute frenzy was something familiar in an unfamiliar situation. The winter weather was awesome, but I was used to warmth and palm trees during the holidays. I was living in a different house, in a whole different part of the country. My friends were new. I didn't know a single one of my friends last Christmas. I barely knew Percy then and didn't know my grandparents much better.

Everything was strange, and I felt a little lost. Mostly, I missed my mom and dad.

I talked Brayden into going Christmas shopping with me. I had already made plans to go shopping with Tyler the next day, but I needed to shop for my brother's gift while he wasn't around. I figured I'd concentrate on his present, pick up what others I could, and then focus on Brayden's gift while I was shopping with Tyler.

College Mall was filled with shoppers and Christmas music. It was the middle of the afternoon when Percy dropped us off, but it was crowded as if it was a weekend, even more so.

"I haven't bought anything for anyone yet," I said.

"Me either."

"Sick! You are a fellow Christmas procrastinator."

"It's just so hard to find things my family will like. How am I supposed to know what my mom wants?"

"Uh. Ask her?"

"That's cheating."

I laughed.

"I am not above cheating and I hate to admit this, but I never thought of asking Percy or the others what they want."

"Well, you are blond."

"Grrrrr!"

"Percy is a writer. Buy him a pen."

"Oh, that's original! He uses a word processor anyway. He almost never writes anything by hand. His handwriting is so bad he should be a doctor."

"You'll find something."

"Yeah. You know something I don't like about Christmas shopping?"

"Spending your money on others?"

"Screw you. No. I have to go into stores I would not otherwise be caught dead in."

"Like?"

"Hollister, Abercrombie & Fitch..."

"I like Aeropostale myself."

"No!!!! Don't say that!!!"

"Why?"

"That's where preppies shop. It's almost as bad as A&F and Hollister."

"Do I look preppy to you?"

"No."

"So calm down. You're as hyper as Dylan."

"Those are fighting words."

"I just mean you're too intense. You've been toning down your Goth-ness anyway so why are you complaining?"

"The whole Goth thing is getting a little old, but I do like my collar and wristbands still. I just don't wear them all the time."

"Maybe I'll buy you something in pastels..."

"I will kill you!"

"Oh, that's a nice Christmas spirit."

"Pastels are for guys like Dylan. I only like dark colors."

"Insecure, are we?"

"Nope, I'm gay. I just don't like dressing like an Easter egg."

"I think I'll buy you something in light pink."

"You're not funny," I said.

"I am to me and that's all that really matters."

We neared Abercrombie & Fitch. I checked the crowd and wished I'd brought sunglasses.

"Expecting someone?" Brayden asked.

"No. I just don't want anyone I know to see me go into Abercrombie & Fitch."

"You're openly a homo, but you don't want to be seen going into A&F? What kind of a bad ass are you?"

"Just shut up and come on."

I darted into A&F. Brayden was right behind me. The music was kind of cool and definitely loud. The air was filled with cologne. Big posters of hot guys, most of them shirtless, were on the walls.

The store was filled with the kinds of clothes I did not and would not wear, but I wasn't shopping for me. I checked out a few shirts for Tyler, but they were incredibly expensive!

"If I buy a shirt in here, it's going to blow my budget," I said.

"Come with me, amateur shopper," Brayden said.

"You're a shopping expert now? Is that what you and Dylan do after your dates?"

Brayden punched me in the arm.

"Oww!"

We walked out into the mall and followed the herd of shoppers. Brayden led me directly to Aeropostale.

"This store has basically the same stuff as Abercrombie & Fitch and Hollister, but it's much cheaper."

"You could have told me that before we went into A&F."

"You didn't ask."

I glared at Brayden.

After looking around at polo shirts and sweatshirts I wasn't sure I wanted to get Tyler clothes at all. Clothes are the most dreaded gift for kids, but Tyler wasn't a kid. Still, clothes did seem a little boring. That's when I spotted the cologne. I'd seen some in A&F and it was about $70 a bottle! At Aeropostale it was $20. I tried some. It smelled much better than the A&F stuff.

"I found something," I said.

"You're welcome," Brayden said.

I gave Brayden a dirty look and then purchased the cologne.

We wandered back into the mall and then slipped into The Indiana Shop a few doors down. The Indiana Shop sells nothing but Indiana University stuff. I bought my grandfather an IU sweatshirt. It would be a Christmas gift and souvenir of Bloomington, too.

A few doors up, Yankee Candle was having a buy-one-get-one-free sale, so Brayden and I teamed up. He would buy a candle for his mom and I'd get one for Grandmother. Yankee Candle was another of those stores I didn't go in, but it smelled really good inside. The decision to purchase a candle was easy, but picking out which candle was hard. I opened the lid of a Home for the Holidays candle first and took a sniff. It smelled so good I almost picked it, but then I tried a Banana Nut Bread candle and it smelled even better. I went around the store smelling one candle after another. Brayden was having the same problem. He sniffed candle after candle and couldn't decide.

I thought maybe the store clerk wouldn't like two teenage boys smelling candles, but not only didn't she mind, she brought us candles to try. When I took a whiff of the Red Berry & Cedar candle, I was sold. Brayden decided on a Hazelnut Coffee candle. We pooled our cash and bought our candles. They were expensive, but at half price they weren't so pricy.

The mall was decked out with lights and oversized Christmas decorations. Christmas music played and Santa Claus was sitting in a huge red chair up by Macy's. I wasn't a fan of shopping, but I did like the hustle-bustle of shopping for Christmas gifts at the last minute. The Christmas decorations and music added to the fun.

I liked shopping with Brayden. He had the same "get it done" attitude I did. Sure, we smelled half the candles in Yankee Candle, but mostly we were all business. We looked around in American Eagle where I noticed Brayden eyeing boxer briefs. They came in really bright colors, which were cool. I could tell Brayden liked them so I decided that's what I'd get him for Christmas. I could even use the age-old threat of "I'm giving you underwear for Christmas" and he'd think I was kidding. The only decision to make was the color. Was I evil enough to buy bright pink?

"That look on your face makes me nervous," Brayden said.

"You should *always* be nervous around me."

Before we left American Eagle, I spotted a deep purple shirt that I thought Daniel would like. It had some kind of crest on the pocket and looked very sharp so I bought it.

We shopped around in the mall some more. Brayden found a cool 8-in-1 screwdriver set in Sears for his dad. I hadn't found anything for Percy, but I'd bought presents for Tyler and my grandparents, plus I knew what I was getting for Brayden. I had decided to get Brayden some Peanut M&Ms in Christmas colors to go with his boxer briefs.

"I am starving!" Brayden said.

"Let's check out the food court."

We walked down to the food court but there wasn't a lot there. I definitely wasn't eating at Chick-fil-A. Percy said they donated a lot to anti-gay groups so they could take their chicken and stick it up their ass. I thought about calling out "your chicken sucks!" but the people working there were just trying to pay their rent. They weren't evil even if they worked for an evil, anti-Christian empire.

"Let's walk over to the China Buffet," I said. "I feel like eating a lot."

Brayden agreed, so we left the mall and walked across the parking lot. The China Buffet was in Eastland Plaza, which was just across College Mall Road. I called Percy on the way and told him he could pick us up there later instead of at the mall.

Once inside the China Buffet we picked a booth, dumped our bags into it, and loaded up our plates with sweet and sour chicken, peanut butter chicken, rice, crab Rangoon and more. I tried some salmon and this cheesy crabmeat stuff and both were delicious.

We sat in the booth and stuffed our faces while we talked. Once, we both got very quiet and just gazed at each other for a moment. We didn't say a word, but I knew exactly what we were saying without words. I hadn't mentioned my parents and Brayden hadn't mentioned Stuart, but we were both thinking that our friendship was making the holiday without those we loved much easier to handle. Together, we were able to focus on what was good in our lives instead of those who were missing.

I called Percy when we were nearly finished. He said he would be about twenty minutes before he could be there to pick us up. I told him if the service didn't improve I was going to use another taxi company, but Percy just laughed.

Since we were too stuffed to eat more and had some time to kill, Brayden and I went next door to the Dollar Tree. I was glad we did because they had cool Christmas stuff including cards. Brayden and I looked around, bought a few things, and then stepped outside right as Percy arrived. I let Brayden ride up front because the front seats in the Prius have butt-warmers; at least that's what I called them.

After Percy dropped Brayden off and drove us home, I grabbed a couple rolls of Christmas paper and locked myself in my room. I wasn't the best at wrapping presents, but the finished packages didn't look too bad. Yankee Candle had given Brayden and me gift boxes, which made Grandmother's candle much easier to wrap. When I finished wrapping, I took my gifts out and placed them under the tree with the others. There was one big box wrapped in green paper covered with reindeer that particularly intrigued me. It wasn't the only present labeled "To: Caspian" but I couldn't begin to guess what was inside.

Our Christmas tree was beautiful. It was a real balsam pine. I breathed in deeply. The scent was wonderful. Percy, Grandmother, Grandfather, and I had decorated it the night after Percy's wedding. Grandmother told me about the Christmas bulbs as we were decorating. Most of them were family pieces and very, very old. Grandfather told me about old-fashioned Christmas lights and how frustrated he used to get with them. I almost couldn't believe a whole string of lights wouldn't work if there was one bad bulb, but I didn't think he was putting me on. I liked decorating the tree with Percy and my grandparents so much that I didn't get too sad because Mom and Dad weren't there. The main reason I didn't get too sad is because I felt they *were* there. I know that sounds a little odd, but I could feel them there with us and I don't think it was just my imagination or wishful thinking.

I looked around the room at the Christmas wreaths with red bows and all the evergreen garland. I couldn't feel my parents with me as I had on the night we decorated the tree, but I guess they had other places to be.

I looked out the window. It was beginning to snow again. The ground was still white from the last snowfall. I walked to the window and gazed out. I loved to watch the snow. I wish Mom and Dad could've seen it, but I guess they had seen plenty of snow. They hadn't lived in California all their lives. At one time, Dad had lived in Bloomington although I'm not sure how long. Percy said Dad moved out on his own when he was eight or nine; when Percy was eight or nine that is, not Dad. My dad was ten years older than Percy.

As I stood there watching the snow come down I caught the scent of sugar cookies. For a few moments I thought I was imagining it because it smelled just like Mom's Christmas cookies. I also thought it was my imagination because Percy didn't bake. If he tried baking cookies the only scent wafting through the house would've been burning cookie dough. The scent grew stronger. I turned and followed it into the kitchen.

As I crossed the living room, the scent of sugar cookies overpowered that of the balsam pine. When I stepped into the kitchen the air was thick with the delicious scent. It made me hungry despite the fact I'd stuffed myself at the China Buffet. Grandmother was cutting out shapes with cookie cutters and placing the cookies on a cookie sheet.

"Would you like to help me by decorating the cookies?" Grandmother asked.

I looked at the finished cookies. They were decorated with icing. There were green Christmas trees with bulbs of different colors and a yellow star at the stop. There were snowmen with black top hats and red scarves. There were Santas dressed in red and half a dozen other kinds of shapes, all decorated well beyond my ability.

"I don't know how, and I'm not very artistic," I said.

"I'll show you. It's not difficult and the best part is you can eat your mistakes."

All the bowls and tubes of icing looked intimidating, but I figured I'd give it a try. I started with a Christmas tree. Spreading the green icing on the cookie with a butter knife was easy enough, but the first bulb I tried to add with a tube of red icing was much too big. Grandmother gave me a few hints, such as not squeezing the tube so hard. My bulbs were misshapen and the yellow star I tried to put on the top was pathetic. Charlie Brown's Christmas tree looked much better than mine. I ate the evidence of my lack of cookie-decorating skill while I gave a snowman a try.

"Percy always helped me make Christmas cookies when he was a boy," Grandmother said.

"Yeah? I bet he didn't do any of the baking! He never cooks."

Percy walked in just in time to hear my pronouncement.

"What are you talking about?" Percy asked. "What about that great Italian meal I prepared last week?"

"You mean the one at DeAngelo's?" I asked.

"Yes."

"That's not cooking. That's ordering from a menu."

"It's my version of cooking and didn't I fix a great lunch the next day?"

I rolled my eyes and then looked at Grandmother.

"He microwaved the leftovers from the night before," I said.

"Microwaving is cooking," Percy said.

"Of course, it is," I said, patting his shoulder.

"Just for that, I'm not helping you bake cookies," Percy said.

"Good! I don't like them black and crispy."

"See what I have to put up with, Mom? He's horrible."

I grinned.

"He reminds me of you at his age," Grandmother said.

"Oh, that's just cruel!" I said. "I'm deeply insulted!"

Percy grabbed the snowman cookie I was decorating and bit his head off.

"Hey, that's murder!"

Percy took another bite of the snowman and made his escape.

I worked on a reindeer next. I was becoming a pro at spreading on icing with a butter knife, but my skill at decorating with tubes of icing lagged behind. My reindeer had some strange looking antlers and the Santa Claus I did next didn't look like any Santa Claus I'd ever seen.

"Did Dad ever help you make cookies?" I asked.

It was hard to talk about Dad sometimes, but then again talking about him made it seem like he was still alive.

"Your father was more interested in eating cookie dough. I also had to keep an eye on him or he'd lick the icing off the cookies."

I laughed.

"He really did that?"

"He was about four at the time, but yes."

"Dad and Percy didn't spend a lot of time together, did they?"

"No. Your father was ten years older than Percy. By the time Percy became old enough that they could do things together, Anthony had moved out on his own. They cared about each other, but they never did that much with each other."

"I'm excited about Tyler becoming my brother, but he'll be going off to college soon."

"You'll likely be closer to Tyler than my boys were because you're much closer in age."

"Yeah, Tyler is eighteen and I'm fifteen, and we're already close."

I didn't tell my grandmother how close. There were some things grandmothers did not need to hear. Besides, the sexual part of our relationship was in the past and I wasn't sorry at all about what we'd done. If anything, it made us even closer now.

I looked out the windows. The snow was falling gently, covering the lilac and rose bushes. Inside, the kitchen was warm and cozy. The scent of sugar cookies filled the room and I could catch a whiff of balsam pine. The radio played Christmas music while Grandmother and I baked cookies. I wanted to hold onto the moment forever for *this* was Christmas. If only...

"I miss Mom and Dad," I said.

"I miss them too," Grandmother said and hugged me to her for a moment.

Grandmother looked like she might cry and I felt guilty for making her feel so sad.

"I have most of my Christmas shopping done now," I said quickly to get Grandmother thinking about things besides her lost son.

"Do you?"

"Yes, I'm going shopping with Tyler tomorrow to finish up. He's better at shopping than I am. I don't much care for it although I do kind of like it at Christmas."

"Christmas is a special time of year. I love baking Christmas cookies, listening to Christmas music, and watching the snow. That's one thing I miss in Florida, the snow. Of course, I don't miss the cold or the slick roads."

"I'd never even seen snow before a few days ago," I said.

"I hadn't thought of that."

"I love to watch snow and I love to go out and walk while it's snowing. I'd always wondered what snow was really like."

"You'll get to see plenty of it in Indiana although the southern part of the state has much milder winters than the northern half."

We didn't talk a lot after that. Grandmother cut out cookies and put a new tray in the oven whenever one batch was finished. She helped me decorate when she wasn't busy with the mixing. My cookie-decorating skills improved with practice, but my cookies never looked as good as Grandmother's. At least they would taste the same.

The best part about making cookies was sitting down and eating some when we were finally done. I'd devoured my worst mistakes while decorating, but after we were finished, I targeted a rather pathetic wreath, a sorry-looking reindeer, and a candy cane that looked... well, not like a candy cane at all. Percy and Grandfather joined us when the work was all done and helped us eat a few cookies. Percy said it was the least he could do.

***

Tyler picked me up the next afternoon so we could both finish our Christmas shopping. We went to the mall first, which was even more crowded than the day before. I stopped in American Eagle and picked out two pairs of boxer briefs for Brayden. Purchasing a bright pink pair was an incredible temptation, but I settled for just thinking about it. I selected a bright blue pair and another pair in light neon green.

I tried to find something for Percy as Tyler shopped, but what could I buy him? I knew he was into Star Trek, but as sure as I bought him a Star Trek novel, he'd already have it. I was pretty sure he had all the DVDs too. A horrible thought entered my head. I might have to go to the antique mall to look for his present. Percy liked old stuff even more than Star Trek.

"What's wrong? You look depressed. Come on! Tomorrow is Christmas Eve!" Tyler said.

"I was just thinking I might have to go to the antique mall to find Percy a gift. It's a fate worse than death."

"It is not, but I know the perfect place to look for a present for Percy. It's across town. Are you done here?"

"Yeah. I only have Percy left."

"Good. Let's get out of here."

I helped Tyler carry his bags out of the mall. Once we navigated our way out of the too-crowded parking lot we were on our way to the west side.

Bloomington isn't all that big, so getting to one side of town from the other took fifteen minutes at most. Even with the holiday traffic the trip wasn't bad. It wasn't like we were in a hurry anyway.

In only a few minutes, Tyler parked the car in front of a store called T.J. Maxx. We got out and he led me inside. The first things I saw were purses and a perfume counter.

"I'm supposed to buy Percy a purse?"

Tyler gave me a "you're too stupid to live" look and led me toward the back.

"T.J. Maxx has things for men too. It's a great place to look for clothes, but I have something else in mind for Percy."

We passed small items of furniture and some kitchen stuff. I became more hopeful as teapots and cool looking mugs came into view. Maybe I could get him some nice mugs for tea.

"This is the gourmet food aisle and if we're lucky, we will find..."

"Tea!" I said as I spotted it. "Perfect!"

"Finding it is hit or miss. This is where Percy buys his tea, and you know how he loves his hot tea."

"He should be forced to attend Tea Drinkers Anonymous meetings," I said. "He seriously has a problem."

"Exactly, so it's the perfect gift for Percy."

"What are you getting him?"

"I bought him a tea pot here a couple of weeks ago. His current one is looking a bit sad."

I picked out a couple of tins of Scottish Breakfast, a tin of Edinburgh Blend, and a set of four little tins of different teas. That pretty much used up the rest of my Christmas money, but I was finished!

We were both hungry, so we ate at O'Charley's. Tyler said it was a chain restaurant, but I didn't remember seeing one in California. O'Charley's had something called an endless lunch that included all the soup, salad, and rolls you could eat. Tyler and I both ordered that as well as Cokes.

Our food was delivered fast. The rolls were delicious. We had both chosen Caesar salad and loaded potato soup. The salad was great, but the soup... wow! It was the best soup ever! It had lots of cheese in it and even bacon bits.

The restaurant was decorated for the holidays. Near our booth was a Christmas tree and there was red, green, silver, and gold tinsel draped along the edges of the booths. O'Charley's had a very Christmassy feel to it as I sat there eating with my brother.

So far, I'd enjoyed having Tyler as my brother even more than as my boyfriend although it was quite a different relationship. I did miss certain things, but with any luck, Brayden and I could mess around soon. If I got desperate, there was always Dylan.

Tyler and I sat, ate, and talked. He was obviously excited about Christmas. Tyler and Daniel and Daniel's parents were coming over the next evening, and we were all having Christmas together. I wasn't accustomed to so many people at Christmas. It had always been just Mom, Dad, and me. I think that Christmas would be easier for me with lots of people around this year, especially when those people knew that I missed my Mom and Dad. Tyler and Daniel had never met my parents and therefore couldn't really miss them, but everyone else did. I knew Tyler and Daniel understood. I was glad I'd be around people who cared about me and who understood that Christmas would be a little hard this year.

I must have been looking sad because Tyler reached across the table and grasped my hand. I looked up and he gazed at me with sympathy.

"Focus on the good stuff, Caspian. If you want to talk about your mom and dad, I'm here, but look for things to enjoy."

"Like this soup," I said, as Tyler released my hand.

"It's incredible, isn't it?"

"Yeah. Maybe we should call Percy and Daniel."

"So they can come and have some too?"

"No. To tell them we won't be home for a couple of days. This is all you can eat, right?"

Tyler laughed.

"I think they close at ten and you can't eat *that* much soup."

"I can try."

"I plan on a second bowl, but that will be as much as I can manage."

A wave of sadness hit me. From out of nowhere, it came.

"I wish I could tell Mom and Dad how much fun I've been having," I said.

Tyler nodded, but I wondered if he really understood.

"I want to tell them about seeing snow for the first time. I want to tell them about Jesse and Dylan and you. I want to tell them about all the wonderful places to eat in Bloomington. I want to tell them about Brayden."

"You like Brayden a lot, don't you?"

"Yeah. I like him a whole lot. That doesn't make you mad, does it?"

"No. Why should it? You're my brother, not my boyfriend," Tyler said with a mischievous grin.

I leaned in closer.

"I liked him a lot when you were my boyfriend."

"I had that figured out."

"I still liked you, and Brayden and I didn't *do* anything."

"You mean you didn't do anything that would be considered cheating on me. You did a lot of stuff."

"Yeah, that's what I mean. I still felt guilty. I felt guilty because I really liked him and I was having fun with him."

"You shouldn't have felt guilty for that, Caspian. There is nothing wrong with liking someone or having fun with them. Now, if you'd had sex with him..."

"I didn't."

"I know that. I trust you. You have no reason to feel guilty. Even when we were dating, I was glad you befriended Brayden. I was so busy with school and planning the commitment ceremony I didn't have much time for you.

"You're very good for each other. If you're worried that you'll hurt me if you begin dating him, don't. We're brothers now. I want you to be happy."

"I'm not sure the whole dating thing is for me," I said.

"Bad experiences with your last boyfriend?" Tyler teased.

"No. The whole commitment thing is so 1950s. I want my freedom."

"Going to give Dylan some competition?"

"That would be exhausting! I don't mean I want to be a slut. I just want to be free to do what and who I want."

"There's nothing wrong with that."

"I do *really* like Brayden, but I'm thinking friends with benefits. I want some benefits *very* soon."

"That's the Caspian I know." Tyler laughed.

"How about you? Have your eye on anyone?"

"Not really. I have my eye on about two dozen hotties at school, but that's just lust."

"There's nothing wrong with lust," I said.

"Mmm. Yeah. We better talk about something else."

"Why, Tyler?" I grinned mischievously.

"You know exactly why. I want to be able to stand up when we're finished eating."

I laughed.

The topic of our conversation had shifted, but that was okay with me. Tyler was right. I needed to focus on the good stuff. It was Christmas. This was going to be a rough one, but there was no reason it couldn't be a good one too. The more I focused on the fun, the less sadness I'd have to endure. I felt a little guilty for having a good time when Mom and Dad were gone, but I knew that my parents wanted me to enjoy my life so that's exactly what I was going to try to do.

# Chapter 17

Christmas Eve was given over to getting ready for that evening. Grandmother spent most of the day cooking. Percy had tried to talk her into having our meal catered, but she wasn't having any of that. Percy was absolutely useless for any cooking task, but he did make a couple of runs to Kroger for Grandmother. I wasn't much help either, except for pulling out whatever Grandmother needed from the cupboards.

The aromas in the kitchen were absolutely wonderful. The scent of roast turkey mingled with that of sweet potatoes and green beans. Grandmother baked something that looked like an especially deep blackberry pie covered completely by a crust. She called it a cobbler. I thought it a very odd name, but then again these Hoosiers had some strange names for things. I still couldn't get over calling a cap a toboggan. To the rest of the world a toboggan was a type of sled, but not in Indiana or the South. No! Personally, I believed the whole thing was a plot to confuse me.

Tyler, Daniel, and Daniel's parents arrived in the middle of the afternoon and that's when the party really got going. The house looked beautiful and smelled wonderful. The big balsam pine was all decked out with lights and old ornaments, evergreen swag and Christmas lights surrounded the windows, and the scent of pine and dinner was in the air. Snow was falling yet again and even though it was afternoon it felt later. *Silent Night* played through the Bose Sound System when Daniel and Tyler stepped in the door and the music perfectly fit the atmosphere.

Tyler looked very handsome in a green sweater with red reindeer. It was a bit hard to see him because a stack of Christmas gifts mostly hid him. I helped him put them under the tree with all the others. I was very excited to see how everyone liked the presents I'd bought for them. I wondered what I'd get too, of course, but stuff didn't matter as much to me anymore. Maybe because Percy had already bought me so much stuff since I came to live with him. There wasn't much else I needed!

The Christmas music kept playing, the snow kept falling, and dinner called to me from the kitchen. I knew Grandmother had Christmas cookies, fudge, and divinity hidden away, but she wouldn't get it out until after we ate. My pleading that I might die of starvation before dinner was served only got me one cookie.

I wished Mom and Dad could be with us and once again I felt like they were. I hoped so because I didn't want them left out. As I looked around the room, I was reminded that I was very lucky. I could have been stuck in a foster home or out on the streets doing unspeakable things just to survive. Instead, I was safe with a family that was my own. I even had a brother!

Grandmother finally announced that dinner was ready. Percy and I had set up a makeshift dinner table at one side of the living room so we could all eat together. Tyler and I helped Grandmother carry out big bowls of mashed potatoes, corn, green beans, sweet potatoes, stuffing, cranberry sauce, and more. Percy carried out the turkey, but let Daniel carve it because he didn't know how. What a shocker! Grandmother brought out hot yeast rolls and we all took our seats. We immediately began passing around bowls and dishing things out for each other. At last, everyone's plate was full and it was time to eat!

Maybe it was because I was starving, but Christmas dinner was the best meal ever! I normally wasn't a big fan of green beans, but even they were delicious. My favorites were the stuffing and the broccoli casserole, which I almost didn't even try because who likes broccoli? Grandfather said the broccoli casserole had always been a favorite at family get-togethers so I tried some just to humor him. It was cheesy and delicious! I'm not kidding! This isn't an attempt to trick you. If you have a chance to try broccoli casserole, do it!

I tried not to overeat, because I wanted to try all the desserts and Christmas goodies. In addition to the cobbler thing, there was cherry cheesecake, a beautifully decorated Christmas cake that Percy claimed he baked but that really came from a local bakery, and all kinds of candy. There was a box of chocolate-covered turtles that Percy also claimed he made. I asked him why they were in a sealed box with "The Chocolate Emporium" printed on the lid, but he told me that creating the box was the hardest part. I rolled my eyes at that.

It wasn't time for dessert yet and it was hard to save room. Percy and I ate out a lot and the restaurants in Bloomington were awesome, but Grandmother had them beat. If only we could convince her to stay in Bloomington...

There was a lot of talking going on, sometimes a few conversations at once. Percy's parents talked to him about his books. They encouraged him to do book signings in Florida and to visit. I forgot Percy was an author sometimes. I knew he was a writer but I didn't think often about the fact that people actually bought and read his books. It's just too bad he wasn't a cool writer like Rick Riordan or J.K. Rowling. Imagine living with one of them? Then again, it wouldn't be cool if Percy was famous. He'd probably never be home.

The time for dessert had come. Percy said he was assembling "the dessert sampler platter" which must have been some kind of inside joke because he and Daniel laughed about it, but Tyler and I didn't get it. I dismissed it as yet more evidence of Percy's strangeness, but it wasn't a bad idea. I took a plate and got a little bit of everything.

The cobbler was better than blackberry pie although I always thought cobbler was an old-fashioned name for someone who made shoes. The cherry cheesecake was so good it almost made me moan and the fudge and divinity... yum! The cake that Percy "baked" and the chocolate covered turtles he "made" were incredible too. I wanted to go back for more, but a second helping had to wait. If I took one bite more, I might've exploded and that would not have been a pretty sight.

Soon, we settled around the Christmas tree. The task of handing out presents fell to Tyler and me. We handed out some my grandparents had brought first. Mine was in a box about a foot square all wrapped up in stripped red and green paper. It was really heavy so there was no way it could be the usual gift card, which was too bad because I always liked those. The good news is it was too heavy for something like socks or boring underwear.

I ripped away the paper, opened the box, pulled back tissue paper and was dismayed. It was socks and underwear! Worse, it was old-man jockey shorts and socks so long they'd probably go to my knees. Below these was the world's most hideous shirt. I tried to hide my reaction so my grandparents wouldn't feel bad, but I wasn't very successful. That's when first Grandmother and Grandfather then everyone else began laughing. I knew I'd been had. I reached into the box and pulled out two bricks. Attached to each was a gift card, one to Amazon.com and another to Barnes & Noble. I released a huge sigh of relief.

"That's just cruel!" I said. "I was trying to figure out how to act like I loved this shirt," I said, holding it up. It was lime green with big pink dots and sickly orange kittens.

Percy was laughing the loudest so I turned on him.

"Just for that. You're getting it for your birthday!"

I didn't realize it then, but a tradition had been born. I did give the shirt to Percy for his birthday. He gave it to Tyler the next Christmas and after that it got passed around for years. Just when I had nearly forgotten it, the shirt was back, showing up as a birthday, graduation, or Christmas gift. It was the gift that kept on tormenting.

I got some cool stuff after that, but the most fun was handing out my presents. Percy loved his tea and Tyler loved his cologne. Grandmother said Red Berry & Cedar was her favorite Yankee Candle scent so I knew she liked her candle. Grandfather's eyes lit up when he opened his IU Sweatshirt and Daniel really liked his shirt too.

Near the end, Tyler opened a box from Percy and Daniel that had a new iPad in it. I would've been jealous, but I had a kickass laptop already. Then, Tyler pushed the big box I'd been wondering about toward me and I ripped away the paper. This present was from Percy and Daniel too. I feared it might be another trick, but there were no old-man underwear or ugly shirts inside. Percy and Daniel had bought me a Bose Surround Sound system for my TV. My games would sound incredible on the sound system and so would my music. I hugged both of my new dads and kind of got watery eyes when I realized I'd thought of them as my dads. I knew I was lucky for a lot more than getting cool Christmas presents.

By the time the presents were all unwrapped, I was ready for another round of desserts. The snow kept falling outside and the music kept playing inside. At the moment, "Christmas Time Is Here" from *A Charlie Brown Christmas* was playing. I loved that Christmas special the best of all, even though it was so old Dad and Percy had watched it as kids.

We all sat or stood around talking and laughing. I tried to get embarrassing stories about Percy as a boy out of Grandmother, but she wasn't talking. Percy caught me and tickled me, but not for too long.

We spent the whole evening and into the night talking and eating. I think I ate my weight in dessert. I missed Mom and Dad and I wished they could be there, but I was sure they were happy for me. My first Christmas without them could have been much harder. A couple of times I got really sad thinking of my parents and almost cried, but both times someone was there to save me. Once, Grandmother noticed and gave me a big hug and told me how her son was with her through me. The other time, Percy wrapped his arm around me and guided me to the couch where I sat between him and Daniel. They both put their arms around my shoulders and it made me feel a lot better.

Mostly, it was a great Christmas. I got kind of hyper after a while, but that was probably all the sugar. When Tyler and Daniel went home at eleven, I went straight to bed and fell asleep. Having fun was exhausting!

The next morning, I awakened to find my stocking had been filled with candy and little presents. It was almost like Mom and Dad had been there during the night. That thought made me remember a dream I'd had. In the dream, I was sleeping in my bed back in California, but I was in Bloomington too. I got up and crept into the living room and it was the living room in both places, which made sense in the dream, of course. I saw Santa Claus filling my stocking and when he turned around he was my Mom and Dad. That one person turned into two didn't bother me in the dream.

I know it's kind of crazy and I know Percy filled my stocking during the night, but I had the oddest feeling that it was my Mom and Dad who did it instead. I almost asked Percy about it, but I liked believing that my parents had filled that stocking for me. I couldn't truly believe it and yet, who knows?

Not much was going on for Christmas Day and that was fine by me. Tyler came over and we hooked up my sound system. Tyler wasn't a big video gamer, but I did get him to play *Need For Speed* with me. He liked racing, but he wrecked a lot! After that Tyler insisted we watch *Scrooge*. It was a musical! I protested, but Tyler claimed it was tradition. It was Christmas, so I figured I could tolerate even a musical. It turned out that *Scrooge* was pretty cool. There was too much singing, but I liked Scrooge's "I hate People" song. I could almost picture Percy singing it while walking down the street. I planned to tell him that later.

I called up Brayden to see if he was doing anything, and he came over to hang out with Tyler and me. I was extra nice to Brayden by not inviting him over until the musical was over. I didn't think it would be cool to torment him on Christmas Day.

Brayden was kind of down when he arrived, but we cheered him up with a game of "Bull Shit." I couldn't believe Percy and my grandmother played with us. It was pretty funny to hear Grandmother say "bullshit," especially when she caught Percy bullshitting and he had to pick up all the cards. Grandfather would have played, but he said he had to rest his eyes, which I had learned meant he was taking a nap.

Later, Tyler, Brayden, and I went outside and built a snowman. Brayden and I told Tyler about the snowman we'd built to freak out Percy. Tyler was sorry he'd missed out on Percy's reaction. Since there were three of us, we set out to build an extra large snowman. We used up a lot of snow just creating the base. It was probably about four feet across. The next section was a good yard across and we struggled to lift it into position. The head was a couple of feet across and while much lighter than the other sections had to be lifted up over our heads. We just about lost control of it but managed to get it into place. The only way we could get the eyes and mouth into place was for Brayden to sit on my shoulders. Ours wasn't the finest snowman around, but I was sure it was the biggest.

"I bet our snowman can kick any other snowman's butt," Brayden said when we'd finished.

Tyler laughed at Brayden's comment. Brayden pretended to be offended and used it as an excuse to hurl a snowball at Tyler. That led to an everyone-for-himself snowball fight that was a blast. We darted around, dodging and launching snowballs for several minutes. I learned quickly that it was dangerous to use tree trunks for protection. Tyler hurtled a snowball not at me but at the tree trunk beside me. When the snowball impacted, snow exploded all over me. Some of it even got down my shirt. Tyler nailed Brayden with the tree trunk trick too.

After several minutes of fighting, we were freezing. We'd each taken hits that sent snow under our shirts. I loved snow, but boy, was it cold on bare skin! We called a truce, went inside, got out of our coats, and shook the snow out of our shirts.

Grandmother offered to make hot chocolate for us and we gratefully accepted. The three of us sat at the kitchen table while we waited. One of Brayden's sad expressions crossed his features and I knew he was thinking about Stuart. I stuck my tongue out at him to divert his attention and he smiled.

Grandmother's hot chocolate was a lot better than what Brayden and I had once made. I'm not quite sure what she did to improve it, other than to add mini-marshmallows, but it was delicious. We had some sugar cookies to go with it. Brayden held up a sorry looking Santa Claus and looked at me.

"You decorated this, didn't you?"

"How could you tell?" I asked, trying not to laugh.

"Because it's pathetic. Don't worry, I will put Santa out of his misery." Brayden bit Santa's head off.

"Hey, I decorated all of these. Some of them look pretty good," I said.

"Yes, I have to admit they do, but Santa had to be put down."

The three of us spent the rest of Christmas day together. We mostly stayed inside since the temperature decided to plummet. Daniel came over and with everyone there it was like Christmas Eve all over again, except that the presents had already been opened. I told Brayden I had him a present, but that he wouldn't want to open it in front of witnesses. He looked a little scared, but I assured him he'd like what I bought him. He told me he couldn't think of what to get me at all so he was taking me out to eat sometime before the end of Christmas vacation. We made a date for the very next day. Brayden told Tyler he was welcome to come, but Tyler declined and then gave me a wink behind Brayden's back.

# Chapter 18

Brayden took me to DeAngelo's, which I thought was rather extravagant. I would have been happy with Fazoli's. I took along Brayden's Christmas gift when Percy drove us to the restaurant. I couldn't wait until I could drive! Percy was very good about carting me around, but I would have much rather driven myself.

DeAngelo's wasn't too busy and we were shown to a somewhat secluded booth. Jazz played quietly in the background as our waiter gave us menus and took our drink orders. I looked over at Brayden for a moment. He was quite handsome and definitely sexy. I lost myself in a daydream about making out with him until Brayden noticed me gazing at him and grinned as if he knew what I was thinking.

I wasn't quite sure what I wanted, so I ordered cheese ravioli. Brayden ordered a calzone with pepperoni, Genoa Salami, and extra mozzarella.

When the waiter departed, I pulled out the Christmas gift I'd brought for Brayden.

"Since my present is being prepared in the kitchen, here is yours," I said, handing him the package.

Brayden eyed me suspiciously.

"I thought you said I shouldn't open it in front of witnesses."

I looked around.

"No one can see. Go on. I promise it won't explode."

Brayden tore open the paper and pulled out the two pairs of boxer briefs I'd bought at American Eagle.

"Nice," he said.

"I resisted the urge to buy you a bright pink pair."

"I would have killed you."

I laughed.

"Do you like them?"

"Yeah. I love boxer briefs."

"Maybe you'll model them for me sometime," I said.

"I will," Brayden replied. The tone of his voice made my heart beat a little faster. We both grew silent for a few moments.

"Thank you for my present and thank you even more for making me rejoin the world. I'm not sure how long I would have lingered on the sideline if you hadn't butted in."

I grinned.

"You don't have to thank me. I was returning a favor. It wasn't all that long ago that Tyler butted in on my brooding. I was angry at first and well... I was angry at the whole world and mostly at myself. Tyler made me see that all my anger wasn't getting me anywhere. All it was doing was causing me pain. So, when I saw myself in you..."

"You knew I needed some compassion and a kick in the ass."

"Exactly. Uh... I have another present for you," I said.

"The boxer briefs were more than enough. You didn't have to get me anything."

"I wanted to get you this," I said, pushing a large envelope toward him.

Brayden took it and opened it. He looked inside and then looked back up at me with wide eyes.

"How did you get this?"

"I paid a visit to your parents. I figured it was a long shot, but they'd kept the pieces. I took it to a photographer's studio and they were able to restore the photo."

Brayden took the photo of Stuart and himself out of the envelope and stared at it. Tears came to his eyes. He got up, walked to my side of the booth, scooted in beside me, and kissed me on the lips. It wasn't just a friendly kiss either. Brayden slipped his tongue into my mouth.

"Thank you so much, Caspian. You don't know how much this means to me, but then again maybe you do. I wish he was here, Caspian. I miss Stuart every day, but I know I can make it now because you're here with me."

"I need you as much as you need me. This Christmas has been wonderful, but it's also been hard. I miss my parents every day. I try to make the best of things, but sometimes..."

"Sometimes you feel like you can't go on. You can't stand that they are gone. You feel like you can't last another second."

I nodded.

"See, I do need you. You understand in a way no one else can," I said.

"Let's make a pact," Brayden said. "We'll always be here for each other, no matter what."

Brayden and I clasped our hands, smiled at each other, and then kissed once more. I didn't know where the future might take us. I didn't know if we'd end up dating or if we'd just remain friends, but I did know we'd keep our promise to each other. Brayden and I would be a part of each other's lives forever. I, for one, couldn't wait to see what the future had in store for us.

**The Gay Youth Chronicles**

**Listed in suggested reading order**

## *Also look for audiobook versions on Amazon.com and Audible.com*

*Outfield Menace*

*Snow Angel*

*The Nudo Twins*

*The Soccer Field Is Empty*

*Someone Is Watching*

*A Better Place*

*The Summer of My Discontent*

*Disastrous Dates & Dream Boys*

*Just Making Out*

*Temptation University*

*Fierce Competition*

*Scarecrows*

*Scotty Jackson Died… But Then He Got Better*

*The Picture of Dorian Gay*

*Someone Is Killing the Gay Boys of Verona*

*Keeper of Secrets*

*Masked Destiny*

*Do You Know That I Love You*

*Altered Realities*

*Dead Het Boys*

*This Time Around*

*Phantom World*

*The Vampire's Heart*

*Second Star to the Right*

*The Perfect Boy*

*The Graymoor Mansion Bed and Breakfast*

*Shadows of Darkness*

*Heart of Graymoor*

*Yesterday's Tomorrow*

*Boy Trouble*

*The New Bad Ass in Town*

*Christmas in Graymoor Mansion*

*A Boy Toy for Christmas*

# Also by Mark A. Roeder

*Homo for the Holidays*

*Ancient Prejudice**

*Ancient Prejudice is an early version of *The Soccer Field Is Empty*, which is recommended by the author instead of *Ancient Prejudice*.

Information on Mark's upcoming books can be found at markroeder.com. Those wishing to keep in touch with others who enjoy Mark's novels can join his fan club at http://groups.yahoo.com/group/markaroederfans.

Printed in Great Britain
by Amazon